BREATHE

THE CRESCENT LAKE WINERY SERIES

LUCINDA RACE

Betty —
I hope you love
Tessa & Max's
Story
Lucinda

MC TWO PRESS

Breathe

The Crescent Lake Winery Series

Book 1

By

Lucinda Race

INSPIRATION

Enjoying fine food and wine at the family table,
surrounded by your loved ones and friends, is not just a joy –
It's one of the highest forms of living.
Robert Mondavi

This is it, Tessa thought and rose to her feet, ignoring the heavy pounding in her chest. The sound of her chair scraping across the hardwood floor was muted by the buzz of conversation around her parents' enormous dinner table.

She cleared her throat and said in a loud, clear voice, "Can I have everyone's attention? I have some exciting news to share." Eight pairs of eyes with laser-like focus rested on her. For a second, she wondered if her family would throw her out of the house after they heard what she had to say.

"Tessa?" Dad's deep baritone cut the din with quiet authority. He sat at the head of the table with her older brothers, Don to his right with his wife, Kate, and Jack to his left. He sat back in his chair, his fingers curled around the base of his wineglass as he casually swirled the burgundy-red liquid. Dad's deep-brown eyes were fixed on her, his expression unreadable. Despite having had a serious heart attack over a year ago, he was a formidable man. Tonight, he reminded her of a king holding court.

"I hope you'll understand what I'm about to say." Her heart continued to race as the beeswax candles flickered in the center of the table. Her voice seemed to echo off the high coffered ceilings. "Crescent Lake had a great year and the winery is flourishing." Her gaze moved over her family and came to rest on her sister, Anna, who sat beside her and gave her an encouraging nod. "This was my last harvest with Crescent Lake Winery." Before anyone could speak, Tessa's next words came out with quiet confidence. "I've purchased and closed on Sand Creek Winery."

The silence was deafening. Don, her oldest brother and president of the family's winery, slowly shook his head and scowled. "Did you know anything about this?" he asked their father, his voice flat and his mouth in a thin line.

Dad shook his head; his eyes searched Tessa's. "Why would you do such a thing?"

Standing tall, with her back ramrod straight, she said, "It was my dream to manage CLW, until Don moved home and you turned the reins over to him. I realized then the only way I would ever run a winery would be if I struck out on my own."

"How long have you been thinking about this?" He deliberately enunciated each word, his body rigid.

"Nine months." Tessa studied his expression as he came to terms with her announcement.

Don and Jack had been researching the purchase of Sand Creek for the last six months. And while the family had always put their cards on the table when it came to business, she hoped this time, they would understand why she had put the brakes on CLW purchasing the floundering winery. She understood they would feel she had gone behind their backs, but she still hoped they would be excited for her anyway.

Anna sent Don a censuring look before she turned to Tessa and clasped her hand. "Congratulations. You must be very excited."

Tessa sent Anna a small grateful smile. "Thanks, sis."

The youngest of her siblings, Leo and Liza, also offered

their congratulations but otherwise remained silent. They weren't actively involved in the winery.

Mom pushed back her chair. She picked up two empty serving bowls. "Tessa's news calls for a celebration. Will someone please help me pour the sparkling wine?"

Everyone but Don, Tessa, and her father picked up their empty plates and followed their mother into the kitchen. Tessa appreciated a moment to talk more with them alone.

"I'm surprised you did this without talking to us." Dad looked her in the eye.

"I had assumed Don and Kate would stay in Loudon and I'd be the one to take over, Dad." With her head held high and her voice unwavering, Tessa said, "I've been considering a winery of my own since Don returned and became president." She looked at Don. "To be clear, I'm angry with the way things evolved, but I understand. You were groomed for this job since you were a child. I worked hard to become a good marketing manager. I know what I'm capable of, and I want more." She tapped her red-polished fingernail on the table. "You weren't here to run the winery, Don. I was. But then the prodigal son returned, and it became apparent the only way to achieve *my* dream would be to strike out on my own."

Don stood and paced the length of the dining room. "Tessa, think of Sand Creek differently. We could fold the new winery into CLW as part of our expansion plan. The cost is higher doing it your way. I had hoped to buy it from the bank at a lower price than you likely paid."

Stunned by his presumption, Tessa just stared at her brother.

Dad nodded and ran his thumb and forefinger over his chin. "You might be right." His face turned contemplative. "Why don't you go to the winery tomorrow with Tessa and take inventory of what they have? We can have an impromptu board meeting on Tuesday. We'll go over the details of the acquisition."

"You two are forgetting a very important point." She addressed them with a sharp inflection to gain their attention, but also because their plotting was making her blood pressure spike. "Sand Creek Winery belongs to me. I have no intention of merging it with the family business. If that's a problem for you, I'm prepared to sign over my interest in CLW if you think that is best."

At that moment, Mom entered the dining room holding a tray of glasses. "You will do no such thing." She shot her husband a sharp look. "Isn't that right, Sam?"

Without looking at Don, her father said, "Your mother is correct. Your share of CLW is yours. But I want you to think about this. Kevin Maxwell has proven he didn't know how to handle a winery. You may have assumed a mountain of debt. Suppliers and small business owners might be reluctant to do business with a new owner despite the Price reputation."

Tessa fumed.

Anna returned to the dining room, Jack at her side. Kate, Leo, and Liza followed and they all sat down.

"Dad," Anna said, "Do you remember when Leo was in a similar situation after he bought the garage? He does quite well now. Tessa is honest and I'm sure vendors and store owners will give her a chance. She's going to be an excellent wine mogul." She gave Tessa a quick wink.

Tessa looked at Jack. "You know the vineyard. What do you think?"

"When we were considering buying Creek, I inspected the fields. You're getting good vines. If you need to make personnel changes, I'd be happy to make some recommendations, but I'm sure you'll hire good people." He leveled his gaze at her. "What about Maxwell? He's hardheaded. You've got a tough road ahead of you if he stays on. I never understood why he never joined the wine growers council. We could have offered him support." Jack glanced around the room. "Then again, you've got the courage to make this announcement in front of the entire family. I think you can handle Maxwell."

She clasped her hands behind her back, tilting her head to one side. "Thank you, Jack. I'll be fine, but I appreciate your support." She couldn't help but notice Don and Dad looked less than enthused. "I hope you can try and be excited for me."

"Sis, I think you're in over your head." Don crossed his arms over his chest. His voice was flat.

"Don." His wife, Kate, spoke for the first time, her voice sharp. She glanced over her shoulder at the kids watching television and then back to Don.

Tessa could feel heat burn her cheeks. "I'm not a novice in this business. And while you were off cutting trees, I was here working and learning as Dad's right hand. I'm better prepared than you give me credit for."

This was what she had expected from the men—zero understanding, at least not today or maybe ever—but the women in her family were thrilled. With a heavy heart, she pushed her chair back so that she could step away from the table. "Since I put a damper on the evening, I'm leaving."

Dad looked at his dessert plate and pushed around the remnants of his pie. "Come by my office tomorrow. Don and I will discuss your exit from CLW."

He had dismissed her. At least she had expected it. In a quiet voice, she said, "I'll be in at nine."

Dad gave her a curt nod but didn't look at her. With her head held high, she walked out of the room. Her heels clicked against the floors. She paused in the front hallway as the swell of voices reached her ears. She put her hand on the doorknob.

"Tessa, wait."

Kate hurried toward her and gave her a squeeze. "I'm

really proud of you. Following your dream can be tough. But you'll prove to all of them that you've got the grit needed to be a smashing success."

"Thanks, Kate. I knew it would be a shock, but Don acts as if I'm destined to fail."

"You know he wants us all to be pulling in the same direction. His opinion is family first and always."

"I didn't disown the family. I want to have something of my own. Succeed or fail, it will be a direct result of my hard work. Leo did it."

"I get it."

She pulled open the door. "I'm exhausted. I'll talk to you tomorrow."

Kate said, "I'll walk out with you."

Tessa knew she was doing the right thing for her future, and if the family couldn't see that, it was their problem and not hers.

Kate closed the door behind them and smiled. "For the record, I think the guys were overly harsh on you."

Kate's support meant even more. "I'm pretty excited."

"You're fearless and more than ready to run your own business." Her eyes grew serious. "I'm sorry you feel Don took away the opportunity you really wanted when we moved back."

"The experience helped me to realize I want to be in charge of my destiny, not merely working in the shadow of my father and brother." She looked at Kate, who had become like another sister. "I'm sorry how that sounded. But it's a fact."

Kate nodded. "I get it. When I opened the bistro, I had to make it clear to Sam it was my business. He gave me complete control over every facet and never tried to influence me in any way. I had the experience of running a kitchen when I worked for my mom at her coffee shop, but it was never really mine. No matter how many changes I made to the menu, it was always her vision. I admire you. Hell, you jumped off the cliff when I stepped off the sidewalk!"

Tessa laughed. Her heart felt lighter than it had all evening. "Good visual." She added, "The bistro has really helped the winery grow and it's given the family amazing opportunities." She gave Kate a quick hug. "I really appreciate your support. Thank you."

Kate nodded. "And if there is anything I can help with, don't hesitate to ask."

"I have to talk to Kevin Maxwell tomorrow and ask him if he would consider staying on and working with me."

Kate winced. "That will be awkward. He's not exactly a fan of the Price family. Do you want him to stay?"

"Other than what happened to the business, he has good instincts and an excellent palate to make good wine. I firmly believe that long term, he'll be an asset."

"Have you thought about what you'll do if he doesn't want to work for you?" Kate asked.

Tessa gave a one-shouldered shrug. "If he doesn't, I have a few people in mind."

Kate pointed to the house. "No matter what their initial reaction was, you know the entire family is behind you."

Tessa gave a snort. "Once they get over the shock." She walked to the steps. "I'm going to take off. Big day ahead. Wish me luck."

"Want to meet after work tomorrow and we'll have a glass of wine? You can share all the details of your conversation with Mr. Maxwell."

With a grin, Tessa said, "Meet me at my house at seven and I'll bring the wine."

_____

2

The moment Tessa opened the heavy wood and glass door, her eyes were drawn to the tall, open stairwell. Kevin Maxwell leaned against the steel and glass banister, watching her.

He greeted her with a flat smile. "Good morning, Ms. Price. Welcome to Sand Creek Winery."

The glass door closed behind her with a small whoosh. She squared her shoulders and walked into her winery. "Please call me Tessa."

He gave her a half nod. "Tessa."

"I'm glad you're here. I wanted to talk with you."

"I've been clearing out my"—he gave a slow shake of his head—"your office. I won't be long."

She ascended the stairwell. "Wait."

Kevin's cool blue eyes met hers. He was dressed casually in a crisp, cream-colored shirt, the cuffs rolled back, which highlighted strong hands and muscled forearms. He had high cheekbones, a long, thin nose, and was more handsome up close. She guessed he was around her age.

"I'd like to start our relationship on the right foot."

His eyes never left hers. Challenging her.

She had been right that he wasn't thrilled to see her. She had negotiated the purchase through a broker since she suspected he wouldn't sell to a Price, no matter how much money was involved. She'd made a fair offer and he'd accepted it.

She pointed to an open door. "After you."

He did a one-eighty and strode through the doorway.

The large room was dominated by a long maple conference table and several leather chairs. In front of her was a wall of windows that looked out over acre after acre of vines. Pride surged in her. It already felt like she belonged. Several boxes were strewn about, in various stages of being packed. Not seeing a desk, she set her black leather briefcase on the table and walked to the windows.

"Quite the view." Kevin had come to stand next to her. He was so close, she could feel the waves of indifference radiating off him.

Without looking at him, she said, "It looks completely different from this perspective. The virtual tour didn't do it justice."

"When I built this building, my intent was to be able to look out and witness nature as it nurtures the vines. Watching the vineyard throughout the seasons gives me hope for the future. There's nothing like it." He turned away as if he couldn't bear to look any longer.

"Impressive." She was reminded of the view in Don's office. It was strikingly similar. She turned from the window and gestured to the chairs at the table. "Please, can we talk?"

He dropped to a wooden stool, leaving the executive chair noticeably empty.

Unsure where to start, she said, "You can trust me with Sand Creek Winery." She empathized with how it must feel, forced to sell his business.

When she sat down, he gave her a curious look. "It was

either accept the blind offer or let the bank take it. I'll admit if I had known it was a Price, I might have reconsidered."

She cocked her head to the side and let that comment slide. "I have a proposition for you." She wanted to rephrase that, but it was already out there.

His eyebrow rose and his chin dropped a fraction of an inch. "I'm listening."

"I would like for you to stay on as the general manager."

She could have heard a pin drop.

"And why would I want to do that?"

She leaned forward and clasped her hands, resting them on the polished wooden surface. "You're a good winemaker. I suspect a good marketing campaign can change sales. I happen to excel in sales and marketing."

"You think very highly of yourself."

She thought she saw a glimmer of humor in his crystal-blue eyes. "You know how to manage the field workers. You have a couple of excellent wines, but I want to hire an enologist to work with you, someone who is interested in growing this business."

Kevin leaned back in the chair and crossed his arms over his chest. "What's in it for me besides a paycheck?"

She suspected she had captured his interest. "If after the first year we exceed our profit by twenty percent, I will give you an additional bonus." She held up a hand before he could speak. "That would be in addition to the profit-sharing plan I'll be rolling out to all full-time employees."

He gave a snort. "Your staff consists of Brad, who manages the warehouse and is laid off every winter; Mrs. Hanley, who works part time in the tasting room, and we bring on seasonal workers in the vineyard."

"Maybe that's it for now, but I'll grow the staff as well." She lifted her chin. "I plan to turn this winery around and make this region take notice."

His eyebrow cocked. "You're rather bold. Do you have a concrete plan to back up your words?"

She smiled at his assessment of her. "I do."

"Care to share with me?" he challenged.

She slowly exhaled the breath she didn't realize she had been holding. She had definitely captured his attention.

"If you agree to stay on, we can talk specifics. After we come to terms, we'll draw up a one-year contract."

He stood and shoved his stool under the table. "Are you ready to tour your property?"

This was the day she had been dreaming of for the last three months. "This will be my first full tour. I'm curious to see the improvements you've made with the new holding tanks, and I would like to see the vines." She rose. *This must be his way of saying he'll consider my offer.*

He glanced at her slacks, black cashmere sweater, bold red silk scarf, and short black designer boots. "Any chance you have something less *indoorsy* to wear?" He looked at her. "Unless you want to just walk around the buildings."

She smiled, feigning patience with the man she hoped would ease her transition at Sand Creek. "I have hiking boots and a down jacket in the car."

With a shrug like it didn't matter to him, he headed through the office door.

She picked up her bag and then set it on the chair. This was her office. She stowed her cell in her slacks pocket while Kevin waited on the landing. "Ladies first."

They descended the stairs without speaking until they reached the bottom. Tessa said, "I'll get my boots and coat and meet you at the bar."

"You're the boss."

She could feel his eyes on her, watching as she crossed the gravel parking lot. She retrieved her hiking boots and coat from the trunk, pausing to take note of the circular driveway in front of the well-maintained white farm house that had

11

morphed into the contemporary building she had just left. Was this the best flow for customers to enter and exit the tasting room before touring the warehouse? Maybe Kevin hadn't allowed customers a full tour like they did at CLW.

Tessa took a few minutes and walked around the circle. She could envision climbing roses in full bloom tumbling over a split rail fence and people milling the grounds, drinking wine from glasses etched with Sand Creek's logo and carrying reusable tote bags sporting the new brand. The walkway would look stunning if the brick was replaced.

"Tessa!"

Hearing her name snapped her out of her vision. She whirled around and bumped into Kevin. He grabbed her arms to steady her.

He scowled. "What are you doing?"

Where his hand held her arm, she felt heat build.

"Thinking." She took a step back from him. "I might replace the walkway with slate and add a split rail fence along the stone driveway."

He dropped his hand. "You might want to hold off remodeling plans until you see what improvements are needed to actually produce next year's wine."

"I'm one to keep the ideas flowing." She held up her boots. "I'll need a minute to change."

Kevin followed her into the tasting room. He tapped the toe of his boot impatiently, but she refused to allow his sour mood to overshadow her excitement.

She shrugged on her jacket, and when she was ready to go, she said, "Let's see what we've got."

He pointed to the back door. "We'll go this way."

Outside, she stopped next to the pickup truck near a storage building.

He walked another twenty feet and stopped next to a golf cart. "We'll take this."

The cart was wide open with zero protection from the wind. "Shouldn't we take the truck?"

He flashed her a look of annoyance. "We can't drive between the vines in the truck."

"I've been in fields before; a truck will fit. You just need to drive slowly."

His eyes narrowed as he gave her a frosty look. "Not in my fields."

There wasn't anything different about *her* vines; he was just being irritating on purpose. Given the circumstances, she let it go and settled into the passenger seat. The electric golf cart hummed to life.

Kevin jerked the cart forward. He smirked. "Hang on."

Sarcastically she said, "Maybe I should drive?"

He looked straight ahead. "I know where we're going."

The air was crisp and cold as the cart zipped along. Kevin was rattling off details about different varieties as they flew down the gravel lane. Tessa had studied all the pertinent details in the prospectus, but her ears picked up an interesting tidbit. "Did you say the vineyard has twenty acres ready for planting in the spring?"

"Yes."

"On top of the thirty already producing?"

"Yes," he said, his expression deadpan.

"Did you also say you retained another forty acres of prime vineyard acreage as yet unplanted?"

"Yes."

"Can you answer me in more than one-word sentences?"

With a wide grin, he said, "Yes."

Giving him a wide-eyed look, she said, "Do you know what this means?"

"No."

She smiled at the prospect she had in mind. "That means there is huge potential for growth. No pun intended."

"Yes. You have a lot of potential to expand the business, but *I own* forty acres. Not you."

She didn't miss the emphasis he put on the ownership of the land. Her mind was spinning with possibilities. "Can I see that land too, and would you be open to a long-term lease?"

He took a quick left and she slid across the short seat, bumping into him unintentionally.

"You have more to see that you *already* own."

"Another time then." She could see the vines were well maintained. If Mother Nature was benevolent, they'd have a good harvest next year. "Tell me, how was the crush this year?"

"I'll show you."

They drove for twenty minutes in almost complete silence. He pointed to areas of interest and would say a few words, but otherwise there was little conversation, which suited Tessa just fine. She was busy making quick calculations in her head about yield and the potential for bottling and of course marketing the final product.

When they got back to the winery, she could tell from the irritated expression on his face that something bothered Kevin Maxwell—but that was his business, not hers. He pulled up short at a side door of the warehouse.

Chilled to the bone, she was happy to get inside. Touring the fields hadn't been on her agenda for today and her jacket hadn't been quite warm enough. The only time she had felt pleasantly warm was when she nearly ended up in Kevin's lap.

He opened the door and let her step inside first. "We'll go into the fermenting room."

"When will we begin aging the juice?"

"The white will be aged in stainless steel and bottling in a few months. The red from this season, maybe eighteen months, but we'll be bottling a cab next week."

"You seem well-suited to running this part of the business." She had been right in her assessment about Kevin's importance to the success of Sand Creek.

"It's part of the job."

She gave him a sidelong glance. "Have you thought about my proposal yet?"

He gave her a level look. "It's been less than two hours but I'm mulling it over."

It didn't escape her notice that he held the next door for her as they entered the large warehouse that soared two stories high.

There were enormous silver metal holding tanks lined up one after the other down the length of the building. He said, "After this, we'll go to the bottling room and you can inspect the labels. If you want to make a brand change, you'll need to do it quickly."

It was as if he read her mind. But changing the brand would be a logical step for any new owner. As she toured the space, Tessa was pleased to see it was immaculate. She noticed he was studying her, and he didn't disguise his interest. What was going on behind those blue eyes?

"I'd like to see the labels now." For today, she was starting with her strength. Marketing.

3

*M*ax—which was what Kevin preferred close friends call him—wasn't sure what to make of Tessa yet, so he just went through the motions. "You can see the labels in the tasting room." He pointed straight ahead. "Through that door."

With a nod, Tessa led the way. He couldn't help but notice how her tailored pants hugged her shapely backside. Her long auburn hair cascaded in waves down the back of her cashmere sweater. Even wearing hiking boots, she looked every inch a successful businesswoman. *Snap out of it. For the moment, she's your boss.* He shook his head and put his game face back on.

"I must say I'm impressed with the operation. You've done a good job breathing life into the old place." Tessa's roving eye didn't miss the smallest detail, including the new digital gauges that had been installed on the tanks. She tapped the keys to fire up the computer and he was pleased when she gave a half nod as she discovered the latest software had been installed.

"Thanks. I thrive on challenge." Everything he had instituted here could easily be replicated in a new location.

"Who designed the current label?"

"I worked with an in-house designer at the printer." Max liked the label. It was simple and straightforward. But it'd make sense she would ask. At least she didn't say it was horrible, but he was mildly curious what she had in mind.

They reached for the doorknob at the same time.

She withdrew her hand and glanced at him. This close to her, he could smell the light floral scent of her perfume. He had assumed she'd select something bold, but this suited her. He pushed the door open and stood back so she could go through first.

She said, "Thank you."

She surveyed the spacious, open floor plan with a wall of windows overlooking the vines. He looked at the room through fresh eyes, her eyes. He was proud of the honeyed oak wood floors he had refinished himself. It wasn't cold and sterile like some of the tasting rooms in the area, with cement floors and a slab bar lining the perimeter and huge displays of wine bottles in the middle. Here, he had small tables scattered around the space. If someone wanted to sit and enjoy a glass of wine, they could. "Did you see the patio area?"

She crossed the room and looked through the glass door. She smiled. "That is unexpected and charming."

He wasn't sure what the tone of her voice meant. Would she want to rip it out? It had taken him weeks to lay the stone. "Does that mean you approve or it's something you'll want to change?"

She walked in a circle and crossed her arms over her midsection. "It's different from what I'm used to. At CLW, we have a more"—she paused—"traditional approach to tastings."

He leaned against the bar, studying her. *Was Creek about to become CLW two-point-oh or, worse, an extension of the existing business?*

"I'm not looking to change everything about Sand Creek.

17

But I'll be honest. If I don't think something will work, it will evolve to fit my vision."

The tenor of her voice didn't leave room for discussion. But he did admire her confidence. If a Price had to buy his winery, he was, at this moment, pleased it was Tessa. It might be interesting to see where she planned to take the place. And for now, Max had nothing better to do than hang around and maybe he'd be able to preserve some of what he had accomplished while he was the owner. Well, at least until he figured out his next step.

"If the offer still stands for me to stay and work together with you, I accept." He deliberately added the *work together* part. He might have failed on the business side, but she'd need his expertise about the wines.

Looking pleased, she stuck out her hand. "Excellent! I have the contract in my bag. I give you my word it is straightforward, with no tricks. You'll find that's my style."

He liked the feel of her hand in his; her grip was firm. "No offense, but I'll have my lawyer look it over, and if it's in order, I'll sign it."

She smiled. "Good. Now let's see the labels lined up."

❦

*T*essa was relieved when Kevin finally said he wanted to work with her. She stopped feeling anxious about how much wine was in the fermenting tanks; she needed them to be at full capacity for the next bottling. She needed inventory for sales, and sales to pay the bills. She was beginning to wonder if she had imposter syndrome, thinking she could take on a floundering business and make it a success.

She took a seat on a barstool. He lined three bottles up in front of her. She could feel her heart drop as she scanned from right to left. The labels were dull and unappealing. Basic font, no color, just white on a dull black background. "I thought there were more than three varieties?"

"I had a fourth, but it wasn't selling. I plan on discontinuing it."

She knew there were six varieties. But two could play this game. "And it was?" Tessa was sure the fun, unpretentious picnic wine was missing from the lineup, along with his special blend.

"A semisweet light summer red." With a nonchalant shrug, he said, "It never caught on."

She took a deep breath. He'd put up barriers to the winery's success. "Do you have any bottles?"

"Yup."

She pushed back from the bar. "After lunch, I'd like to do a tasting of all the varieties we have in the stockroom."

"Suit yourself."

She strode from the room knowing he watched her as she walked up the stairs. She needed to get out of the hiking boots and back into full business attire. Something about this man put her off her game.

*T*essa opened her laptop, intending to launch a graphic design program. She wanted to play around with a few ideas, but the real design work would be handled by the Buffalo-based advertising agency she'd hired. The screen remained blank. Why would Kevin have taken a good product with serious sales potential off the market? She tapped a few keys to bring up a sales report from the files she had received at closing.

Scrolling through data, she found what she was looking for. Sales were decent for the initial launch on the summer red. Could she rename it, change the label, and launch it next April? She made some notes on her ever-present legal pad.

First question: Was there still inventory that could be relabeled? A second question was if Kevin had juice for the summer red in any tanks for next year. She didn't think this was the type of wine that would be aged in barrels. She added: *stage of wines, types?* She tapped her pen on the paper. She had many questions. Hopefully Kevin had the answers.

She turned back to the computer. A poor or downright bad label could kill the success of the best bottle of wine. She knew better than anyone that labels initially sold the product. All a winery had was the span of a couple of seconds for the label to tell the story and convince the buyer to pick it up. After the customer bought it, Tessa was confident the taste would keep them coming back. She had sampled the wines before buying the winery, and Kevin was talented in creating wine.

She closed her eyes, leaned back in her chair, and thought about the Sand Creek label, letting her mind drift and taking her time to really think about how the bottles would look in a store when compared to other wineries' products. The current Creek labels were drab. They bore a dark rectangle and the wine name in bold block text. The CLW logo, by contrast, was oval. At the top was the logo, with the type of wine listed below. The label reflected her father in every way. Traditional, classic, and timeless. Just like their wines. She wanted something different for Sand Creek.

Trying to clear her head, she unpacked a small box of personal mementos. When she was finished, she was satisfied with the way the room reflected a bit of her. She sat down and swiveled in the chair. She was breaking away from the Price family business. *I want to attract a younger customer base and develop brand loyalty.* Vibrant colors with accents of gold in a bold but easy-to-read font. A logo with a capital S and C would be a good backdrop. She had to get this right. With that decided, next was the website.

Making a snap decision, she grabbed her cell phone and scrolled through her contact list.

On the third ring, she heard, "Pad Stone."

"Hi, Pad. It's Tessa."

"Hey, this is a surprise. What's going on?"

She propped her feet up on another chair. "I'm curious what it would take to get you to come to Crescent Lake for a photography gig."

"For your new winery?"

"Yes. I guess the news hit the grapevine like wildfire."

"Did you forget your sister-in-law is my wife's sister? It was big news over the breakfast table."

She couldn't help but laugh. "If you're free, I'd like to have pictures taken for the website."

"Ellie and I were just talking about making the drive out to see Kate and Don. Ellie's had a little bit of cabin fever since the baby was born. Being with her sister might be just what she needs. Why don't you give me a few details, and then I can figure out how much time I'll need." With a laugh, he said, "Once I tell Ellie we're taking a road trip, our bags will be packed."

Tessa smiled into the phone. "I'm sure Kate will be thrilled to see you. Ben is growing like a weed and I bet he'd love to see his new baby cousin too."

"Why don't you tell me exactly what you have in mind."

She got up from the desk and walked to one of the large windows overlooking the vineyard. "Originally, I wanted some pictures to help me design a new label, but I've already gone in another direction. However, the website is outdated, and it could use an update. Tasting room pics, maybe some exterior seasonal shots, the warehouses. Think of it as a visual walk-through, but I don't want video, only still images I'll be able to switch out with the seasons."

"Don't you want me to give you an estimate?"

"No, that's not necessary. I want the best, and that's you." She thought about the cost but knew she needed a quality website to bring people in; it was her twenty-four-seven storefront. "What do you say?"

"I think we can get out there in a couple of days. Will that be too late?"

"No, and the long-range weather forecast looks good."

He chuckled. "Leave it to you to have checked everything."

"When your livelihood depends on the weather and land, it's something you keep close tabs on."

A cough drew her attention. Kevin was leaning against the doorjamb, hands stuffed into his jeans pockets. His eyes roamed the room and took in her advertising awards hanging on the wall along with the crystal wine bottle on the table, presented to her during a national wine conference.

"I need to run, but call and let me know when I should expect you."

"Sounds good. We'll talk soon."

She walked to the table after the call ended.

Kevin gave her a look she couldn't read. Was he disinterested or impressed by her accomplishments?

"Looks like you've been busy." He nodded to the wall.

"I did a little decorating."

He strolled over and studied each plaque but didn't say anything more about the specific awards.

He pointed to her cell phone. "Sounds like you've jumped in with both feet."

She settled into a chair at the long table. "How much did you hear?"

"You're bringing in a big-time photographer to update the website and you're hot on the trail of a new label design."

"There's work to be done." She gestured to the chair across from her. "Will you sit down?"

He crossed the room with a slow walk.

Tessa felt heat flush her face. Damn, he was good-looking. She dipped her head, withdrawing another pen from her briefcase. She knew his eyes never left her and she had an unusual response. Her pulse rate had definitely quickened.

*H*e sat in one of the leather armchairs at the other end of the office, one leg crossed over the other knee as if he didn't have a care in the world. Except the woman who bought his company was sitting in his office. Well, at least it had been his until two days ago.

She crossed the room and handed him a set of papers. With a cursory look, he set them aside and waited. Wasn't she supposed to start the conversation?

"Thanks. I'll look at them later."

"Do you think you can have it back to me by Friday?"

"Shouldn't be an issue. I have an appointment with my lawyer tomorrow."

"Good."

He pointed to her pad on the table. "Mind if I have a look?"

She picked it up and handed it to him. "Not at all."

He cocked a brow as he scanned her list. "You have a lot you'd like to discuss. Do you have a particular order for your extensive list, or should I talk and you take notes?"

"I'd like to start with a question not on that page and I hope I don't offend you."

He gave her a forced smile. "Try me."

Tessa picked up her pen and held it over a blank page. "I know for a fact you can produce an excellent wine. What went wrong?"

He cocked his head to the side as if challenging her. "Why don't you put the pen down and I'll tell you."

4

_____

*T*essa settled into the chair and crossed her long legs. "What happened with your business?"

God, this woman could be infuriating. She didn't waste any time going right for the messy details of its failure.

Should he be honest? He looked at Tessa, really looked into her doe-brown eyes. Under the façade of a tough-as-nails businesswoman, he suspected there was a kind heart. He could share some of what had happened without invading Stella's privacy.

He waited until their eyes met. "My sister got sick and didn't have health insurance. I wanted her to have the best care, so when it came time for the business, I was, well, distracted. The winery suffered."

Empathy flashed across her face. "How is she now?"

There it was, the confirmation he had been looking for. He could see the concern in her eyes and hear it in her voice. She wasn't just a shrewd business executive; there was a softer side. "Better, thank you. She's in remission."

"I'm so sorry you both had to deal with that." She didn't hide the compassion in her eyes.

"As much as I hate to admit it, you buying the winery

loosened up my cash flow, so I'm in a better position to continue to help her if needed." His eyes never left Tessa's. She reached across the space between them and barely touched his hand. It wasn't out of pity but, he thought, to show she genuinely cared.

"If you need anything at all, please let me know. That includes time off. Family is always the priority."

"I figured with the Price family, it's business first."

She withdrew her hand as if he'd just insulted her. "Not at all. With my parents and siblings, our family is the most important, before business. We just happen to work well together."

That—family first—hadn't been his impression on the few occasions he had bumped into Sam Price, although he'd never had the opportunity to meet Don. And this was the first time he had been up close and personal with Tessa. Not that he minded. She was stunningly beautiful and her voice was like honey. Plus, she was smart—a triple threat. "But you walked away from your family business unless your plan for Creek is to become part of it at some point."

"It was time to make a change and let me guess. You thought I was a coldhearted businesswoman without an ounce of compassion."

He could see her eyes flash, more from frustration than anger. "To be honest, we've never met. Your father and I haven't been on friendly terms." He'd be damned if she was going to make this his issue.

"You never became a part of the wine growers association."

He heard the accusation, maybe even blame for his failure, in her voice. "I went to a couple of meetings. It wasn't my style. Too cliquey, if you ask me." He could hear the defensive tone in his voice and made the conscious decision to tamp it down. He needed to remain in control. She wasn't going to get under his skin. "I was competition." He wouldn't make that mistake again. If he purchased a new winery, he'd get involved with other growers in that region.

She sighed. "I'm sorry you didn't feel welcome. But I get it. Some of the members are so insecure about their wines, they don't realize competition is good for everyone in The Valley. It makes us strive to grow, bottle, and sell high-quality wines, which leads to success for the entire region."

He was surprised to hear Tessa's insight. Could he have unfairly put her in the clique? "Thanks."

She gave him a small, tentative smile. "For the record, I have a feeling you brought some of your bias to the table too."

"That's possible." He pushed off the chair. "What do you say we go to the tasting room and I'll give you the full experience?"

She stood. "Lead the way."

*T*essa trailed behind Kevin, surprised at what she had learned about him in their brief conversation. She admired anyone who put family before the job, even though in this case, it all but killed his business. It had put him in the position of working for her instead of being in charge. However, she never would be a heavy-handed boss. She preferred they work collaboratively.

He led her down a back set of stairs and past a large door, which she guessed led to a storage room. She noted it would provide easy access during a busy weekend. She was pleased to see they were entering the tasting room from a well-equipped commercial kitchen.

He pulled out a barstool and stepped behind one of the bars and, with an easy smile, said, "Have a seat." He placed ten classic wineglasses on the bartop. If he noticed her eyebrow arch, he didn't react. Next came a box of plain crackers that he poured into a small bowl decorated with a vine pattern around the edge. Based on the pretty bowl, he seemed to understand that details mattered.

Finally, a corkscrew and four bottles of wine. One white, a blush, and two reds. But where was the Picnic Basket and the sixth variety? She had heard he'd developed something amazing. She'd wait to see how this played out and then try to figure out why the mystery of number six. With flair, he popped each cork with a *gloop* and placed the cork in front of her, lining them up in a row.

She had to wonder why he hadn't brought out six bottles. "Are we tasting the picnic wine too?"

With a gleam in his eye, he withdrew another bottle from under the bar and presented it over his arm for her inspection. It was simply titled *Picnic Basket*. "Madame, you asked, so I grabbed a bottle and chilled it before I went upstairs." He put the bottle in a granite chiller sleeve on the bar and picked up the bottle of white.

Tessa watched him pour a partial glass of the white into two glasses. "This is from a Cayuga grape." He nodded and placed the open bottle in a chiller sleeve.

She studied the color, swirled the wine, then held the glass to her nose. She cocked her head and looked at him.

"I get a hint of pear and apple." She closed her eyes, took a small taste, and paused. "Slightly dry. A touch sweet and very enjoyable." She opened her eyes.

He nodded with appreciation as he sipped the wine. "Good nose."

Tessa bit into a cracker. "They taste a little stale."

With a short laugh, he said, "They'll clear your palate."

She grimaced and tapped out a note into her phone. "I'm ready for the next one."

He poured the blush, adding some to a glass for himself.

She picked the glass up by the stem and swirled the pale-pink wine. "It has a nice color." She took a sip. "This is a blend. Correct?"

He smiled. "Yes, a Fauch grape and our Cayuga. I think it gives the wine a more complex flavor, with a hint of the sweet from the white." He leaned casually against the bar and sipped the wine. His eyes had a spark of amusement. "You seem to know a bit about wine."

She noted the touch of humor and was happy he was beginning to soften a minuscule bit. "You do know you can get a blush by removing the skins early in the fermenting process, keeping whites and reds separate."

A flicker of annoyance flashed over his face. "I do. I happen to like this blend. And up until two days ago, it was my decision."

"You're right. I was thinking at CLW, we create our blush from reds, not a blend."

He stepped back from the bar and downed the last sip of the blush before setting his glass on the bartop with a thud. "I like this version better."

She could hear the exasperation in his voice. "Yes, I know what you're implying. Creek is a different business."

"We should stay the course and not have Creek become an extension of your family's winery." His eyes narrowed. "Unless that *is* your intention."

She sat up straight. "Sand Creek Winery will be independent from the Price family business. It doesn't matter what my last name is. This is my business to grow or fail." She held up her glass in his direction. "With your help, of course." She wasn't about to tell Kevin that was exactly the conversation she'd had with her family when she announced her ownership of Sand Creek.

"You're saying for the foreseeable future, we're in this together." Giving her a half-smile, he said, "Good to know. I assumed your family sees profit with every bottle they sell. My vision has been to produce and bottle an excellent wine."

"You don't have a very high opinion of my family."

"As I said before, I have only had the pleasure of meeting your father."

It didn't sound like it was a positive experience. She knew Sam could be difficult, but that was a conversation for another day. She waved her hand over the glasses and said, "Let's continue." She broke a cracker in half. "What's next?"

He poured a translucent red wine in the next glass. "This is the picnic wine. It can be served chilled or at room temperature. It doesn't have a long shelf life once it's opened, and it won't last long, even in the refrigerator."

She sipped and her lips twitched. "This is really good." She reached for the bottle. "I've never even seen this in the wine section at any of the local stores."

"I wanted it to be exclusive to customers who came to the winery."

"Oh, Kevin." Her breath came out all at once. "It's like you've kept this fun, unpretentious wine a secret." She took another sip. "It's fruity and refreshing. I bet it would be perfect in sangria." She set the empty glass down.

At last, he picked up a bottle of red, a shiraz. Red wines were her favorite. She was looking forward to tasting it and the cabernet.

He handed her a glass. "Try this."

She swirled the wine. "It has a nice ruby-purple color. Aged in oak?"

"Yes. Alcohol content for the shiraz hovers near sixteen."

She took a sip and held it on her tongue before swallowing. "It's smooth like velvet. Do I detect notes of blackberry and pepper?"

"You do."

She sipped the shiraz. "Why did you pick these varieties to start the winery?"

"I think the white and blush are self-explanatory; they

belong in any portfolio. My favorite is a shiraz or cab, and the picnic was for fun."

She tapped her glass to his. "The base on which to build our empire."

He shook his head. "Your empire now." Maybe he shouldn't sign the contract and just bide his time until he found the right opportunity.

"When you sign the contract, we'll be in this together." Munching on the stale cracker, she asked, "I know I just handed you the contract, but I'm curious if you glanced at it and were there any points we should discuss?"

"I'll let you know after I've read it." He leaned on the bar. "Here's the fifth wine we'll taste today, a cabernet."

"Has it been aged in oak?"

"For over eighteen months." He poured and slid the glass across the glossy bartop.

Tessa studied the rich burgundy color in her glass. "Visually stunning." She let the aroma fill her senses. "Cabernet is my favorite, but I do like all red wines."

She watched as Kevin held up a glass, brought it to his nose, and closed his eyes briefly while he inhaled the aroma, then he swirled the glass and studied intently the way it moved and clung to the sides. She didn't interrupt him, as she enjoyed watching him revel in the moment; it mirrored how she savored this experience. Kevin's intensity for the wines was not something she had expected. This wasn't his hobby or just a job, but his passion.

The longer she held the glass to her lips and let the rich wine linger on her tongue, it seemed her taste buds almost sighed. "This is amazing. I love the rich but subtle dark cherry flavor that seems to dance across my tongue." She set down her glass. "I wish we had more to taste. This has been fun, and you did an excellent job."

"Do you want me to pour you something more?"

"No. Go ahead and recork." She stood up. "I'll take the

Picnic Basket home with me unless you want it. No sense in wasting a good bottle of wine. And by the way, the wines are excellent and probably the best-kept secret in the region. I want to hold an event for local businesses, both restaurants and shops. Let's see if we can stir up some sales for the upcoming holidays."

"Sounds like an interesting idea. But expensive."

"We have to spend money to make money, and to keep this place running through the winter could be challenging if we don't get some incoming revenue. Besides, if people don't know how amazing Creek wines are, they'll never buy them."

He started the process of recorking the open bottles. "Are you going to keep the tasting room open during the winter months?"

Did she hear a challenge? "The tasting room will be open until the weekend before Christmas, and the shop will be open until Christmas Eve. Then we might shut down for the month of January and resume the first of February, hopefully to pick up some Valentine's Day sales. We'll really kick off the spring season with a big splash for our grand reopening, with tours and expanded tasting room hours."

She spouted ideas, but it would have been nice if she had actually fleshed out the concepts first. She was faking confidence she didn't feel at that moment. Her chest tightened but she kept her face neutral.

"Sounds like a big bite from the elephant."

For a split-second, she was confused. "Ah, I get it. You've been building the business slowly and you think I'm just diving in for a smorgasbord?"

"Well, you've just rattled off several special events, including keeping the shop open for the holidays. In the past, we closed down for several months, so to me, that is ambitious."

"If we work together, I know we'll see a spike in sales."

"And who's going to plan your tasting event?"

She tapped her temple and smiled. "I have an idea but need to make a couple of phone calls. I'll get back to you with an answer by tomorrow."

She turned toward the front stairs, where she stopped and pivoted, pushing up the sleeves on her sweater. "First I'm going to wash our glasses." She stopped mere inches from him.

He took her shoulders and turned her around to face the stairs. "I've got this. You go ahead and create the wonderful world of wine events."

She wasn't sure what he meant. Was he saying working together was a good idea? "Are we in this as a team?"

He shrugged. "I'm not saying a word other than deferring to your marketing expertise."

She laughed over her shoulder and walked up the stairs, pausing midway. "We're going to wrap the year up with record sales." She flashed him a huge grin. "Trust me."

"What's with this *we* stuff?" he called out to her.

When she got to the top, she hung over the banister. "Sign the contract."

5

"*R*obert, I've looked at the real estate listings you sent over, but none of them seem like a good fit. Have you toured any of them in person?" Max had wanted this video call. He never trusted anyone with his money unless he could look them in the eye. Under the circumstances, with Robert Haskins living near wine country on the West Coast, this was the best option to read his face.

"Kevin, I've come across a winery that I didn't email you. I'm not sure it's what you're looking for, as it is in rough shape."

"The vines or the grounds?"

"Both. The vineyard has been neglected for a few years and the buildings need work."

Max shook his head. "No way, man. The vines could be diseased. They'd have to be burned and I'm surprised neighboring vineyard owners aren't up in arms. Disease can transmit to their land."

"Do you want me to keep looking?"

Max's eyes drifted to the window overlooking his backyard. Even though the past few days working with Tessa hadn't been as bad as he had anticipated, there was no reason he couldn't explore other opportunities. His sister could move with him. All he had to do was talk to her and ask.

"Scope out Oregon and Washington for me. They're good options too."

"We're done with California?"

"Yeah. Unless something else comes along. Let me know when you find something that reminds you of the Finger Lakes."

"Think about Michigan, too. Winters can be harsher, but there are some good vineyards. I'll be in touch."

Restless after the call ended, Max changed into running clothes. The best way to work out any problem was to sweat.

*

*D*on's office door was open and Tessa could hear Dad's deep voice but couldn't make out specifically what he was saying. Not wanting it to appear she was eavesdropping, she called out, "Don, Dad."

Her brother answered, "We're in my office."

Tessa entered the office. She was on a mission. She had dressed in a pale-gray suit and white blouse to project a strong and confident image. Grandmother Price's ruby studs graced her ears, which she always believed brought her luck. She had wanted an extra boost of confidence when she met with her brother and their father.

They both stood as she entered her brother's spacious office, with its panoramic view overlooking the vines. It reminded Tessa of her new office at Creek.

She smiled at Don and her father.

"Thanks for making the time to meet with me." This was her first meeting where Don and she were on equal footing as presidents of wineries.

Dad pulled out a chair next to the large wooden conference table. "Have a seat."

Don sat across from her. "I was happy to get your call."

She looked between her father and Don. "It's only been a day." She relaxed. Nothing had changed between them.

With a slight shrug, Dad said, "How are things going with Maxwell?"

She felt a familiar flash of annoyance, the natural response when Dad questioned her abilities. "Everything is good." She pulled a pad of paper from her briefcase and then set a pen on it. Doing this helped her remain focused on her goal. She leveled her gaze between these two strong men.

Don let out a snort. "We're family. You don't need to be so formal."

"Don." Dad's voice held a low warning tone.

He dipped his head to one side. "Please continue."

"I see a lot of promise at Creek with a little focus on marketing."

Dad nodded. "A mistake made by so many people who start a winery or any other business is poor marketing. A good product doesn't translate into success if no one knows about it."

"Exactly." She continued. "I don't want to go behind your back, but I'd like to hire Liza to plan a tasting event for local shops, restaurants, and wine distributors." She looked at Don. "I would also like to ask Kate if she could give me some pointers on what food to pair with Creek wines. She knows how to bring out the best in a wine with food." She didn't need his permission to talk to Kate but again was trying to be transparent to avoid conflict later.

He gave her an encouraging smile. "Solid ideas. Kate is the best chef in the area and giving Liza more exposure will expand her client base." Don looked at their father. "Any concerns?"

Dad asked, "What do you hope this will accomplish other than spending your money?"

She had done her research and facts supported the expenditure. "One store carries our line in the area." She felt a burst of pride as she continued. "This event will showcase each wine. I'm confident I can get placement in more stores and restaurants. By pairing our wines with food, it will introduce area chefs to the subtle flavors. With more potential customers trying them, I believe they will see that carrying Creek wines can only enhance their current wine lists."

"Do you have a projected ROI?" Don's lips tipped up.

Inwardly she relaxed and continued. "Have you ever known me to not have run all the numbers every which way?"

Don leaned back in his chair. "I wouldn't expect anything less."

Dad looked out the window. The minutes ticked by and the silence was becoming oppressive.

She turned to Don for support and when he dropped his eyes, she said, "I came here to be open about my plans, but maybe I shouldn't have bothered." She jammed her pad in her bag and pushed back her chair. The chip on her shoulder just got unbearably heavy. "This was a mistake."

"Tessa. Your impatience is getting the best of you. Please, sit down." Dad's words stopped her midstep. She waited for him to speak. Quietly, he said, "I've been in the wine business my entire life, and there have been times when I've stepped in to help other wineries, but this is the first time I'm going to put a condition on my response."

Her body was taut. She couldn't imagine what he might say.

"If Liza wants to work with you and Kate decides she's going to jump in too"—he paused, and it was then she saw his brown eyes had softened—"I expect the family will receive an invitation to your event."

She swallowed the lump in her throat. "You'd want to come?"

"Of course. We want to support you, even if I'm not happy you've left Crescent Lake. You're my daughter."

She eyed him cautiously. "Is this because you're hoping I'll fold my company under the CLW brand?"

Dad frowned. "Even if that had crossed my mind the other night, I want you to be successful and build Sand Creek up to be a fierce competitor. There is plenty of room in the marketplace for good wines." He lifted his eyes to hers. "And top-notch winery owners."

Don said, "Liza should be in her office. Your sister took the one next to Anna's. You've got an event to plan." It broke the tension in the room.

"Why the change of heart from two days ago?"

Dad clasped his hands together. "Everyone has the right to reach for their dream. Even if I don't agree."

She nodded. It was the best she was going to get from him. "Thank you."

Tessa's head spun with ideas for the event as she left the room and poked her head into Liza's small office. It was empty. Pictures of her boys and late husband Steve were sitting on the corner of her desk. Tessa had begun to scrawl a note when Liza came up behind her.

A smile tipped the corners of her mouth. "Tessa, this is a nice surprise. What are you doing here?"

She could smell the tantalizing aroma of fresh coffee. It reminded her she was a few cups shy today. "Hi. I had a meeting with Dad and Don, and I wanted to stop in and talk to you about something. I was surprised when they told me you set up an office here."

"I wanted to have a specific place to work instead of the kitchen table with two boys running around all day or a basket of laundry staring me down. This is so peaceful; I can concentrate and make phone calls uninterrupted." She gestured to the chair. "Have a seat."

Tessa set her bag on the floor next to the chair in front of Liza's desk. "Have you booked any more events for this fall?"

Liza sipped her coffee. "Not yet, but I do have two deposits for next summer."

"That's awesome." She leaned forward and rested her elbows on the desk. "Are you interested in a gig separate from CLW?"

Liza's eyes twinkled. "Now you've piqued my curiosity."

Tessa's smile spread over her face, relieved Liza was ready to jump on her party train. "I'm hosting a tasting event at Sand Creek and inviting a wide variety of people from the area. It will introduce the winery to local businesses. I was wondering if you want to plan it."

"Tell me more."

Encouraged by Liza's enthusiasm, she said, "It will be a cocktail reception. I'm going to ask Kate what I should serve."

"I happen to know she's in the bistro. We should ask her to come up." Liza picked up her cell. She tapped out a message and set the phone on the desk.

"I was going to stop down and talk to her."

"Now you don't have to." Her cell pinged and Liza glanced at the screen. "She's on her way."

This was what Tessa loved about the women in her family. They pulled together. She could hear the clunk of clogs banging on the steel stairs.

In a moment, Kate poked her head in with a smile. "You pinged?"

Without giving Tessa a chance, Liza said, "Tessa needs our help."

Kate perched on the corner of the desk. Her dark hair was pulled off her face in a messy bun, highlighting her high cheekbones and deep-emerald-green eyes. She was an amazing chef and if she was willing to give some advice, Tessa was sure the event would be a smashing success.

"I'm planning an open house at the winery. I'll invite lots of local business owners and have everyone taste the wines."

Without hesitating, Kate said, "That's a great idea. How can I help?"

Tessa was thrilled by Kate's enthusiasm. "I was hoping you'd come over, taste the wines, and give me an idea what I should serve for appetizers. You instinctively know how to pair wine and food."

Kate gleefully rubbed her hands together. "This sounds like fun, but I'm not just going to suggest what you can serve. I'll do the cooking. What do you have for a kitchen over there?"

"Kate, that is very generous of you but..."

Liza piped up. "I'll talk with Peyton; she hires all our extra waitstaff and bartenders."

Tessa said, "I'm hiring you, Liza; you're not working for free. It's a win for both of us. I'll have a great event and people will see how talented you are. It will drive more business to you and build your client list up for event planning."

Kate suggested, "Text Peyton. She can make a list for us and I'll pick it up before I come over."

Before Tessa could protest, Liza rapidly tapped the keys, and then Tessa heard the familiar ping of a message sent.

Another ping followed the first. What the heck? Was Peyton sitting on her phone?

Liza turned the phone around so Tessa and Kate could see the response.

"She's said it'll be done within an hour." Kate exchanged a mischievous grin with Liza and then smiled at Tessa. "So pull out that pad I know you have with you at all times. We have an event to plan."

Tessa looked at Kate. "This is above and beyond. I wanted your advice. I didn't expect you to cook."

Liza's grinned filled her face. "You're paying me, and I'll give you lots of direction. And if Kate wants to help, accept it graciously. After all, she's the best chef in the area. You'd be a fool to turn her down."

Kate nodded. "I'll give you an invoice for food plus my team. Besides, why would you want to hire another chef when you have me?" She winked. "I just received an excellent recommendation from a talented event planner, which is why you should allow me in your kitchen. Per Liza, I'm the best chef in Crescent Lake."

With her palms held up and out, Tessa chuckled. "Alright. I'll accept your help. Since you're all in, we can head over to Creek. We'll look at the space and the kitchen facility. Liza, what if we meet tonight at my place for girls' night? Do you think Mom will take care of the boys?"

Liza glanced at her watch. "I'm sure she'll jump at the chance. I'll let you know if she can't."

Tessa was thrilled Liza was eager to get to work.

Kate said, "Don can have Daddy-little guy night. We'll be over by six?"

Tessa felt her smile slip. The only sister not in on the act was Anna.

As if reading her mind, Liza held up her cell. "I've texted Anna and she'll be there too."

"Liza, you do think of everything." Tessa picked up her bag. "I'll see you then. Put your thinking caps on. We have five wines we'll showcase."

"When will we meet Kevin?" Liza asked.

"I'm not sure. Soon."

Kate said, "I'll follow you over now if that's okay and take a tour of the kitchen."

"Sounds good." Tessa stepped into the hallway.

Liza called after her, "You didn't say when we're holding the event?"

Tessa looked over her shoulder and grinned. "In two weeks."

The girls looked between each other and Kate said, "Not to worry. We'll make it happen."

Tessa had a spring in her step. If Kevin had doubted her before, he surely couldn't now.

⁂

"*H*ey, Tessa." Max stood on the front step of her condo and held up a cardboard box. "I brought the wine."

"Come in."

He entered the small foyer. A large vibrant abstract painting dominated a taupe wall. He would have thought she was more of a classic art lover. "I can put it on the counter for you."

"This way."

He followed her into a large room that ran the width of the place. The furniture was an eclectic mix of contemporary upholstered pieces with a few antiques. His gaze swept over the group of women in the living room area and he set the box down. "Is this the team helping to plan our event?"

She beamed. It was the same look she'd had yesterday when she launched the cocktail reception idea. He knew it meant she had something going on in that beautiful head.

"Kevin, let me introduce you to the Price women." She pointed. "Liza is an event planner. Behind her is Anna; the two of you have a lot in common. You're both the genius behind the wines." Last, she gestured to Kate. "This is Don's wife Kate. She owns the bistro."

He walked over and shook hands with each woman as he was introduced. "Nice to meet you." He smiled at Tessa. "I'll set the bar up and take off."

Kate wandered over to the glass doors. "Tessa, come here a sec."

"What's up?"

Kate looked over her shoulder in his direction. "He's cute."

Max pretended to be engrossed in the task at hand and that he couldn't hear the conversation. He was curious what Tessa would say in response.

"Forget that *he's hot.*" Tessa dropped her voice, but it carried.

Kate's eyes popped open. "That's a first."

He smiled to himself when she said, "Let's talk later."

Speaking louder, Kate said, "I couldn't help but notice, when I was at the tasting room, the bottles on display. If you reorganize those shelves by type, not a hodge-podge, people might buy more. If people think they can't get more than a bottle or two of a single variety, they might hesitate. People like what they like and want plenty of supply."

"Dad has said the same thing forever." Tessa frowned. "I hadn't noticed the display."

Max bristled. There was nothing wrong with the way the shelves were stocked. He had hoped it would get customers to purchase more than a single bottle or two of one variety. "Tessa, I'm all set."

She flashed him a killer smile that touched her deep-brown eyes and caused an unexpected shock wave to ripple through him. How the hell did she do it? This was the second time her smile had stopped him in his tracks.

"Come on, ladies." Anna sat down at the bar first. "Tessa, we should make notes."

"Good idea."

With a practiced hand, Max uncorked the five bottles. "If you run out of wine, give me a call. I'll be around." He smiled at the women, who were paying close attention to him. "Ladies, I'll leave you to enjoy your evening."

With a lopsided grin, Tessa said, "If we polish off five bottles of wine, we'll be having a pajama party."

The women laughed with her and invited him to stay but he declined.

"I'll walk you out." Tessa led the way to the front door.

Max had to wonder why some of her family, the competition, would want to help Tessa have a successful event. Did they have an ulterior motive? Were they hoping to sabotage the event? Unable to let his winery be made a laughingstock, he said, "Can I talk to you outside?" He'd clear the air before he let any of them trash *his* wines.

She told the women she'd be right back. She closed the door behind her. "What's up?"

He stuck his hands in his jacket pocket. "I'm not comfortable with what you're about to do."

Her brow furrowed. "What do you mean? Is there something wrong with the wine?"

"Sabotage."

She rolled her eyes. "You can't be serious?"

For a split second, he wondered why he cared. Tessa owned the winery. He plowed ahead anyway. "We're opening ourselves up to the competition."

Surprise flashed across her face. "You're all over the place. First you act like you're all in, and then you jump to these unfounded ideas about my family." Her eyes grew wide. "Are you insinuating my family would do anything to harm my business?"

He didn't miss the inflection when she said the word *my*.

"Yes." The word hung heavy in the air. Max could feel the temperature drop to freezing. "Tessa, I've got to say what I think and…"

Before he could finish his comment, her hand flew up. "Stop. My family would never do anything to hamper a business venture, whether it was mine or another competitor's. That is not how we conduct ourselves. And if you think for one minute anyone in my family wants me to fail, you're dead wrong." She put her hand on the doorknob. "Thank you for bringing the wine over. Have a good night."

He touched her arm. "I've poured my heart and sweat into this business. I was forced to sell or watch my work go down the drain. It was like drinking vinegar. I'm glad you bought it. You know how to market and sell wine. I know how to grow grapes and make a good vintage. Together we can be unstoppable." He was conflicted; there was a part of him that wanted to stay and watch his winery grow into its full potential, but he also didn't want to be a witness if she turned it into a CLW extension.

Her gaze slipped to his hand on her arm and then back to his eyes. He removed his hand. "I'm sorry."

The ice thawed slightly. "Thank you." Then her voice softened and she turned her head in the direction of the house. "They're not the enemy. Trust me. I know what I'm doing." She looked at where he had held her arm. It still tingled.

"You're right. Sabotage wasn't the right word." He hesitated. What could he say to make her understand it was agony to have to step aside?

She studied his face. "I'm going inside."

His shoulders sagged. "You're really sure this is the right thing to do?"

She touched his hand. "Yes."

He took comfort in the simple gesture. For a half a second, he wanted to pull her in his arms. He was unsure where that came from. Maybe it was the stress of keeping the winery afloat for so long. Alone, it had been a heavy task. It had never seemed a burden but now, just maybe, sharing the process of a relaunch would make it somehow easier if it failed. He quickly pushed that thought to the recesses of his mind.

He watched her walk in the house, her head held high. Confidence oozed from her. *She's going to be an amazing winery owner and she doesn't need me. If I leave, I'll be sorry I won't be able to see her enjoy success.*

✹

essa plastered a smile and walked inside. Working with Kevin was an emotional roller coaster. What the hell had he been thinking, insinuating her family would try to derail her success? Sand Creek was more than a viable operation. If he couldn't trust her instincts, maybe they couldn't work together.

Yes, her father and brother cast long shadows, but they thrived on strong competition. She had observed and learned from the best. Sand Creek would find its A game. The roots were strong; she just needed to nurture it for it to thrive. She studied the women who had interrupted their evening to come here. Not a single malicious thought among them. She'd show Kevin who they could trust.

Tessa was eager to see what each one of them thought. "Okay, ladies, are you ready to get your taste buds working? Oh, and I want detailed notes. This will help me write copy for a new brochure and the website."

6

---

*H*er first two weeks owning the winery had flown by and express shipping had just delivered her first purchase—new logo wineglasses—in time for the reception. The extra cost for expedited production had been worthwhile, as they were just what she wanted. While filling the sink at the bar, Tessa opened up the first box. It was a simple pleasure, sinking her hands in hot soapy water and washing the new logo glasses. Kevin sauntered over and opened the top of a box sitting on the bar.

"These are nice." He held one up. "You do know we have a glass dishwasher in the kitchen?"

She pushed her hair off her face and smiled. "I do, but there is something very satisfying about washing glasses by hand. It goes back to my first job at CLW. I was the chief glass washer."

"You started from the bottom?"

She straightened and dried her hand on a cotton bar towel from the stack. "We all did. Dad is a firm believer that we know every facet of the business. I've also worked with the vines, the crush, bottling, and the tasting room."

"What about creating the wine?"

She wrinkled her nose. "I was horrible at that. Anna, on the other hand, has a gift. I dare say there isn't anyone in the region who's better at blending wines."

He lifted a brow. "Really. Is there a challenge in there somewhere?"

Her lips twitched. "I didn't mean to bruise your ego; I'm just proud of my sister. Anna has been doing this since she was a teenager. She doesn't have to taste it. What she can do by smell is a gift."

"Tessa, my ego's intact. You've spent your career immersed in CLW, and now you're undergoing a deprogramming of sorts." He chuckled. "This time next year, you'll be fully versed in all things Creek."

She liked how his laugh softened his eyes. They might become friends. She held up a freshly washed glass.

He took the glass. "The logo is nice. I like how the S and C kind of swirl around the W. You did a nice job."

"Almost everyone has said yes for tomorrow night."

He nodded. "Good. Maybe we'll get a new contract or two."

"*A*im higher than that, Kevin. I'm going for *ten* new contracts." She plunged another glass in the water and rinsed it.

He looked at the stacks of boxes. "Did you order too many glasses?"

"I don't think so. People can take one home if they want." She tilted her head to the side. "Want to know a secret?"

He leaned closer. "Sure."

"I have a collection of wineglasses from other vineyards. It's sort of my thing, checking out wineries whenever I'm on vacation."

"Do you travel much?"

"I try to take off for a couple of weeks midwinter. I come back recharged and ready for a hectic season."

"I haven't taken a vacation in over five years."

"This year, you need to plan one."

He gave her a long look. "Maybe a change of scene would be a good idea."

*A*ctivity buzzed around them. Liza was directing a group of men to position the last of the tables. Everything was coming together, and it looked better than Tessa had envisioned.

Kate sailed through the door carrying Ben, who was in the midst of a temper tantrum, on her hip, a huge tote bag over the opposite shoulder. Don crossed the room and took their son. He kissed her lips and Tessa couldn't help but sigh.

Kevin gave her a quizzical look.

Choosing to ignore the question on his face, she turned to Kate and smiled. "Hi. You're right on time as always."

"I've got a couple of boxes of tools I need. They're in the car if you want to give me a hand." Kate looked between Tessa and Kevin.

"Sure, I'll get them." Kevin walked through the swinging door into the kitchen.

Kate gave her a curious look. "Did I interrupt something?"

"I'm not sure." She and Kate walked into the kitchen. The hub of activity faded away. "I just don't know what to make of him."

"Meaning?"

"He's frustrating and hardheaded. He loves this business and borrowed against it to take care of a situation to the point of losing it." She swung her gaze back to Kate. "He's upset he had to sell but knows it was the only way to keep it alive."

"Like some guys, still waters run deep."

48

Tessa folded her arms across her chest. "I want him to want to stay."

Kate nodded. "I'm not surprised. He's very talented."

Slowly, she said, "He is. At first, it was because I wanted to keep his talent within the business but now..." She could see him approaching the back door through a window, his arms full. She rushed to open the exterior door. Kevin balanced a box under each arm. He placed them on a stainless-steel table and went out again. She was still holding the door when he returned.

Tessa said, "Thanks."

"Not a problem."

She slid one of the boxes to the center of the table. "Kate, do you need these someplace special?" She glanced at her watch. "The food delivery truck should be pulling in any minute." She peered out the small side window with a view of the driveway.

Kevin propped open the door with a large brick. He looked over his shoulder at Tessa but directed his question to Kate. "Do you need me to hang around?"

"No. I've got this covered." She waved her hand toward the tasting room. "Out of my kitchen." She softened her comment with a grin. "Anyone hanging around will be put to work."

Tessa held up her hands. "You do not want me in here. I can't cook."

Kate popped her hands on her hips. "I happen to know that's a lie. You're decent in the kitchen but choose to leave it to others."

"Well," Tessa began, "I don't starve."

Kate turned to Kevin. "Do you cook?"

Tessa felt her face grow warm. She knew what Kate was up to.

"I do. If I can grill, I'm all in. My specialty is a good porterhouse."

Kate flashed a Cheshire cat smile. "Isn't that a coincidence? Tessa adores a good steak paired with an excellent red wine."

"Kate," Tessa warned.

Her eyes widened. "It's a true statement. Am I wrong?"

"No," Tessa drawled. "But we're not talking about my dinner preferences."

Kevin said, "Maybe sometime we can all get together for a cookout."

Tessa wondered what he was thinking. He hadn't seemed to want to be anywhere near her family until this exact moment, and then she wanted to sink through the floor when Kate said, "That sounds like fun. I'm sure there will be one or two warm evenings left before it snows."

"Kate, we can plan a dinner party another time. I need to get upstairs and check on—" She struggled to think of how to finish that sentence.

Kevin flicked his thumb toward the door. "I'm going to get back out front and stock the bar." He looked at Tessa. "If you need something, just holler."

She mumbled, "Thanks," as he walked out.

"Do you want an honest observation?"

"Sure, why not?"

"He's a great guy and you're attracted to him but don't know what to do about it."

"I'm going to my office. Shoot me a text if anything comes up."

Tessa crossed the room and went up the back stairs, deliberately avoiding the tasting room. She needed to stop thinking about Kevin other than as a valued employee. Nothing more. Tomorrow night was all about creating awareness for the winery and the excellent wines they produced. She still had to decide what she was going to wear. After all, this was the first time anyone would see her as the owner of Sand Creek, and she was determined to make her mark.

After about an hour, her phone pinged with a text. It was from Kate. *Delivery truck delayed. Don't worry, I'm on it. Just wanted you in the loop.*

Her fingers hovered over the keys. *What do I need to do?* Whoosh.

Before she could get out of her chair, Kate answered, *Nothing. I've got this.*

If the truck didn't show up in the next sixty minutes, she'd go to the grocery store if necessary. She dropped her head in her hands. *Please let this be the only hiccup.*

---

*M*ax hovered at the bottom of the stairs. Should he go up to the office and give Tessa the signed contract? He had been making her wait until it dawned on him that the only person bothered by his not returning the contract was him. She had extended a generous offer. After reviewing it with his lawyer, Max knew he'd be a fool not to sign. He would make a good salary and the bonus potential was excellent if they had a good year. But if he up and left before the year was up, well, he'd feel like a heel. Tessa hadn't done anything but ask him to stay.

It still surprised him that her family had shown up and pitched in to organize the tasting event. He had to wonder if he had tried to become a part of the wine growers association, would things have turned out differently? Would he have had to sell his dream?

"Hey, Kevin."

Don's voice brought him back to the present. There wasn't any point in wondering what might have been. All he had was now.

"What's up?"

"Liza seems to be done ordering us around. I'm going to take Ben home."

He stuck out his hand and Don clasped it and gave a firm shake. "Thanks for helping us out."

"My sister has a way of getting people to do exactly what she wants or needs."

Max wasn't sure if that was a joke or a warning.

Don slapped him on the back. "She has an amazing intuition when it comes to business. It was our loss when she announced she bought this place. But don't tell her I said that."

"Should I be concerned?"

Don chuckled. "No. I'm just telling you to be ready. Forewarned is forearmed." He slung Kate's tote bag over his shoulder. "See you tomorrow night."

"Thanks again for your help today."

"Think nothing of it. When you meet our dad tomorrow, you'll understand this won't be the last time you've got a bunch of Price family members wandering around the premises."

Max watched Don and Ben walk into the kitchen. What the hell? Was this winery going to become an extension of CLW? Taking the stairs two at a time, he strode into the office.

"We need to talk."

7

"*T*essa." Her name came out as a growl. He watched as a flash of confusion appeared on her face.

She looked up. "Is there a problem with our plans for the event?"

"Have you lied to me?" It didn't matter if she had the marketing know-how. He was the one who developed the wines, and they were damn good.

She pushed her chair back and stood up and looked him square in the eye. "I don't lie." Her voice was cool. "What are you talking about?"

He couldn't help himself. "Are you going to sell Creek?"

"We've had this conversation." She crossed her arms across her chest. "And I'm not going to dignify your question with an answer. I don't have to explain myself to you."

He paced the length of the room. Was he annoyed with Tessa or himself? Obviously, he had issues about the sale. But she was right that she didn't owe him any explanations. It was her company.

"I have no idea what you think you might know, but I can assure you Sand Creek Winery is going to remain my company. Not that it's your concern, but I've poured all my personal savings and mortgaged my condo, among other assets, to purchase this business. It will not become an extension of my family's winery."

"Don just said I'll been seeing a lot of your family around from now on." He could hear the indignation in his voice.

"Do you often jump to conclusions without facts to back you up?" Her lips thinned. "You really do have a huge chip on your shoulder, don't you?"

She gestured for him to sit down. As if explaining to an unreasonable child, she said, "My family will be around more because they're my family. As much as you don't seem to believe me, they'll respect the boundaries of Creek. They want me, us, to be a smashing success."

The band around his chest eased with her simple answer, maybe because he wanted to believe her. He grimaced. "Maybe I did jump to conclusions." He needed to consider why it mattered if she did sell the winery. He was still thinking about a fresh start far away from this place.

For the first time since he burst into the room, she seemed to relax. "There is one thing you have to learn. I'm brutally honest. Sometimes it's going to tick you off, but that's how I roll."

"I can accept that." It was a quality he admired.

"Now, to change the subject"—a smile graced her lips—"have you given any thought to what you're wearing tomorrow night?"

"Pants and a shirt?"

"Would you be opposed to me picking out your shirt, and can you wear dark slacks, perhaps a suit?"

Now this was an odd turn of events. "Why?"

"I want us to project a very specific image."

"Branding?"

With a sharp clap of her hands, she laughed. "Now you're starting to figure out how my brain works. Every step we make for the winery is planned. I leave nothing to chance."

"I don't mind you picking out clothes. Saves me the trouble." He was curious to see how this played out.

"When we finish up here, can I follow you back to your place?"

"You want to do it tonight?"

"If you don't have anything that will work, we still have time to shop tomorrow."

"I don't shop."

Her eyebrows shot up like she was daring him. "Fine. I'll shop for you."

Rather than coming off as a jerk, he decided this might be interesting. "Why don't we head to my house in a little while? I should be finished here in about an hour."

She glanced at her screen and said, "Perfect."

Feeling like he'd just let her win their first skirmish, he leaned forward and pulled the contract from his back pocket. "Here."

"Did you sign it?"

"I did."

The smile reached her eyes. She jumped up and moved around the desk to give him a firm handshake. "Kevin, I promise you won't regret it."

The tingle he got from clasping her hand was unsettling. "I hope not." Their eyes met. "And for the record, call me Max."

*

*T*essa was pleasantly surprised when he asked her to call him Max, but she masked her reaction. It was a sign their friendship was progressing.

He led the way to his place after work. His home was set at the very edge of the winery, and it hadn't been part of the purchase. She noticed the lawn was well maintained and there were pots of mums in a riot of colors and pumpkins placed on either side of the front door. The house had a nestled-in-the-woods kind of charm, but it was much larger than a cottage.

He waited as she parked her BMW in the driveway, then walked with her up the flagstone walk. "Welcome to my home."

"It's lovely. I don't remember there being a house here when Mr. Fletcher owned the winery."

"I built it after I purchased the place. I thought about renting, but there is something about owning your space. You can do whatever you want with it, hang pictures or paint the walls hot pink if that turns you on."

She gave him a side-eye glance. "Hot pink, huh?" They strolled up the walk and Tessa stopped and looked back at the rolling acres of vines. "Now I see why you picked this location. The view is spectacular."

"The best." He saw his home through her eyes, and it was like he was looking at something he wasn't allowed to have anymore. It would be hard to leave here after building his home, on the edge of his real dream, owning this winery. He pushed open the door and gestured her into the spacious front entrance. "You can leave your bag on the bench."

essa looked around his tidy home. To the left was a small wooden bench and a coatrack. To the right and front was a high-ceilinged living area open to the kitchen, and she could see a large deck beyond French doors and a wall of windows. Farther left, she guessed, was Max's office and a short hallway leading to a closed door. Directly in front of them was a staircase.

"Upstairs are the guest rooms." He hung their coats on the rack and said, "My bedroom is at the end of the hall."

Tessa's stomach flipped. She was suddenly surprised she

had the nerve to invite herself into his home to select his clothes and he was actually letting her.

"Why don't you bring a few shirts out here and I'll take a look."

"You can come in the bedroom. I won't bite."

Her laugh was tinged with nerves. "I didn't say you would."

He walked away from her. "Come on."

She dropped her black leather satchel on the bench and followed him down the hall, her heels making a distinct clicking sound on the polished red oak floors. She admired his taste. His home was lovely.

He opened double doors to the suite.

She took a tentative step into another large room with a long wall of windows and a glass door overlooking a small stone patio.

"This is gorgeous," she breathed.

He gave a low chuckle. "I designed it for the views." He gestured to an archway. "The closet is in there."

She crossed the room, the deep-pile beige carpet silencing her shoes. She stood at the windows. "This is a perfect place to sit and have morning coffee." Over her shoulder, she flashed him a smile. "You need a small bistro table and a couple of chairs right over there." She pointed to the left corner of the patio.

"Maybe." His voice lacked warmth and she silently admonished herself that she had tried to impose her ideas on him.

"Lead me to your closet."

"I'll warn you now I've been told most women would kill for a closet like this." He grinned. "At least that's what my sister told me when she saw it."

He walked through the archway and a light came on automatically. He opened one set of double doors to expose rods of neatly hung shirts and pants. Shoes and sweaters were meticulously folded on shelves, and there was a small section for what looked to be casual clothes.

"Your sister was right." Tessa instantly had closet lust. What she could do with a space like this. She peeked through the next door and saw a large bathroom. She was curious to see what he had done in the bath but instead of snooping, she stepped deeper into the room-sized closet.

She pulled out a charcoal-gray suit first. "This is perfect." She then rifled through the button-down shirts and selected a light-blue shirt. "What do you have for ties?"

He pointed to a fold-out door. "Everything I have is hanging in there." If he was annoyed or amused, he wasn't letting on.

She selected a blue tie with a small geometric pattern and from the short stack of pocket squares selected a pale gray.

"There you go." She presented him with her selections. "The perfect outfit."

He leaned against the doorjamb. "Now that you've picked out my attire for the evening, may I ask what you're wearing? If the goal is to present a complimentary look."

She noticed a hook on the wall and hung the suit and shirt and arranged the pocket square in the coat pocket. "I've got a tan dress. Simple and tasteful."

He gave a single nod. "Okay then."

What she didn't say was it was an off-the-shoulder velvet dress that skimmed her knees while hugging her curves. She always went for elegance at these types of events.

"I'm sure you'll look pretty."

She felt a flash of warmth as he studied her. Maybe she should rethink her dress choice and go for something with more fabric.

*H*aving Tessa in his home was eye-opening. He wasn't sure if he wanted to throw open the doors and show her every detail or hustle her out as fast as he could. No one was more shocked than he when he suggested she stay and have a glass of wine. And then she actually said yes.

She strolled through his bedroom. With a quick look back through the glass doors, she said, "It really does scream for a small table and two chairs."

He could picture her sitting across from him, sipping a steaming cup of coffee on a cool morning, her face soft from sleep, her thick, dark auburn waves tumbling over her shoulders and framing her face. Where the hell had that image come from? With a shake of his head, he refocused on what she was saying.

"This space is amazing." She walked into the great room and crossed to the fireplace. Her fingertips trailed over the smooth fieldstones. "This is stunning. Excellent craftsmanship."

"I got lucky. I wasn't sure if I should go for brick or stone, but it turns out I made the right choice. It works."

"Gas?"

"Yeah. There's a switch to the right. Would you like to turn it on and have our wine there?" He uncorked the bottle.

She flicked the switch. The flames whooshed and illuminated her face in the soft glow. He uncorked a bottle of red.

"Cheese?"

"Sounds good. Can I help?"

"If you want to grab the glasses"—he pointed to the cabinet she was standing beside—"I'll bring in cheese and crackers."

Holding the glasses in one hand by the stems, she crossed the room and picked up the bottle of wine. She studied the label and looked at him.

"I didn't see this in the tasting room." She poured wine into each glass.

"It's something I bottled last year. It was a very small batch."

"The secret sixth variety." She swirled and inhaled the bouquet. "I detect notes of cherry and vanilla."

A hint of a smile played over his lips. "You knew about Fuse and never said anything?"

"I can be a very patient woman." She inhaled again. "This might have been worth the wait."

"Good nose." He plated some cheese and crackers and sliced an apple. "Ready."

The awkward silence enveloped them.

Tessa perched on the edge of the overstuffed leather chair near the fire. "You have a lovely home." She sipped her wine. "This is excellent."

He swirled the rich burgundy liquid and inhaled. "If we have a good harvest of the Fauch grapes next year, I want to make this again." He was surprised he was talking about next year.

Tessa eased back and crossed her legs. She rested the base of the glass on the arm of the chair. "You should. I think this is by far my favorite wine under the Creek label."

"Thanks." He sipped his wine to hide his crooked grin. Fuse was his favorite too.

"I'm curious."

He gave a low chuckle. "Aren't you always?"

She flushed a becoming shade of pink. "You're a comedian."

"I try." He brought the glass to his lips and took a drink. He liked this side of her, relaxed. "What's your question?"

"Are we going to be friends?"

After a moment of silence, he said, "You don't think we are?"

"It seems like we're at odds most every day, and I'd like to be good friends, not just co-workers."

"We're getting there." He smiled at her again. "Sitting here, sharing a bottle of wine and talking is a good step in our relationship." He cringed. Relationship? That word had way too many nuances to be used in this circumstance.

Slowly she said, "I'm nervous about tomorrow night."

Now, that surprised him. Tessa projected confidence. But like everyone, she must have her moments. "We've contacted everyone within a fifty-mile radius, and it sounds like we're going to have a full house. The rest is out of our hands."

Their eyes met. He felt a strong desire to take her in his arms. Maybe he'd lost his mind. He smothered a snort with a cough, which hopefully she didn't notice.

"I know. It's just the jitters. I want our warehouses to be emptied of inventory so that when we start bottling in February, we have shelves to fill."

"And we will."

A slow smile filled her face. "If we have to build a new warehouse to store our unsold wine, we will."

"That would be a good problem to have." He picked up the plate of cheese and passed it to her. "I'll tell you what. If we don't have great sales after tomorrow night, I'll give up my bonus for next year."

She took a slice of cheese. "In the spirit of optimism, I'll counter that. If we sell half our inventory before January first, I'll give you an additional bonus."

"I do like your confidence."

With a sassy little wink, she said, "You ain't seen nothing yet. I'm just getting started."

He was beginning to believe her.

She held up her glass. "To new friends."

essa looked at her reflection in the mirror. Maybe her dress should have been more conservative. This one was off-the-shoulder and showed more cleavage than she had realized. Oh, and it clung to her backside, too. Whoever said tan was boring hadn't seen this velvet dress off the hanger. She glanced at the clock next to her bed. There was no time to change. She took one last look, noting that she and Max would look sharp as they worked the room tonight.

She closed the door to her condo and drew her cashmere pashmina around her shoulders to ward off the early evening chill. The stars were just starting to make an appearance and she could see her breath on the air. Thank heavens it wasn't raining or, heaven forbid, an early snow. Just as she opened her car door, an SUV pulled up.

She glanced over. She didn't want to be late tonight. A window slid down and her eyes caught his. "Hi, Max."

"I thought we could ride together." His voice was smooth like a fine merlot.

"You don't mind bringing me home?"

With a lazy smile, he said, "I always bring people home when I drive."

She instantly thought of him dropping off a woman and wondered if he kissed on the first date. She pushed the question from her mind. This was business.

"Sure." She shut her car door and chirped the locks.

From inside the SUV, he stretched across the passenger seat to push open the door and she climbed in. "Nice perfume."

She flashed him a smile. "I'm not wearing any. Plain old soap and water."

He seemed to be at a loss for words and she felt bad that she made it awkward between them. He was just being nice.

"I don't wear perfume to these types of events. There will be enough scents in the air with flowers, food, and wine."

"That makes sense."

He drove through the twisting side roads. As he turned into the winery, the building awash with lights came into view. He stopped the car.

"Before things get crazy tonight, I wanted to say thanks. With your determination to put Creek on the path to success, I know tonight is going to be a huge hit."

"Thank you." She touched his hand. "We're going to make it a success."

He took his foot off the brake and eased down the rest of the driveway until he reached the back of the building where he parked. The door to the kitchen was propped open.

Tessa could see the waitstaff, dressed in all black, milling around inside.

"I hope the ties I bought arrived this afternoon."

He glanced at her. "Ties?"

"I bought each staff member a tie for tonight. A deep burgundy background with small grape clusters in purple with a dash of green for the leaves." She gave a one-shoulder shrug. "What can I say? They looked fun."

He gave a snort. "Who'd have guessed the proper vineyard owner would go for a whimsical tie?"

"I just hope they look as good in person as they did online." She pushed open her door. "Are you coming?"

"Of course. I can't wait to see the ties." He gave her a side-long look. "Does this mean I'm wearing one too?"

She tucked her long dark hair behind her ear, feeling her eyes twinkle. "Not a chance. I'm partial to blue."

✷

*H*e followed her through the back door and into organized chaos. Kate was giving directions in a firm, authoritative voice. "Everyone, doors open in thirty minutes, and we will be ready."

Tessa crossed the room and had a quiet word with her. Kate gave her a nod, and then she looked at Max. She gave him a quick thumbs-up as if to reassure him all was good.

His nerves were not as steady as he pretended. Putting himself out in front of a bunch of strangers was not his idea of a fun evening. However, watching Tessa move with confidence in that killer dress was worth it. He knew she was beautiful, but the way she looked tonight did nothing to keep him from thinking about her, and not like his boss.

She chewed her bottom lip as she moved around the tasting room, making slight adjustments to the vases of flowers. He stayed within easy reach in case she needed him to do anything.

She stopped and did a slow three-sixty. "This room looks better than I had hoped." She couldn't contain her smile. "Max, do you think you could check with the bartenders? Make sure they're prepared to answer all questions on each wine we're serving tonight." She waved a hand in the air. "Scratch that. I'm pulling everyone together for a quick review." She hurried to the kitchen and pushed open the door. "Can I have your attention? Meeting in the other room in two minutes." Without waiting to see if anyone heard, she went into the other room, confident people would follow her. She was like the Pied Piper.

Tessa stepped behind the bar and held her hand out for Max to join her. She was a whirlwind and he was fascinated to see what she was going to say next.

"Thank you, everyone, for working tonight. We're expecting approximately two hundred guests this evening and it's important you have a basic line or two for each wine." Her gaze roamed the group. "Kevin will give you a few pointers and if you have any questions during the evening, please ask. Giving a guest the wrong information is worse than having to get either me or Kevin. We'll be working the room and available at all times."

As Kevin gave a few tips about the different wines, her family drifted in, her parents in the back of the group. Anna waved in greeting. Without missing a beat, she and Liza came to the bar.

Tessa continued. "In addition to us, anyone in the Price family can answer questions. They've tasted the wines and know exactly how to respond."

A heavy weight filled Max's gut. He was going to hope for the best where Tessa's family was concerned even if they were like ants at a picnic. She was right that families did support each other. Hers wouldn't be an exception.

Her intense look bored into his eyes. She mouthed *relax*. It did little to quiet the churning in his gut.

Don stepped forward and gestured for him to go outside. Curious, Max wondered if he should follow or stay and support Tessa. She deserved to have a great night.

Max stepped through the front door. Before Don could speak, he said, "Thanks for coming to support your sister tonight."

Don's dark-brown eyes were steady. "That is exactly why we're here."

Max glanced over his shoulder. "Tonight is about Tessa's success. She's worked hard."

"You don't need to remind me. She left a huge hole at CLW. We'll get through it. Dad's stepped in to keep the sales team motivated and mentor Barb, our new marketing manager, but it's going to take a while." Don raked a hand through his hair. "I wanted you to know we're not the enemy, but your ally. And there is not one member of my family who would ever hurt another vineyard owner, let alone my sister. Tessa thinks she has something to prove to our father and me. She thought she was going to have CLW until I came home." His voice softened. "I'll do all I can to help her if for no other reason than I took her dream from her."

Max said, "We should go inside." He gave Don a firm handshake.

"She's lucky you have her back."

Tessa stuck her head out the door. "Guys, are you coming?"

"Right behind you, sis." Don followed her inside.

Tessa grinned. "Max, it's showtime!" And then the building went dark.

9

"*Max*, what happened?" she groaned. "We will have guests arriving in thirty minutes or less and we can't be without lights."

Max hurried to the door. "I'll check the breakers." Using the light on his phone, he raced to the storage room. Tessa stood by and felt helpless until she remembered she had seen a box of candles on a shelf in the kitchen.

"Liza, I'll be right back, but see if there is a way to put a candle in the middle of the flowers or somewhere on each table."

The emergency lights gave her enough illumination to get into the kitchen. Kate was still cooking, using cell phones for light. "Kate, what do you need?"

She was chopping parsley. Without missing a beat, she said, "If we keep the refrigerators shut as much as possible, the food will stay cold, but without hot water to wash dishes, we might have some issues."

Thinking fast, Tessa said, "If we run out of small plates, we'll need to use napkins. We won't have a choice. Hopefully it won't come to that." She moved a box aside and found the candles she was looking for.

Max rushed into the room. "Good news. It's not us and I've called the electric company. Bad news. No idea when we'll get electricity back."

She held up the candles. "We'll have light in the main room, but I'm worried about the water heater and the refrigerators." She looked at the swinging door. "I'll go find Don. Maybe he'll have a good idea."

"Hold on. I have a generator out back. I can hook it up and we'll be able to keep them running."

She gave him a momentary look and relaxed. Max had everything under control. "I'll take care of the candles and you'll get the generator." She flashed him a smile. "Meet you in the tasting room when you're done."

Tessa wished she could quiet her nerves. What if this had been a colossal mistake? The room was washed in candlelight and she never had to convince people to purchase CLW wine. She only had to entice new customers; building a business from the ground up was uncharted territory for her.

She smoothed the front of her dress and plastered a huge smile on her face. *Fake it till you make it* was the motto for tonight. She could feel Max's presence behind her as she made her way to the front of the room to address the staff. She glanced at him. For the record, the man sure knew how to wear a suit and handle a crisis. Anna was talking about the cab franc and one waiter asked her a question.

"What's the difference between this cab and a sauvignon?"

Tessa watched as Max acquiesced to Anna. Good for him. He was beginning to trust someone in her family.

"The franc has a lower acidity and tannins and is a lighter color. Although it's aged and will develop complex flavors, often it's more floral in nature. A key advantage for Sand

Creek, the franc grape grows well in the region and the sauvignon grape is more temperamental. This particular vintage is excellent." Anna smiled at Max. "Do you have anything to add?"

"No, that about covers it."

Tessa held up her hands. "Alright, everyone, it's time to put a smile on your face. Mix and mingle and make sure our guests have wine and something to nosh on. Be careful walking among the guests; the candles aren't as bright as I had hoped, but it does create an intimate setting. But most important: If anyone asks to place an order, get Kevin or me."

Kate called out, "Trays are ready."

Tessa held up her hand and Max gave her a high five. For her ears alone, he said, "You look beautiful."

Her cheeks grew warm at the compliment. "You're looking sharp yourself." The main door opened and leading the throng of people was the owner of Sawyers, one of the best restaurants in the region. Tessa walked over with her arms open and a welcoming smile.

"Alan, thank you for coming."

"Anything for you, Tessa, and besides, I'm excited to see what Kate's cooking up. And glad to see the power outage didn't cause you to cancel. I've been looking forward to tonight."

It didn't bother her that people came for Kate's food. She was confident they'd order the wines. Tessa laid her hand on his arm. "You won't be disappointed." She handed him a card. "We're suggesting you start with the white and finish with the cab franc."

With a laugh, Alan said, "Tee, go fuss over a novice. I know which wines I want to taste."

She gave him a quick peck on the cheek and went to greet the next couple coming through the door.

*M*ax wasn't about to let the current situation slow him down. He stuck out his hand. "Good to see you, Alan. How's business?"

"It was a good summer season. We'll have a lull before the holidays, and then I'm shutting down for January to recharge the batteries."

"I hear ya." A waiter was coming in their direction. "Since you seem to be on a mission, which wine do you want to try?"

"All of them." He flashed Max an amused look. "I've known Tessa all our lives and she likes to be in control. I like to keep her on her toes."

"Step up to the bar and I'll give you a personal tasting, but only if you give me some insight on my boss."

Alan slapped him on the back. "You're on."

The men made their way through the growing crowd to the long polished bar. Max was pleased so many people had turned out and maybe, he thought, this wasn't such a bad idea after all. It did sound like Alan might be placing an order. He hoped for a case.

Alan eased onto the barstool as Max took his place behind it. He set up five logo wineglasses. Alan picked one up and smiled.

"I see Tessa's handiwork."

"She did a great job. I have always hesitated to put the brand on everything, but she's right. They look great." He held up the bottle of white. "Interested in starting here?"

Alan slid his glass closer. "Absolutely."

Max poured about an ounce of wine. "I'll be right back."

He stepped from behind the bar and into the semi-darkened kitchen. "Kate, can you put together a plate of apps for me? I'm doing a tasting at the bar for Alan Waters."

She gave him an air high five. "Nice going. Give me two minutes."

"Thanks." He turned back to the tasting room and was stunned to see more people had arrived. He went back to Alan, who was sipping the white.

"I have a plate coming out—" But before he could finish his sentence, Kate set the plate down in front of Alan. *That was fast.*

"Kate, it's good to see you."

She took his hand. "You know the Price kids. All for one and one for all."

He gave her a wide grin. "How well I know."

She turned the plate around. "I have this set up in a clockwise pattern. Start at twelve and work your way around like the hands on a clock and for each wine, you'll have the perfect bite."

He peered closer. "I'm not even going to ask what it all is. I'm just going to savor the flavors." He gave her a sidelong look. "You know my offer stands. Anytime you want to throw in the pots at the bistro, I have a place for you at Sawyers."

"I'm happy right where I am, but thank you." She pointed back to the kitchen. "If you'll excuse me, I have work to do." She winked at Max and said to Alan, "Enjoy."

Alan stabbed a tiny meatball with a petite fork from the plate. He popped it in his mouth and closed his eyes. "Oh," he groaned. "Sweet, spicy, and a hefty punch of garlic."

Max hoped it wouldn't overpower the blush to come. *Kate knows what she's doing and is a well-respected chef.* He had to let go of some of these residual suspicions.

Alan finished the last drop of the white. "I want this on my order. Let's start with six cases."

Max didn't betray his surprise and nodded. "We can do that." After he'd tasted the blush, Alan increased his order.

Next on the plate was the barbeque chicken stuffed wonton paired with the Picnic Basket. He could see that Alan held the wine on his tongue before swallowing.

He nodded and wore a half-smile. "I'm not a fan of

sweeter reds, but this is interesting. I have been mulling over an idea. Next summer, I'd like to put together baskets for customers. This wine would be a nice change of pace from a white. People like to buy a complete basket for when they go to the lake or an open-air concert. Can you do me a favor?"

Max had no idea what he was going to ask but after committing to ten cases of the white and blush, he'd agree to just about anything.

"In April, can you bring a couple of bottles to the restaurant? We'll do some food pairings, and then I'll place an order. If they sell well, it will turn into a nice offshoot for both of us."

He had never had this much success so easily. "Not a problem." Tessa had been right about this event. His admiration for her grew.

Alan finished the last appetizer and the red wines and placed the napkin aside. "Each wine is excellent and I'm not sure which one is my favorite."

"I hope the food didn't overpower the wine."

"Kate did an awesome job. I wonder if she'd share any of these recipes with an old family friend."

"Speaking of old friends, you were going to give me the skinny on Tessa."

Max looked over Alan's head and his eyes met hers. She smiled in his direction and mouthed, *All good?*

He gave her a wink.

Alan turned around and then looked at Max. "I don't think you're going to need my help. It's easy to see you're getting along just fine."

Max tore his gaze away from Tessa. "Thank you for coming in tonight."

Alan said, "Kevin, I'd like to order six cases of the reds."

"And four of the whites?"

He picked up his glass. "Let's make it six cases of each of the four wines. When can I expect delivery?"

"Tomorrow?" He couldn't believe it had been this easy to sell cases of wine. If the orders stayed this strong, they might just have a great night, especially if Tessa was taking orders too.

"Alan, I'm curious. Why haven't you ordered before?"

He seemed to size Max up before answering. "It's about a relationship. Other wineries make the effort to stop by and share different wines with me. This is the first time I've been invited to try anything from Sand Creek."

Humbled, he said, "I appreciate your honesty."

"And Tessa... She's smart, trusts slowly, and is one of the hardest-working people I've ever met." He turned to walk away and then as an afterthought said, "She's loyal, almost to a fault."

He watched as Alan walked away. Family loyalty is strong, so where would that leave him?

---

*T*essa watched the exchange between Max and Alan. From the look on Max's face and the notes he was jotting down, it had been a productive conversation. She was dying to know how many cases Alan had ordered, but that would have to wait.

She worked the room, pleased to see her parents walking around with bottles of wine, refilling glasses. Dad might not say it, but this was his way of showing support, and he firmly believed in putting the customer first. Anna was passing food and sharing her thoughts on Creek wines. Don, Jack, and Leo weren't in the main room, but Tessa knew they were making themselves useful. And then there was Liza, constantly in motion, checking in with the waitstaff and bartenders. No detail would be overlooked while she was working, and the lack of electricity hadn't caused a misstep with guests at all.

Tessa was thrilled. This was the beginning of a turning point for the winery.

Max slid up beside her. "How's it going?" he asked softly.

"Better than I had hoped. We'll get some nice sales tonight, and then it will be up to us to keep filling the pipeline." She placed her hand on his arm. "Did it go well with Alan?"

"Twenty-four cases to start, and he wants to do picnic baskets in the spring and summer featuring a white and Picnic Basket."

"That's awesome." She kept her voice low to control her exuberance. "He's well respected and once other restaurant owners catch wind he's carrying our wines, they'll order just to stay on the same playing field."

"He's a trendsetter. Interesting."

Tessa suggested, "At the end of the evening, let's take a bottle with us. We deserve a nightcap."

"Sounds good. I'll see if Kate can put a few apps aside for us too. I don't know about you, but I'm starving."

Tessa couldn't help but notice how his blue eyes sparkled. She reached up and pushed a lock of dark hair away from his forehead. Her eyes slid to his mouth, which was sexy as hell. She wanted to see for herself if they were kissably soft. "I like how you think."

Softly, he said, "Until later."

10

*O*ne by one, Tessa's family made the rounds to say good night as the last of the guests' taillights disappeared down the drive. Tessa longed to slip off her heels and massage her aching feet. Taking halting steps, she sank to a barstool. The electricity came on, washing the room in bright light. *Perfect timing.*

Mom and Dad were headed in her direction with their coats on. They looked as fresh as they had six hours ago.

Mom said, "Sweetie, you look exhausted."

Tessa looked at her dad. "You two look like you're ready for a night on the town. How do you do it?"

"Easy," Dad said. "It wasn't our party, so we didn't have any stress. All we had to do was enjoy ourselves."

"You worked the room like pros."

"Talking with friends is hardly work." Dad gave her a hug. "I'm proud of you, Tessa. I overheard Kevin talking to Alan, and your delivery people are going to be busy."

"I'd better wear sneakers tomorrow. I'm pretty sure we have one guy and he'll never get everything delivered in a timely manner."

"It's a good problem to have, Tee." Mom kissed her cheek. "We'll talk tomorrow."

Dad patted her shoulder. "You're on track for success."

That was high praise from her father, but there was a part of her that wished he'd come right out and say he was proud of her. "Thanks, Dad. And you too, Mom."

Max walked in from the storage room. "Mr. and Mrs. Price. Thank you for your help tonight."

Mom said, "It's Sam and Sherry."

Tessa held back a grin. Leave it to Mom to put Max at ease.

Mom continued. "No matter what, our family supports each other. We only want what's best for our daughter."

Max shook hands with both of Tessa's parents. "Thanks again."

Dad shook his hand. "I'm sure we'll be seeing you again."

Mom piped up. "Come for dinner on Sunday. The whole family will be there, and we always have room for more. Although be warned. We're a loud and noisy bunch."

"Thank you," he said and paused. "Sherry." He hesitated before giving Tessa a small smile. "I might take you up on that."

"Good night," Dad said. Hand in hand, her parents walked out the door.

It filled Tessa's heart with happiness. After all these years, her parents were a strong team. She could feel Max watching her watch them.

"So, what do you think of them?"

"In all honesty, not what I expected. The few times I met Sam, he was less than friendly."

"Mom softens him. He's a marshmallow when she's around." She yawned. "Are you ready to hit the road?"

He held out his hand to help her off the stool. "Do you want to hold off on the celebration drink?"

With a shake of her head, Tessa said, "No. I've been

looking forward to it. Besides, I'll catch a second wind from the fresh air." She took one last look around the room. "The staff did an excellent job cleaning up."

He withdrew his car keys and depressed the button on the key fob. "The car is warming up and I'll lock up the front and we'll go out the back."

Tessa placed the rest of the empty glasses on a tray and hobbled into the kitchen. She wasn't surprised to see it was spotless. A plate covered with foil sat on the counter. Kate had remembered.

"Everything's all set out front." Max came into the kitchen. "We'll finish cleaning up tomorrow. Did Kate leave..." His voice trailed off as Tessa pointed to the foil-covered plate.

"I can't wait to try everything she made tonight. I don't even remember if I ate lunch." She drew her shawl around her shoulders, grateful she didn't have to climb the stairs to her office to retrieve it. "I can't wait to get these shoes off and put on a pair of soft thick socks."

Max held the door open for her and Tessa stepped outside. The chilly temperatures cooled her exposed skin after the warmth of all the people at the party and she shivered. "The temperature's dropped." She looked at the star-filled sky.

The frost-covered grass crunched under their feet as they walked to the car.

She inhaled the crisp air. "I just love this time of year. All the vines are drifting into a long nap, giving us time to plan for what comes next." She touched Max's arm. "Don't you think?"

"I never really thought of it like that, but I guess you're right." He opened the passenger door and Tessa climbed inside.

"Thanks for warming up the car. It was very thoughtful."

He closed the door and strolled around the back. Glancing at the vines, he felt a surge of pride. Whatever happened in the future, he had a hand in it. But did he really want to leave all of this behind and start over? The prospect of a new beginning was daunting.

During the drive, they talked as if they had been friends forever instead of mere weeks.

"Tonight was fun." She pulled her shawl close to her throat.

"Are you cold? I can turn up the heat."

"We're almost to my place. The turn is just up ahead." She pointed to a small driveway on the left. "Turn here. It's the back entrance to the complex."

He flicked on his blinker and slowed the SUV. The road was deserted, and the full moon was high.

He parked next to her car. "Are you sure you want me to come in?"

"Yes." She tilted her head. "Did you remember the wine?"

"It's in the back. I snuck it out during the party."

"Were you afraid we wouldn't have any left?" She winked.

With a low chuckle, he said, "The way those people were drinking, you never know."

She pushed open the door and winced. "My toes are weeping. I needed to get my shoes off, like an hour ago."

"Don't let me slow you down." He leaned over the console and grabbed the bottle and plate.

Tessa waited for him on the walkway and took his hand. She wasn't surprised at the warmth that emanated from him. If she hadn't known better, this might resemble a date.

As they approached the door, he took her house key from her, unlocked the door, and pushed it open. "I've never seen a grape cluster key ring before."

She dropped the key ring in her bag. "It's fun and I can always find them in any of my bags." The instant she stepped on the tile entranceway, she flicked first one shoe and then the other off. Max couldn't close the door, as Tessa stood in the doorway and sighed.

"Are we going to stand here for a while?"

She gingerly walked into the great room. Max joined her. She took the bottle of wine. "Make yourself comfortable and I'll pop the cork." She glanced at the label. "Fuse. This is your special reserve."

"I thought it was a good choice for us to celebrate."

Tessa watched as he wandered around the room. "Your home is nice. The fireplace is unexpected."

"It's one of the reasons why I bought it. Well, that and the deck."

He stood by the glass door. She flicked on the light switch and the deck was illuminated. The glow extended just past the steps. He gave her a knowing smile. "I see you have a small table."

"Guilty as charged." She uncorked the bottle and poured two glasses. "Now you can see how nice it looks."

Max flipped the lock and stepped into the frigid night air. He walked to the railing and looked around. "It's nice out here," he called over his shoulder. "Join me?"

She put the plate of food in the middle of the coffee table and, still barefoot, stepped onto the deck, moving from one foot to the other. "It's freezing."

"Convince me I should get a table." His smile grew wide.

"Now?" She felt herself get pulled into the fun and literally tiptoed across the deck to a metal chair and carefully perched on the edge. "Have a seat." The cold metal was like ice against the back of her legs and derriere.

He eased into the other chair. Surprise flitted over his face. "Chairs are a bit cold."

"Lean back and look around. Imagine this at your place. Sipping a hot beverage, maybe mulled cider. Just think of the romantic possibilities."

What did I just say, talking about romance?

He cocked his head. "You make a good point."

Tessa felt a deep shiver stretch from her freezing toes to the tips of her hair. She couldn't help it. It was frigid out here in no shoes and a cocktail dress. Even if it was velvet, there was a lot of exposed skin.

"Let's go inside. You're freezing." With his hand on the small of her back, he guided her inside.

They stepped into the warmth of the living room area and she took a throw from the back of the chair and draped it around her shoulders.

"Are you warmer now?" His voice was gentle.

"Much." She looked through her lowered lashes. She didn't name the feelings that were becoming stronger each time she was with him. *Did he sense it too?*

His voice broke the spell that was spinning around her. "I'll get our wine."

She tucked her feet under the plush velour throw as she sank deeper in the sofa cushions and watched as he poured the wine. This reminded her of when her parents would come home after an evening out and unwind, sharing a glass of wine together.

Max handed her a glass. "You still look cold."

"I'm going to turn the fireplace on."

She had started to get up when he said, "I've got it."

She pointed to the side of the mantel. "Thanks. The switch is on the right."

Within seconds, the flames came to life, giving the room a soft glow and a cozy feel.

He eased onto the sofa. "Try the wine."

She took a sip. The warmth spread through her. "It's very good."

He clinked his glass to hers and gave her a crooked smile. "I want you to know I was wrong. The event was amazing and by what I booked alone, we have a lot of new customers."

With a laugh, she tilted her head and cupped her cheek in her hand. "Did I just hear you say you were wrong?"

"Hey, I can be a man and admit it."

"Good." She felt a slow smile ease across her face. "Sales were exceptional tonight. Better than I expected."

"If there is one thing I've learned in the last few weeks, it's that you make things happen."

She sipped her wine. "This really is delicious."

"It's a specific blend of grapes, and I played around with aging. It didn't hurt that it was an exceptional growing season."

Tessa set the plate on the couch between them. The firelight reflected in his glass. "What's our next step?"

"As far as?" Max looked deep in her eyes.

Her heart skipped. She steered the conversation to business. "Is there Fuse in the tanks?"

"I never really thought anyone would like this blend, but I'm glad you do." He bit into an empanada.

"This would be a bestseller." She inhaled the bouquet and then tasted it again. "The tannins mellowed, and it has a very smooth finish." She repeated her question. "Is there any in the tanks?"

He gave her a slow nod. "There is."

"How many gallons?" Her marketing ideas began to churn. "We'll develop a campaign to launch this in, what, two years?"

"Well, actually, I have about sixty-five gallons, one oak barrel. Which will give us…"

Tessa interjected, "Approximately three hundred fifty bottles. That's not a lot, but that makes it scarce, and scarcity drives up the price." She tapped her finger on a soft cushion. "How much is bottled?"

He didn't answer her. "I'm not sure if we should do an aggressive marketing campaign."

She felt her eyes go wide. "Why not? We're in business to

turn a profit, and if Fuse can help us do that, why wouldn't we?"

"The other wines we produce are better suited for restaurants and stores. Fuse isn't the right blend to put a ton of money behind."

"Then why did you bother to make it?" She arched a brow. Curious, she asked, "Max. Did you make more this year?"

"I did. We have about a hundred thirty-five gallons in steel. Soon to be transferred to oak and we have another thirty gallons that will need to be bottled late winter."

"Then it makes even more sense to create a slow burn kind of campaign."

He set his glass on the table. "I know you own the company, but I respectfully disagree. This shouldn't be commercially available. I created this blend as my first attempt at something unique." He stood up. "I'll see you tomorrow."

Tessa's mouth fell open as she watched him walk through the door. It closed with a soft thud. What had just happened? They went from celebrating to a minor disagreement, and then he leaves? *I just don't get him. And he never said how much was actually bottled, and if it was not to be sold, why did he make so much of it?* Her intuition screamed Fuse was their golden ticket.

The house felt empty now that she was alone.

⁓

*M*ax didn't know what to think. One minute they were having a nice conversation about the future of Creek, and the next, he was in a cold car alone. What was Tessa's problem? Trying to take something that wasn't meant for the public and release it. The wine was a work in progress. Maybe next year it would be ready, but he needed more time. "Will I even be here next year?" His breath came out in puffs of frost. The pull to stay was getting stronger than the push to leave.

He smacked the steering wheel with the palm of his hand. He needed to talk to Stella, but it was way too late to call her now. Now that the reconstructive surgery and radiation were behind her, she had to rebuild her strength.

Oh, Stella. He groaned. Maybe he should have talked to her before he signed Tessa's contract. On top of all of that, he wanted to dislike his boss, but instead he was having intense feelings for her. He shook his head. *Talk about being conflicted.*

He had been lucky to purchase a healthy vineyard as far as the vines were concerned, but it was the process of making the wine that had been difficult. He had learned so much and now should be the time he was reaping the rewards. If he were to leave now, he'd never get to do that. But maybe, just maybe with Tessa the future could be different.

He gave a snort. "Fruits. Grapes. Wine. Repeat."

Here Tessa had swept in with marketing know-how, but he was the one who had developed the wines, and they were damn good. He slammed on his brakes.

A deer stood in the middle of the road. With a flash, it was gone, unscathed. He eased his foot from the brake and looked right and left. The road was clear. Exhaustion overwhelmed him. He'd call Stella tomorrow. And from experience, he had faith things usually did look better in the light of day.

$\mathcal{T}$he next day, Max took the stairs two at a time. He needed to talk to Tessa. He could hear her talking, but to who? He knew he shouldn't but he stopped to listen.

"I don't understand why he's fighting me every step of the way. I want this business to thrive, and after last night, it's obvious we have a fantastic product."

She grew silent. He could hear her pencil tapping on the tabletop. He had discovered it was her habit when she was oblivious to anything around her and engrossed in a conversation. Should he walk in or continue to eavesdrop?

"I know it has to be hard for him. But I didn't put him in the position of having to sell out." Another brief pause. "It's not my story to tell."

Whoever she was talking to must have asked why he sold the business. Alan had said she was loyal to the people in her life, and it seemed she was now extending that him. He was stunned she was keeping his confidence and he had to admire her. He cleared his throat and stepped into the office.

She glanced up. "I gotta go. I'll talk to you later." She set her cell phone on the table. "Good morning." Her voice was clipped.

He deserved the icy tone after his behavior last night. "Morning."

She pushed back from the table and picked up her coffee cup.

He couldn't help but notice she was dressed in jeans and a deep-purple button-down shirt. She padded across the room in socks. Her hair was pulled off her face in a clip, with waves tumbling around her shoulders. She was as pretty in casual clothes as she was dressed up. But he had to take care of business first before getting sidetracked by her beautiful face.

"Listen, about last night."

Without looking at him, she fixed herself a cup of coffee. She didn't ask if he wanted one.

"I'm sorry for being an ass. And not just last night, but since you walked in here from day one. You did nothing wrong except purchase the business, and you've given me an opportunity to fulfill my dream of making wine."

She pressed her lips together and turned away before lifting her eyes to his. "I'm not the enemy hell-bent to destroy what you've built."

"I know." Stella had been right. He needed to give Tessa a chance before he jumped to conclusions. She hadn't done anything to indicate she was going to sell out. Did he think because he hadn't been successful that she too would fail?

She quirked her eyebrow. "What changed?"

He held up his hands. "My sister gave me a different perspective."

Tessa smiled for the first time since he walked in. "You mean she doesn't pull any punches?"

"Something like that." He felt his shoulders sag into a more relaxed posture.

She absentmindedly swirled her spoon in the mug. "Does this mean you're ready to talk about our next step?"

"If you haven't decided to fire me."

She crossed the room and sat down in her chair. "No, I

haven't. We've got work to do." She gestured to a spot across the table. "Take a seat." She was all business, and this was the Tessa he knew.

She passed him a printed copy of the orders they had taken last night. They had orders similar to the one Alan Waters had placed, plus a few smaller ones.

"We have commitments for over one hundred and thirty cases."

"Not bad. Best single day of sales in the history of Sand Creek."

She gave him a sidelong look. "And it's just the beginning. About fifteen percent of the businesses who came ordered, so there is still a huge opportunity."

A flash of surprise passed over his face. "Are you disappointed? What did you expect?"

"Ten percent."

"Really?"

She gave him a grin. "Aim high but be realistic." She slid another paper across the tabletop. "There's a food and wine event in March. We should rent a booth."

"What does it entail?" He scanned the vendor application. "How come it's only a couple hundred bucks?"

She flipped him a grin. "It's just to get the space. We'll be giving away samples, and then we hopefully make sales. We also will have travel expenses. It's in Boston. I already called and we're on a wait list."

"They have a waiting list."

She nodded and said, "There's another one in New York City in April that has space."

He handed Tessa the paper. He wasn't sure if she expected him to challenge her, but he was willing to give it a go. "I've never had time to go to those events. Sounds interesting."

Her eyes widened. "You're full of surprises today."

"I want this new iteration of Creek to be a success. For both of us."

"Well, good." Her cell rang and she answered it. "Tessa Price."

Max left the office and went to the tasting room. He could finish getting everything cleaned up. The first thing he started with was the dishwasher, and then he moved on to gathering the linen bags for pickup. The kitchen was spotless, thanks to Kate. He marveled at how well everything had gone, and sales had been better than he had imagined.

"Max, are you down there?"

He jogged to the bottom of the stairs and looked up. "Looking for me?"

"You're never going to believe what just happened!" She was beaming.

"Don't keep me hanging. Spill it."

"Have you heard of Edwards in Buffalo?"

"Yeah. I've eaten there a couple of times. It's top-shelf."

She did a happy jig on the landing. "Well, I know the owner, Charles, through my dad, and we were just asked to bring a case of each wine for a meeting tomorrow."

"You're kidding. How did they find out about us?"

"I hadn't called him yet, so my guess is that someone who was here last night must have tipped them off." She began to turn and then stopped. "We're taking two cases of Fuse. Charles will go nuts over it." She gave him a pointed smile before disappearing from view.

He sank to the step. Damn. Things were changing at lightning speed. They might just make a dent in the inventory before the holidays. He wondered what else they could do to boost sales. Maybe special case pricing for the remainder of the year; he'd ask Tessa what she thought. He'd work the tasting room to keep the overhead cost down.

His cell phone pinged. It was his real estate agent. He'd call him back later; there was too much to do to get ready for tomorrow.

He finished up in the tasting room and realized it had

been pretty quiet upstairs since Tessa had announced their meeting.

He stood in the doorway and watched her for a few moments. She had her sock-clad feet propped up and her eyes closed. Was she sleeping or thinking?

Without opening her eyes, she said, "I know you're there."

"What are you doing?"

"Plotting."

He laughed at the truth of her simple word. "To conquer the world of wine?" He walked in and took his usual chair.

Slowly, she opened her eyes. "Has your brain been spinning?"

"Yes, and I have a few ideas. Nothing as grand as last night's event, but what if we run a special on full cases of wine from now until the new year? People love to give alcohol for gifts; it's easy and universal, and if we give an incentive to buy, we can see trends for next season and what locals seem to prefer."

"I like it." She dropped her feet on the floor and sat up. "I'll place a few ads in the local paper and see what that drums up." She snapped her fingers. "You know what else we could do? A toy drive! For every unwrapped toy that someone deposits in our donation box, they get a ten percent discount off a case. I might even try to get radio coverage for the first Sunday in December."

"Ambitious, but I like the way your brain works. Do you think a toy drive is appropriate for a winery?"

She flashed him a killer smile. "When people feel good about giving to those in need and they get a benefit, everyone wins. Including us."

He admired how she added giving back to the community with an idea to boost sales. She wasn't all about profits.

"I've got everything set for tomorrow," he said. "Instead of driving the delivery truck, we'll take my SUV. We'll be more comfortable."

"Good idea. Also, I checked the weather earlier and there's a chance for a dusting of snow late day, but we should be home before it starts." She checked her cell and set it aside. "The forecast hasn't changed."

"If it goes well, we should go out for dinner to celebrate. I could make a reservation at Sawyers."

She shook her finger and head. "Don't jinx us. Let's get a commitment from Charles first, and we can always walk in midweek. The restaurant will have open tables or we can always sit in the bar."

He really wanted to spend more time with her away from the winery. "Want to grab a quick dinner tonight?" It was important to determine if these feelings that were simmering had something to do with the winery or with the woman.

Without hesitation, she said, "I could go for Italian."

Unprepared for her to agree so quickly, he said, "I haven't had pasta in ages."

She looked at her watch. "Now? We can have an early dinner so I can get home. I have a few things to do tonight."

"Sure, we can leave now. I'll meet you at Anthony's. Unless you want to ride together."

Tessa closed her laptop and slid it into her bag. "You'll just have to bring me back here, so I'll drive."

"I live around the corner so it's not a problem." He didn't want to push it and make things awkward between them. They crossed to the doorway and she turned off the overhead lights.

"Max, have I turned you into a believer yet?"

"That Sand Creek Winery is the next hottest venture in the Finger Lakes?"

The smile she flashed said it all. She was sure they had just tapped the tip of the opportunities. "We are." She touched the center of her chest. "I can feel it in here."

The temptation to kiss her was strong. Instead, he said, "If sales continue to roll like they did last night, you'll put Creek on the map."

She laughed. "We're on the map, but at the moment one of the best secrets in the region."

"Not anymore. Tessa, you changed that last night."

She gave him a playful poke in the arm. "Hallelujah. You're starting to see the light."

"Sometimes it takes me a while." They crossed the landing and Max said, "Come on. I'll let you buy me a drink."

A gleam came into her eye. "Beverages are on you, Max. Last night's order exceeded your expectations, so not only are drinks, but I think dinner might be too."

He liked her when she was full of smiles and laughter. He really had come into their situation with the wrong idea.

They reached the bottom of the stairs and he pushed open the door for her. "What do you drink besides wine?"

"Are you mocking me? Because I happen to like so much more. Beer, mixed drinks, and even occasionally bourbon on the rocks. But give me a good dirty martini and I'm all yours." Pink reached her cheeks. She stammered, "Well, you know what I mean."

"Vodka or gin?" Whichever she chose, he was going to make sure he had it in stock at his place.

She opened her car door and flashed him a brilliant smile. "Vodka, and the olives are stuffed with blue cheese."

"Good to know." Now all Max had to do was find out her favorite vodka and see where he could get the olives. "But tonight, it's Italian and red wine."

*T*essa pulled into the winery parking area. Max was closing the hatch on his SUV and he waved. Relief coursed through her. They were ahead of schedule.

"Morning," she called as her feet stepped onto the gravel.

"Good morning, Tessa." His smile reached his eyes and he took her black leather bag. "Do you need to go inside?"

"No. I'm ready." She wanted to squeal to release some of her excitement, but she maintained her professional façade.

"You look nice today." He opened the passenger door.

Always the gentleman. "Thank you. I want to make a good impression even though I've been to Edwards many times. With this being the first time as the president of Creek, I'm looking to set the tone."

She noticed he had on khakis, a navy jacket, and a pinstriped shirt. "You're looking sharp too."

"We're on the same wavelength, and I have something to prove." He closed the door and got in the driver's seat. "Do you have the address? I'll program the navigation system."

She pulled her phone from her coat pocket. "Right here." She read it off to him and he punched in the information.

"We'll be an hour early leaving now." He rubbed the back of his neck.

"I'd rather be early and find a place to get a coffee than stress about the drive." He wouldn't look at her; was he as nervous as she was? "Are you okay with that?"

"Sure. Whatever you think is best." He eased out of the drive, picking up speed on the two-lane road. "Dinner was fun last night."

"It was. I haven't laughed that much in a long time. Your stories of taking over the winery were priceless. And you really had no idea how to make more than a few gallons of wine when you bought the place?"

"Nope. I understood how to grow grapes, but reading online wasn't the best way to learn mass scale wine production. It is definitely not the same as making wine at home."

She laughed and shook her head. "I've never tried."

"Well, you can skip that. We've got it under control now. How did you sleep?"

"Not good. This meeting was so unexpected that I kept trying to figure out how we would present our wines, including Fuse."

He glanced her way. "Do you really think it's that good?"

Tessa turned in the seat to look at him. "You have no idea, do you? If I had tasted it when I worked for CLW, I would have encouraged you to enter it in competitions. In fact, that's something we need to talk about."

He gave her a crooked smile. "Will you always push this hard?"

"When I'm sure of the direction we should be going?"

"Yeah."

"You can count on it. I'm not going to sit around, hoping the buying public will just happen to discover us. I'll use every trick in my arsenal to put and keep Creek on the map!"

Max slowed as they approached the interstate ramp. He merged with traffic and remained quiet. Once he began to pick up speed, he gave her a quick glance. "You can count on me to follow your lead."

She leaned back in her seat. "Why the change of heart?"

"I want Creek to do well. Obviously, I didn't have the marketing skills to make it happen. Whereas you have the drive and determination." He flashed her another look. "And if I'm being transparent, it's the right thing to do for both of us. If you're successful, I am too."

"How's your sister doing?"

His grip tightened on the steering wheel. "Good. It's been a long road and the cancer physically and mentally kicked her butt. However, each day, she gets stronger. She's a survivor."

"Why isn't she here in Crescent Lake?" Tessa couldn't help but push him a bit. She knew firsthand that family support meant everything in a health crisis. Her family had rallied together during her father's heart attack. She couldn't imagine what it would have been like to be alone and dealing with cancer.

"She has a small apartment near Sloane Kettering. When she's ready, I'm hoping she moves to be near me. It's just the two of us since our dad died."

"How old were you when he passed?"

"I was twenty-two and Stella was seventeen."

"That's rough. Can I ask what kind of cancer did Stella have?"

"Breast, like Mom. The biggest differences in their outcomes, our mom put off going to the doctor and my sister was young when she was diagnosed."

Tessa touched his arm. "I'm so sorry."

"Thanks. I'm grateful they caught it early, even though it was an aggressive form. After her mastectomy, she had radiation and an experimental drug therapy. With our family history, she wanted to be close to her doctors."

"Do you get to the city often?" She couldn't help but wonder who Stella had as a support system in New York.

"I was there for surgery and the start of radiation, and we talk almost every day. She had side effects from the medications, so it took some time to work through that." His face brightened. "She's coming for Thanksgiving."

She almost blurted out an invitation to the Price family chaos but held her tongue. Mom knew she was always bringing home an eclectic group of friends for the holiday, but maybe she'd wait to see if this new working relationship continued. Especially since he hadn't gone to Sunday dinner after Mom had invited him.

"That sounds nice." She gazed out the windshield and noticed the signs for Orchard Park. They were making good time.

"Did you go into the city last year for Thanksgiving?"

"I did. Stella is on this kick of doing things we've never done before. She's always wanted to see the Thanksgiving Day parade in person, so we went. It was freezing cold, but her happiness"—his face softened—"was worth every extra layer I had to wear."

"That's something my family would do for one of us too."

Max glanced at his watch. "We're early. Are you hungry? We could stop for a late breakfast."

Tessa pressed her palm to her midsection. "I don't think I could eat, but coffee sounds good."

"I didn't think you'd be nervous."

"It's different this time." She pointed to a sign. "There's a diner at the next exit."

Softly, she said, "My dad paved the way for my success in pitching new wines and the traditional offerings. Don't get me wrong. I still had to know how to market, but I was always propped up by CLW's reputation. This is the first time I'm walking in without history."

"You're wrong. You have your personal reputation and business ethics, and that counts in any business."

She clasped her hands together. "I hope you're right."

He slowed to take the exit. "I haven't seen you in action in front of potential customers, except for the reception, which was impressive. But your reputation is stellar. You have nothing to worry about. Just be you."

His smile crushed her nerves. "Thanks."

᠅

*M*ax waited while Tessa retrieved her bag from the back. He wondered how this woman, who appeared confident and fearless, could think for a single moment that she wouldn't walk into the meeting and emerge successful.

"You look good in dark blue."

"I'm hoping to impress." He winked. "How am I doing?"

"The customers or me?"

Max winked again. "Who knows? Maybe both."

Her eyes twinkled. "Hopefully the customer will appreciate your efforts."

He clutched the middle of his chest. "You've wounded me."

"Come on. After that display of soft underbelly, I'm buying." Tessa held open the door for him. "Gentleman first."

As much as it went against his upbringing, he entered the fifties-style diner first. It was complete with the black-and-white-checked floor, a gleaming stainless-steel-rimmed counter and stools, and splashes of red strategically placed to draw the eye, like the pie case and cake domes. An old-fashioned jukebox stood in the corner, just begging for someone to drop in a few coins. The sign on the podium indicated they could seat themselves. Tessa was one step behind him.

He pointed to a booth in front of a large window. "How's that?"

"After you." They slipped in the booth over slippery red vinyl cushions. She opened up a menu.

Tilting his head to one side, he asked, "I thought you weren't hungry?"

"I'm thinking maybe an English Muffin or something light would be good." She wrinkled her nose. "But no eggs or bacon."

"You don't like them?"

She looked over the top of the large laminated menu. "What's not to like? Thick, crisp bacon and creamy scrambled eggs, with ketchup of course. Add a side of blueberry pancakes with pure maple syrup." She smacked her lips. "Yum."

Taken aback, he grinned. "I take it you like breakfast."

"It's my favorite meal to eat out. Just not before the biggest meeting of my career." She dropped her gaze and groaned softly. "They have the perfect platter."

His eyes skimmed the menu. "Where?"

She tilted his menu down and pointed at the page. "Right here."

"It's exactly what you described." He set the menu aside. "We can stop here on the way home if you want."

The waitress approached their table. She was wearing the iconic uniform: a light-blue button-down dress with a white collar and short sleeves that grazed the elbows with dark-blue piping around the edges. Her hair was pulled up into a high ponytail and she sported well-made running shoes, also in blue.

"Hey there. What can I get ya today?"

"Coffee and a cranberry muffin for me." Tessa handed her menu to the waitress.

Max hesitated. "I'll have the veggie omelet, wheat toast, and coffee."

She didn't write anything down. "I'll be right back with your coffee."

Tessa handed him a paper napkin. "I can't help but wonder. How much white wine did you chill?"

Before Max answered, two beige ceramic mugs were set in front of them, along with a pitcher of cream. Tessa fixed her coffee while looking at him.

"I chilled two bottles of the blush and white and stored the rest of the case in the back. I also brought two cases of Fuse, a case each of shiraz and the cab franc."

"Did you bring Picnic Basket?"

He took a sip of the rich, strong coffee. "I did, but I think we should leave it in the car. After carefully reviewing the restaurant's website, it's not a good fit."

Tessa held the mug between her hands, her elbows propped on the red Formica tabletop. "I think we should bring in a bottle or two. We can leave the rest in the car."

"Why?"

"It's a fun, unpretentious wine and I'd like to showcase all that we have. You just never know if they have a need for something a little different from the norm." She sipped and set her cup down. "Whatever happens today happens. We're on the right path, and that's all that I care about. For our first month, we've come a long way."

"What have you done with Tessa Price?"

The waitress set down his plate and her steaming muffin and moved away.

Tessa leaned into the tufted back cushion. She wore a thoughtful look. "I just might be evolving into the kind of businesswoman I'm meant to be: relaxed, confident, and with a good partner to support the journey."

"You can count on me." Max picked up a forkful of eggs. His eyes twinkled. "Partner."

She cut her muffin in half and added butter. She had thought to wait until later but casually she said, "You know my family has a huge Thanksgiving dinner every year. You and your sister should come."

"I wouldn't want to intrude on a family event."

With a chuckle, she said, "We're not the Norman Rockwell holiday. It's a huge group, loud, kids running around, lots of food, and of course football."

He tipped his head to one side. "It sounds like fun. I'll check with Stella and if she's up for it, count us in." With a chuckle, he said, "I'll bring the wine."

She grinned. "Dad will love that."

---

13

*T*essa rehearsed her opening line, mentally walking through the door right up to her handshake with the owner.

"Max, did you bring a cart so that we can transport the wine in the restaurant?"

"Relax. I have a dolly and I'll make two trips." He gave her a reassuring smile. "We've got this."

"I know. Will you make a deal with me?" She could hear the slight quiver of anticipation in her voice.

"Sure."

"If they buy any wine, we'll definitely have a celebratory dinner." She gave him a wide smile. Her nerves were kicking in again and she really didn't understand why, but she wasn't going to show Max. This should be a cakewalk.

He touched her hand, which was resting on the console. "I thought we had dinner plans, but you're on."

She took a deep breath. "There it is." She pointed to a turn on the right.

"The restaurant is bigger than I thought."

Tessa peered out the windshield and pointed to a spot near the door. "They can seat two hundred people at a time.

Typically, they have a line of customers before they even open the doors, and the reservation list is never-ending."

"Impressive." He flashed her a self-assured smile. "Let's introduce them to some excellent wine."

They got out and Max pulled out the portable dolly and loaded half the cases on it. He slipped the four chilled bottles of wine into an insulated bag and handed that to Tessa. She tucked the strap over her shoulder, and they crossed the parking area.

A tall, thin young man rushed out. He had bright-red hair and a liberal dash of freckles across his fair skin. She guessed he must have a bit of Irish in him, based on his coloring. "Please allow me to assist you." His voice was thick with a British accent. He clasped the handles of the dolly and eased Max from behind it. "Allow me."

"Thank you," Tessa said. "I'm Tessa Price and this is Kevin Maxwell."

Max took the insulated bag from her.

"Gordon, ma'am, but we met once before." He gave her a warm smile. "Would you mind holding the door?"

"I'm sorry for the momentary lapse." She smiled. "I remember now."

Max pulled it open before Tessa's hand could touch the knob. "After you."

Gordon eased the dolly through the front door. Over his shoulder, he said, "Follow me, please."

The front foyer was spacious, with cushioned benches lining the walls. *At least when customers have to wait, they're comfortable*, she thought. The lights were dim. Gordon hurried down a hallway to the right.

"You'll be meeting with Charles in a private dining room." He slipped through a doorway and Max gave her a smile. His eyes twinkled. "Ready?"

She straightened her shoulders. "Yes."

He let her step into the room first, with him one step

behind her. A man in his mid-fifties, wearing dark-blue jeans and an untucked pristine white shirt, rose to greet them. He smiled broadly as he crossed the room.

"Tessa." He took her hand in his and then pulled her into a one-armed hug. "It's been too long."

"You're looking well, Charles." She noted he hadn't changed a bit. His dark hair had a few silver strands and the corners of his green eyes crinkled when he smiled. She gave a half turn and said, "I'd like to introduce you to Kevin Maxwell, the genius behind the wines you'll be tasting today."

Charles shook his hand. "Welcome to Edwards."

Max returned the hearty handshake. "Your restaurant is impressive."

With a casual shrug, Charles said, "Thank you. It's hard work, but it's my passion." He swept the room with his arm. "I took the liberty of having my chef prepare a light lunch. I know it's a bit early, but I knew I'd be tasting your full line, and this would be a good opportunity for us to get to know each other better."

He escorted Tessa to a table set for three. Beyond it were two more tables. One held wineglasses, the standard white and red, and the other had small chafing dishes which Tessa assumed held their lunch. The aromas caused her mouth to water.

She set her leather bag on the floor and had slipped her coat off when Charles said, "I'll have Gordon hang your coat up."

"If it doesn't bother you, I'll just drape it over a chair."

"Whatever you'd like, my dear."

Tessa looked at Charles. "Do you happen to have two ice buckets or chiller sleeves?" Just as she finished asking her question, Gordon came in with a sleeve in each hand. "You read my mind." She reached out and took one from the younger man. "Will you be joining us today?"

"No, ma'am. I have things to take care of before the staff arrives. But thank you for asking."

Charles clapped Gordon on the back. "Join us."

"Thank you. I'll get another place setting."

Charles grinned at Tessa and Max. "He's not much of a wine drinker, but when he likes something, it's a hit with the customers."

"I seem to recall the last time I was here, it was Gordon who selected a couple of the wines."

"Excellent memory." Charles held out a chair for her. "Tell me, how is Edward?"

"The boy is doing well in school. He made the Dean's List last semester. I'm hopeful his sophomore year will be as good."

She turned to Max and said, "Edward is Charles' son and in his second year at Johnson and Wales in Rhode Island, studying hotel and restaurant management."

"Good school." Max took a seat.

Charles rubbed his hands together with anticipation and surveyed the selection of wines. "So, tell me what we'll be sampling today."

Tessa placed her folded hands on the table. "We've brought a white, blush, shiraz, cab franc, and a special red blend, Fuse. Also, we brought a quirky red wine for you to try on the off chance you might host a special barbeque type of event."

"*E*xcellent." Charles turned to Max. "Forgive my bluntness, but I have to ask how it is I've never had the opportunity to meet you before today."

Max shifted in his chair. He really hadn't wanted to get into all of this, and the intensity emanating from Charles was off-putting.

"As the former owner of Sand Creek Winery, my expertise

didn't lend itself to marketing. I struggled to have Creek noticed by restaurateurs such as yourself. Now that Tessa owns the business, she's able to create an awareness that eluded me."

Tessa smiled at his candor.

"I'm new to working with customers and look forward to building a relationship with you."

She leaned forward. "Charles, if I may interject. Max has created something special with these wines. I wouldn't have bought Creek if I didn't believe in them." She gave him a supportive smile. "And…" She paused. "The future of the winery."

He seemed to consider what Tessa had said. "That's high praise coming from a Price. They have some of the best wines in the region."

Max's eyes bored into hers. He had a hundred questions he wanted to ask. He said, "I hope you're not disappointed."

Max was talking to Tessa, but Charles might think it was directed to him.

She looked away and cleared her throat. "May I pour the first wine, or should we wait for Gordon?" She stood and placed a hand on Max's shoulder to stop him from getting up. "You can describe each wine to Charles."

"Gordon will be along, but we can start."

Knowing each wine intimately, his words flowed. "First, we'll taste our white. It's a semisweet wine that features the Cayuga grape. A striking pale blond in appearance, the intense fruit flavor offers versatility to accompany a wide range of dishes. The balanced residual sugar and acidity in this wine coats the taste buds, allowing you to savor its essence. Finally, it can be an excellent base for white sangria, if that's something you'd offer in the summer months."

Gordon sauntered into the room. "What have I missed?"

"We're just talking about the white." Charles took the glass from Tessa and held it under his nose. "Fruity and light." He took a small amount and held it in his mouth before swallowing. Nodding thoughtfully, he took another taste. He set the glass aside. "What's next?" He slid an empty glass in front of him. He watched Gordon take a taste, and he nodded without saying anything.

Tessa went back to the table and poured the blush. "I've never been a fan of a blush, but this is a pleasant surprise."

Charles held up the glass in the light. The subtle pale-pink color danced. "Very nice color."

Max said, "Charles, I think you'll find this blend to be crisp and light with a hint of sweetness but doesn't overpower the fruity taste."

He drank some and bobbed his head from side to side. "You're right." He rubbed his hands together. "Gordon, what do you think?"

He swirled the translucent pink wine in the glass before tasting. "I can see this becoming a favorite. I can't wait to try the reds."

Gordon said, "Tessa, you should join us. After all, this is supposed to be fun." He then took the open bottle of shiraz from her. "Please sit down."

Smoothly, she reminded Gordon, "You're the customers."

Gordon said, "And you've been personal friends with Charles for years."

Max felt the meeting shift to a relaxed and positive direction. Tessa smiled at Charles and took her seat next to Max, bumping her knee against his leg. She seemed pleased with the meeting.

Gordon poured the shiraz and then placed a plate of cheese and berries in the middle of the table. Tessa swirled the pale-red wine in the glass.

Max said, "The shiraz has delicate aromas of cherry, red plum, and a provocative spiciness." If Charles didn't like this one, his taste buds were dead.

Tessa set the glass on the table and watched Gordon and

Charles with interest. Other than Fuse, Max knew this was one of her favorites.

Gordon beamed broadly. "This is good. Really good."

Charles chuckled. "So much for playing it cool." He grabbed the last two bottles, the cab franc and Fuse. He glanced at the labels. "If these are as good as the others, we'll take all of them."

Max looked at Tessa. His face was poker straight. "Do you want to try Picnic Basket? It's a semisweet red blend. There are some people who enjoy a chilled red, and it compliments a barbeque perfectly."

"That sounds like something we'll want for the summer. Charles is planning on doing barbeque catering as a side gig." Gordon propped his elbow on the table. "It's Edwards' expansion."

Max poured the cab franc and Fuse so they could breathe. It was the best way to bring out the subtle flavors.

Charles asked, "Tell me about these."

Tessa picked up a glass and gave Max an encouraging smile. It was her signal for him to close the deal. He played it cool. "The cab franc is peppery, with red and blackberry to the nose. When we get to Fuse, our reserve wine, it's a blend of three different grapes."

Charles swirled the glass of Fuse, forgoing the cabernet. "Tessa, Max, if you can deliver before the weekend, Sand Creek wines will be featured at Edwards. And if you can give me a six-month exclusive in the Buffalo area"—he clinked his glass with theirs—"I promise it'll be worth your while."

Tessa caught Max's eye, and he winked at her. "Charles, I'm sure we can come to favorable terms, and delivery won't be a problem."

14

*M*ax gave her a quick look. "Did it go as you had hoped?" He couldn't believe how well the meeting with Charles had gone. They were going home with an empty SUV and a signed six-month exclusive contract.

Tessa had been quiet for the last ten minutes. Her head was back, and her eyes were closed. Without looking at him, a slow grin spread across her face. "Better."

He could hear the excitement in her voice as he merged into the right lane. Fat white flakes landed on the windshield. "Do tell."

She sat up in her seat, her eyes bright. "My dad started to bring me to Edwards when I was a teenager. I don't remember a time Charles ever asked for an exclusive. We've got something special with the wines you developed."

"Then tonight we celebrate."

"It has been a red-letter day." She looked out the windshield. "The snow is starting to get heavy."

He focused on the road and slowed even more. It had quickly become white-out conditions. "What's up with this weather?" He flicked the wipers on high and checked to make sure his headlights were on.

"I hate when squalls kick up on this stretch of the thruway." Tessa sat up straight in her seat, clasping her hands in her lap. "The road is covered."

He could hear the worry creep into her voice. "I've got good tires, and I've driven this road a hundred times." Despite trying to comfort Tessa, he wasn't a fan of driving like this. He gripped the wheel tighter.

"Are you okay to drive?"

"Yeah."

She pulled out her phone. "The forecast says we should be out of this soon. It's not snowing at home yet."

Her voice seemed to steady. She gave him a tentative smile.

"What is the next promotion plan?"

Taking his cue, she took a deep breath and exhaled. "We'll follow up to make sure all deliveries are received from the cocktail reception. Then we'll make rounds to all the stores and restaurants in a one-hundred-mile radius."

He took his eyes off the road for a second. "We're hitting the road?"

Her eyes grew large like saucers. She screamed, "Max!"

Everything slowed. He swiveled his head forward. A flash of brown and antlers. The SUV was unresponsive under his hands. His instinct was to jerk the wheel, but he held on and prayed he'd maintain control. He steered into the skid. The vehicle wasn't responding and seemed to pick up speed. It was inevitable; they were going to crash into the guardrail. He was helpless to avoid it.

⁂

"*B*uddy, don't move!" a man was shouting at him.

Max's eyes felt wet and sticky. He brushed glass from his chest and ran his hand over his forehead. Blood. His seat belt was unyielding across his chest, pinning him in place. Fear clutched his gut. Tessa. He reached for her hand; it was ice-cold as he squeezed it.

"Tessa, talk to me."

Silence.

His heart constricted. He tried to unhook his seat belt. The whine of police sirens reached his ears.

"Don't move." It was the same man's voice, but Max didn't pay attention. All that mattered was Tessa.

He peered out the shattered windshield. The wipers slapped away falling snow. It was then he saw the passenger side was crushed into the guardrail. The side airbags were deployed around Tessa. He said a silent prayer they had protected her. He croaked, "She needs help."

"Take it easy. Help's on the way."

More sirens assaulted his ears. But it meant people to help Tessa.

"Come on, Tee. Talk to me?" He willed her to say something. Anything. "I'm going to bore you with all kinds of dull stories if you don't answer me." He could see her chest rise and fall. It gave him small comfort.

His door was wrenched open. The man called over his shoulder, "Two. Driver and one passenger."

A fireman leaned in to assess the scene. "Sir, where are you hurt?"

"Take care of her. Tessa hasn't opened her eyes yet."

"We need to get you out of the car so we can help the lady. We'll take good care of her." He moved away from the door and a woman took his place.

"Sir, can you tell me your name?"

"Kevin Maxwell." He noticed the weather had turned again and now the weak sun was peeking out behind fast-moving heavy gray clouds.

"Sir, do you know what happened?"

"It was snowing. I had slowed down. A deer came out of

nowhere." He squeezed his eyes shut. "I lost control. Please help her." He continued to caress her hand and his voice broke. "Please."

Another paramedic reached in through the broken passenger window and pushed the deflated airbag aside. He checked her pulse. Max watched, ignoring the pain in his back. A paramedic continued to ask stupid questions and took his vitals. People and sounds were a blur. She still wasn't moving, and her face was chalky white.

Someone cut his seat belt. "We need to get you on a gurney."

"I'm not leaving her." He watched the fireman cut her belt. "Why is she still unconscious?"

"Is she your wife?"

"No. My boss." Who was he kidding? She was his friend.

"What's her name?"

He rasped, "Tessa. Tessa Price."

The other paramedic said, "Ms. Price, can you hear me?" He carefully wrapped a cervical collar around her neck.

"Is that necessary?" Max looked from one paramedic to the other.

The one closest to him placed a hand on his arm. "It's precautionary. We'll need to immobilize her head and neck before we can safely move her."

"Mr. Maxwell. We need to get you out of the vehicle."

"Is she going to be okay?" His eyes gravitated to her, ignoring the paramedic trying to fasten a cervical collar around his own neck.

"We need to take care of you. We need to put a collar on you, as a precaution, and then we'll ease you onto the backboard. If there's any pain, let us know."

He hesitated, then reluctantly released Tessa's hand. The paramedics reached around him to help him sit forward. "Oh shit." Every muscle screamed in protest.

"Take a deep breath and tell me what's going on."

Through gritted teeth, he said, "Pain in my back." He touched his forehead. When he pulled his hand away, it was covered with fresh blood. "Will I need stitches?"

"They'll decide that in the emergency room. For now, I'll put a pressure bandage on it." Her voice was soothing. "Okay. We're going to ease you to a backboard and transfer you to a gurney."

He gritted his teeth.

"One. Two. Three."

In one smooth motion, he was out of the car, positioned on the gurney, strapped securely to a backboard, and pushed to the waiting ambulance. He strained to see what was happening with Tessa, but he couldn't move his head. Panic strangled his throat. He couldn't help her. "Wait. I need to call her family. My cell phone. It was in the center console."

"Don't worry. We'll find it."

The fireman moved out of his line of sight. A blanket covered him, but he started to shiver. Someone slid the gurney into the back of the ambulance.

"Can you leave the doors open?"

The female paramedic climbed in and sat on the bench next to him. "We need to get you to the hospital."

"I can't leave her." His heart hammered in his chest. "Please," he pleaded with the paramedic. "A few minutes?"

"She'll be right behind us." The woman carefully wrapped his head with a bandage and secured it with a length of gauze.

The police officer handed his cell phone over. "Mr. Maxwell, it's going to be a few more minutes before they get Ms. Price out due to how the vehicle is positioned. She's in good hands."

He closed the doors, shutting out the accident scene. Max's eyelids were lead weights and he fought to keep them open.

"Mr. Maxwell, how are you feeling?"

"Exhausted."

"That's completely normal. The adrenaline rush is over and it's the aftereffects kicking in." She pumped up the blood pressure cuff and listened, then she made a note on the pad next to her. She depressed the button on the mic attached to her coat. "Let's roll."

"Wait, what about Tessa?"

"My job is to take care of you."

She had an unmistakably authoritative tone in her voice. He tried to shake his head, but it was strapped tight. "Not until I know she's out of the car."

She pushed the mic again. "Do you know the condition of the other patient?"

The ambulance began to move. A male voice came over the small speaker. "They are getting ready to move her to the ambulance, and then they'll roll. Ten minutes, tops."

"Thanks for the update."

He forced himself to relax on the gurney. Max was prepared for the sirens and when he didn't hear them, he asked the paramedic why he didn't.

"The only time we use sirens is if we're approaching a lot of traffic or the patient is in critical condition." She gave him a small smile. "Be thankful we're running silent."

His blood ran cold when he heard a siren close by. *Whoop, Whoop.* "Tessa. What's wrong with her?" He could hear his panic-filled voice.

"Mr. Maxwell, please try and relax. I'm sure it's due to traffic, especially with the slick roads."

The trip seemed to take forever. The doors to the ambulance opened and the driver pulled Max's gurney out. He could see the other ambulance pull up next to them. Was Tessa still unconscious? The rubber wheels hit the cement and he was whisked inside. The female paramedic eased the gurney around the wide door into a light-filled corridor where another man met them.

"Head right down to X-ray. They're waiting for you."

The other paramedics with Tessa were right behind them.

How much time had passed, Max didn't know. He was transferred to a hospital bed and a series of scans on his head and an X-ray on his wrist were taken. The radiologist said he didn't need the backboard any longer. He was then moved into an exam room in the emergency department, where a nurse conducted a routine exam: pulse, blood pressure, and a ton of questions. He looked around but didn't see Tessa anywhere. "Where's my friend?"

"She's probably still in X-ray." She tapped the keys, making notes in the computer.

He closed his eyes and waited. A soft *whoosh* caused him to open his eyes. Tessa was being wheeled into an adjoining cubicle. Her face was still pale, with the exception of the purple egg on her forehead. She lay quietly.

He asked a nurse, "Is she okay?"

With efficiency, the nurse took her vitals and made notes in a chart without looking at him. "Are you her husband?"

"No, friends."

"The doctor will be in soon." She left the cubicle without another word.

"Tee." His voice was a hoarse whisper. "Please open your eyes." He hadn't felt this helpless since Stella had been diagnosed with cancer. He squeezed his eyes shut. *This is all my fault. I should have slowed down more or pulled over until it stopped snowing. If only I hadn't been so focused on selling a few cases of wine.*

"Max? Where are you?" she whispered.

He bolted from the bed. His head throbbed. With a few steps, he was next to her. "I'm right here." He took her small hand in his. "Open your eyes."

Her eyelashes fluttered. Deep-brown eyes scanned his

face, and then she gave him a weak smile. She breathed, "Hey. You look like hell."

He clutched her hand to his chest. "Thanks. You're looking beautiful as always."

She gave him a smile and closed her eyes. "Jerk."

15

*J*essa wasn't sure where she was, but when she looked at those familiar crystal-blue eyes, a sense of calm overtook her. Her head hurt like hell and the overhead lights were blinding, and that smell. Antiseptic odors assaulted her senses. She took comfort knowing Max was with her.

"Where are we?" she whispered, hoping to avoid a louder ringing in her head.

"In the hospital." He held her hand. The warmth was comforting.

"At home?"

"No, I think we're about seventy-five miles from Crescent Lake."

"The deer?"

"You remember?" He caressed the palm of her hand. It continued to reassure her. "He missed us. Unfortunately, we didn't miss the guardrail."

She shivered and her teeth began to chatter. "I'm cold."

He tucked the blankets around her. Just like her mom did when she was little.

"You're hurt." She raised her hand. Tears slid back

through her hair. She ached all over. Had she broken any bones, or worse? Her right side hurt.

"You were knocked out for a while, but it doesn't appear you broke anything. Thankfully we were both wearing our seat belts and the airbags deployed. We've got hard heads."

She kept her eyes on him and grimaced. "Not a good sign for your SUV."

His chuckle was low, almost inaudible. "I'm curious to see what the insurance company says about its condition."

"How are we going to get home?" Her brow creased. "When can we leave?"

"I gave the police Don's information. I'm sure by now the cavalry is on their way. I may need a few stitches, but I didn't break anything important."

She forced her eyes open. "Oh, Max." Tears blurred her vision.

"Shh. Nothing to worry about."

A nurse came into the room pushing a cart that held a laptop. "Hello, Tessa. I'm Justin Bach. How are you feeling?"

"I've had better days."

"I would agree," he said. "I'm going to take a look into your eyes; is that okay with you?"

"Can I sit up first?"

He pushed a button on the side of the bed and her upper body rose to a half-reclined position. "Is that better?"

"Yes." She winced while a pinprick of light was flashed in both eyes. He asked for her to follow his fingers only with her eyes and then to squeeze both his hands as hard as she could. He moved rapidly through his exam.

"The side of my head hurts." She touched the large egg on her forehead. "Did I hit the windshield?"

"I suspect you hit the side window a split second before the airbag deployed." The nurse leaned in to take a closer look. "You're going to have a nasty bruise for a while."

With a wry smile, she said, "I'm sure I can cover it with concealer."

"It'll be tender for a few days. You might want to leave it alone." He tapped out some notes into a computer. "I'll be back after I read your scans."

"When will the doctor be in?" She looked from Max to the nurse.

He gave her a smile. "You're looking at him. I'm Dr. Bach."

She felt heat creep up her neck. He responded as if she should have known who he was. "Sorry. You look young."

"I hear that a lot. And I'll take it as a compliment." The doctor addressed Max. "If she needs anything, ring the buzzer."

"Dr. Bach, when will someone take care of Max?" Blood had seeped through the bandage on his forehead. Blood never bothered her, but she was concerned he was watching over her instead of someone taking care of him.

"He's next." Dr. Bach moved through the same exam with Max. After a few minutes, he said, "I'll check the X-ray for your wrist. I suspect it's just a sprain."

"Good." She gave his hand a squeeze. "If you want, I'll hold your hand while they do the whole needle thing for your stitches." Despite her throbbing head, she wanted to support him since he hadn't left her side since she opened her eyes.

He smoothed her hair back, careful not to touch her very tender egg, and gave her a soft smile. "Thanks."

Another man in scrubs came bustling in.

"Hello, I'm Aaron. I'm the physician's assistant. Mr. Maxwell, can you take a seat over here? I'd like to take a closer look at your forehead."

He looked at Tessa and then at the PA. "Is there any chance you can do that here?"

"I'm his moral support. Since I'm supposed to lie here, would it be okay?" She wasn't above begging if it came to that. Even though she told Max she was holding his hand for him, she didn't want to let go. She was scared they'd make her stay overnight in the hospital when all she really wanted was to go home. Now.

As Aaron assessed the situation, he pushed the wheeled tray closer to Tessa's bed. "I can do that."

He pointed to a padded stool. "Have a seat." He picked up round-tipped scissors and cut off the gauze bandage around Max's head. He adjusted the overhead light and peered closer. "This looks a little jagged, but I'll do my best to avoid a Harry Potter-esque scar." He grinned. "Instead of the boy who lived, you'll be the man who survived under Aaron's skilled hands."

Another person came zipping into the area. Aaron said, "Kristy, you're just in time. I'm about to administer the lidocaine."

She wheeled over a tray full of medical supplies. "Glad I didn't miss all the fun."

Tessa liked their attempt to lighten the mood. It must be the small-town hospital charm, to be friendly and diligent.

Max shot back, "Glad we stopped by to add a spark to your day."

Everyone chuckled, and then Aaron and Kristy got down to business. After carefully injecting his forehead with anesthesia, Aaron deftly handled the suture needle. He worked quietly and efficiently until finally, he snipped the thread. "I was able to get in five tiny sutures, so the scarring should be minimal." He pulled off his gloves and dropped them in a covered red can. "Make an appointment with your doctor for five days from now to have them removed. Or you can make the trip back here and someone will take them out for you."

Kristy handed him a hand mirror. Max peered into it.

"Not too bad." He gave Tessa a wink. "Just adds to my rakish good looks."

She chuckled and clutched her midsection. "Don't make me laugh. Makes my side and head ache."

*S*he closed her eyes and waited for the doctor to come back, but when she opened them and looked around, she wondered where Max was. She glanced at the clock. It was almost six. How long had they been here? Confusion clouded her memory as to what time they had left Edwards. She tried to piece together the recent events, but it was foggy. Panic bands tightened around her chest. What was wrong with her?

The minutes dragged. She struggled to push the fear away and clutched the hospital call bell in her hand, ready to depress it. Someone had to know where he was and if he was okay. Dropping the cord, she swung her legs over the side of the bed and waited to make sure she wasn't going to faint.

"Hey, where do you think you're going?"

She raised her head and tears pricked her eyelids. "Is teasing me one of your favorite pastimes?"

With a crooked grin, he said, "I've begun to develop a fondness for it."

The panic eased and she sat on the edge of the bed. When their eyes met, electricity rocked her to her core. "Max, where have you been?"

"The restroom and to stretch my legs." He squeezed her hand. "I wasn't going far."

She relaxed against the pillow. "Do you know when our ride home will be here?"

He pulled his cell phone from his shirt pocket. "Funny you should ask. I got a text before I came in. Your parents just parked the car."

A familiar voice reached her ears. Her mom. She turned her head. It didn't matter that she was a thirty-five-year-old woman; seeing her parents brought tears to her eyes.

"Mom. Dad."

Her mom rushed forward and held her tight. "We got here as soon as we could. The roads were treacherous in parts."

Dad shook Max's hand. "How are you feeling?"

"I'll be fine. Just a few bruises and a potential sprain. Tessa whacked her head pretty hard and was out of it for a while."

Mom perched on the edge of her bed. "How are you feeling now?"

"I'm ready to go home, but the doctor has to release us."

Mom pushed her hair back. "That's a spectacular Easter egg on your head."

"I have a touch of a headache." That was an understatement, but no sense in worrying her parents.

Max stood close to her bed. Tessa eased herself forward, testing to see if vertigo would assault her. Not too bad. He watched her, his hand outstretched.

She gave him a tentative smile. "I'm okay." She leaned against the pillows.

Aaron came in the room. "Good news for you both."

Tessa could only hope it really was good news and they'd be headed east soon.

"Max, other than the laceration on your head, the scans were clear and since you were never unconscious, we're not concerned that you had a concussion. Your wrist has a mild sprain. We'll give you a brace, and that should help. Tomorrow, you're going to feel like you were run over by a freight train, but it will pass. Take some ibuprofen for the aches, but if you start to feel worse, get to your local doctor or emergency room."

Max said, "Thank you." He clasped Tessa's hand and she liked how it made her feel, safe and cared for. "And Tessa?"

"She has a mild concussion, but as long as she doesn't stay alone"—he looked at her parents—"she can go home tonight." He handed her mom a few papers. "Here is a list of things to watch for, but check on her every hour and if you see any confusion, or she won't wake up, get her medical care immediately. We're not anticipating any complications, and she should be fine tomorrow."

Max put his arm around her shoulders and dropped a kiss on her head. Her breath hitched and relief coursed through her. They were going home.

"Again, any questions or concerns, don't hesitate to call or go directly to your local ER. In a few minutes, Kristy will be in with your discharge instructions." Aaron gave a curt nod to Max and Tessa and made his exit.

Mom gathered her handbag and Dad jangled his keys. "We'll wait for you out front, and then we'll head for home."

Max asked, "Would you drop me at the winery? I need to get the truck."

Tessa said, "Can you take me home?"

Mom's voice was sharp. "Did you hear what the doctor said? You need to have someone around, so you'll be staying in your old room for a night or two."

Max ran his hand down her arm. "Tessa, don't argue. It's much better than staying here overnight."

She caught the look her mom shot to her dad. Max was the voice of reason and for all he'd done since the accident, she'd listen.

"You're right. But, Mom, I'm going home tomorrow. Agreed?"

Mom touched her cheek. "I'm going outside with Dad and text the family." She left the room, leaving Max and Tessa alone.

With a sheepish smile, Tessa said, "We've had quite a day, haven't we?"

"We have. Parts I hope we'll repeat, others"—he shrugged —"I can live without."

"Can I ask you something?" Her head cocked to one side. "Why have you been pretty much glued to me the entire time we've been here?"

He leaned in and tucked a lock of hair behind her ear. "You're kinda growing on me."

16

The trip back to Crescent Lake was uneventful. Tessa rested her head on Max's shoulder, their hands interlaced. Dad slowed the Suburban as they pulled up the long driveway at Sand Creek Winery. Tessa sat up. The air was cool against the cheek that had been pressed against Max.

He said, "If you can give me a couple of minutes to unlock the door, that would be helpful."

Dad put the vehicle in park. "I'll go in with you."

Max placed a tender kiss next to Tessa's bump. "I'll give you a call tomorrow. Get some rest."

Warmth spread through her at the sweet gesture. She protested, "I'll be at work tomorrow morning."

"Don't be stubborn. We'll both take the day. Work can wait."

"I'll be fine after a good night's sleep." She reluctantly released his hand.

He gave her an unreadable look. "You're stubborn. Besides, you'll be stiff and sore."

"Look who's talking." She waved a dismissive hand and with a small laugh said, "You'd better get going."

"Good night, Sherry, and thank you."

"If you need anything, we're just a phone call away."

"I appreciate that."

The car door was almost closed when Mom said, "Come for breakfast."

"Mom." It was a good thing it was dark so Max couldn't see the flush that was sure to be on her face.

"Thanks. I'll take you up on that." He gave Tessa one final, intense look. "Shoot me a text later."

Something had definitely shifted between them today.

"I will."

The door closed with a thud.

"I like him." Mom's voice broke the quiet.

Tessa watched as the men stepped into the building. "I think I do too."

---

*M*ax wondered what had motivated Sam to accompany him inside. He didn't have to wait long.

As soon as the door was shut, Sam said, "Thank you for taking care of my daughter today." His voice was strained.

Max tossed the door keys on the bartop and moved around to the other side and clicked on the small light strip. The truck keys had to be here somewhere.

He didn't want to have this conversation with Sam. What could he say, that he felt guilty about the accident? Seeing her unconscious was a sucker punch to his gut? He replied, "You're welcome."

Sam stood in silence. It grated on Max's nerves until he lifted his head and, with his palms down on the polished wood bar, asked, "Was there something else?"

Sam took a step closer. "Is there something I should know?"

"Yes." He wanted to find the keys and go home. But he held Sam's steady gaze. "The accident was my fault. I took my eyes off the road. I lost control."

Sam raised an eyebrow. "It was an accident. The roads were horrible. I know; I've driven them in both directions tonight."

"Yeah, well, I take full responsibility for Tessa getting hurt." He pushed off the bar and shoved his hands into his jacket pockets. His head and wrist ached. All he wanted to do was take a hot shower and have a shot of something to put a fire in his belly. It would help to ease his raw emotions.

"Do you care for Tessa?"

"Of course I do. She's my boss and has become a good friend."

Sam nodded thoughtfully. "She's a good person."

"One of the best." Max didn't look away, but he squirmed inside. He felt as if he were under a microscope and Sam could read his emotions. The last thing he was going to tell Sam was how he might feel for Tessa. It was none of his business.

"We'll see you tomorrow about eight for breakfast."

With a brief nod, Max said, "I'll be there."

Sam cleared his throat and said, his tone gruff, "Are you sure you're okay to drive?"

"Thanks. I'm good."

"Call if you need anything." Sam walked out of the room with heavy steps.

Max couldn't help but wonder what Sam would think if he knew Max was falling in love with his daughter. Until two months ago, he and Sam had barely exchanged two sentences in an entire year and now the other man had attended the winery relaunch, picked him up from a hospital, and invited him to breakfast.

Max turned over a mug and there was the truck key. He

flicked off the bar light. His body ached in places he didn't even think had muscles. Before he indulged in a shot of whiskey, he was going to shower, call Stella, and make a sandwich. If he had been driving any faster, the SUV probably would have flipped. He gave an involuntary shudder. That was not something he would dwell on.

He locked the door and stepped outside. He could see his breath in the air. Stars were pinpricks in the inky sky. No sign of snow here.

In less than five minutes, he was home with the heat cranked in a steam-filled shower. He stood under the stream of hot water and let it sluice over his head and shoulders. His back was so tight. The hot water did little to ease the discomfort.

He dressed in sweatpants and a comfy hoodie, and his belly grumbled. He dialed his sister's number and she answered on the second ring.

Before he could say hello, she said, "Tell me everything. How did the tasting go?"

"Better than I hoped. We got an exclusive contract for six months on the full line." He slapped together a cheese sandwich and poured two fingers of whiskey before sitting at the counter.

She shrieked into the phone. "That's wonderful. Was Tessa thrilled?" She paused. "Wait. What's wrong?"

Did she always have to be so attentive? He pushed the sandwich away and sipped from the glass.

"Don't worry, but on the way home, we drove into a snowstorm and there was a deer. I lost control and crashed."

"Max, did you get hurt?" Without taking a breath, she continued. "Is Tessa okay?"

"I got a few stitches, a sprained wrist, and some bumps and bruises. Tessa was knocked out. She's got an egg on her forehead and a concussion but no other injuries, thank heavens. Her parents came and picked us up. In fact, I just got home."

"How's the deer?"

He grinned in spite of the situation. "Leave it to you to worry about an animal."

"You just said you and Tessa are okay, so the next logical concern is for the animal. Oh, and how's the SUV?"

"The deer escaped unscathed; the vehicle, not so hot. I'm guessing the insurance company will total it."

"That doesn't sound good at all."

He took another drink of the whiskey. "It wasn't pretty."

"Where is Tessa now? At home?"

He could hear the concern in Stella's voice for a woman she hadn't met. "She's going to stay at her parents' tonight in case she has some complications from the concussion. I'll go over in the morning and check on her."

"Max, is there something more going on between you and Tessa that I should know about?"

"We're friends."

"Right."

"I do like her, but I'm not sure what to do about it."

"If you want my advice…"

"I'm not ready to talk about it." He shook his head as if she could see him. "Are you coming home for Thanksgiving?"

"That's my plan. Leave here Wednesday midday and be there in time for dinner."

"We've been invited to the Prices' for Thanksgiving, and I accepted. As long as you're cool with that."

"It's a nice thing for them to invite us. They must be nice people to include a few stragglers."

"You mean like the Maxwell kids?" He chuckled loudly.

"Yeah, a holiday meal for two is a little too quiet. But this sounds like fun. When you see Mrs. Price, ask what we should bring. I can whip up something in that fabulous kitchen of yours."

"Will do. Now, tell me how are you feeling?" It was the same question he had asked for the last fifteen months.

"Still clean as a whistle. If this keeps up, I might just start believing I'm going to live a long and healthy life." Her voice held the distinct impression she was starting to believe.

"You just keep up with the docs and all the tests they want you to do and you'll be doddering around just like Nana did at the ripe old age of ninety."

"From your lips…" Stella sighed.

He looked at the picture on the refrigerator. It was of them when they were kids, sitting on a log at the beach. Simpler times.

"Have faith, little sister. I do."

"You're my hero."

He heard a catch in her voice and swallowed the lump in his throat. "Don't go telling people that. They'll get the wrong impression about me."

She sniffled. "It'll be our secret."

"I'm going to bed now. I'm bushed."

"Pour yourself two fingers of that whiskey we picked up last summer and don't forget to eat something."

"Sure thing." No sense in telling her he already had.

"Call me tomorrow. I want to know how you're feeling. I love you, big brother."

"Night, sis." He set the phone aside and swirled the amber liquid, then tossed back the last of it. It burned going down. He padded to the sliding door and watched as the night grew heavy with stars and the crescent moon crept higher in the sky. What was he going to do about these feelings for Tessa? It would only complicate the entire situation if she knew he was in love with her.

It came as somewhat of a shock, but he was in love with Tessa Price.

Sleep eluded him. He crossed the short distance to the gas fireplace and turned it on. Flames shot up and instantly the warmth reached him. He stretched out on the sofa. Loving the very beautiful and charming Tessa Price was easy, but could he stay and live a life he had only dreamed he'd have?

17

"*M*orning." Tessa's heart skipped when she walked into the kitchen and saw Max sitting at the table with her mom and dad. She moved slowly since her entire body felt like it had been bashed around in a washing machine and her head felt like she had a three-day hangover. He looked handsome, with the exception of the large purple bruise on the left side of his face. She reached up and touched the right side of her forehead. They were a matched set.

She headed for the coffee pot. "Anybody need a refill?" She hoped her cheery voice didn't betray her nerves. Would things be back to the way they had been between them now that the adrenaline rush from the accident was over? She turned with the pot in her hand. "Any takers?"

"I'm all set, thanks." Concern hovered in Max's eyes. "How are you feeling this morning?"

It was the same look he had given her last night. Had their relationship shifted in a mere twenty-four hours? "Slight headache, but nothing a pain pill won't cure. Could be worse." She pulled out a chair next to Max and sat down. Her eyes met his over the rim of the mug as she sipped. "How did you sleep?"

"Not bad. My body feels like I was in a boxing ring yesterday with a heavyweight champ and lost. But I took some ibuprofen."

His eyes said more than his lips did. He was in pain, just as she was. A slow smile spread across her face. "Mom, do I smell cinnamon buns?"

Mom got up and moved to the stove. "They'll be out of the oven in less than five minutes."

Tessa gave Max a sidelong glance. "You're in for a treat. They'll melt in your mouth and there's always extra icing."

"I haven't had homemade cinnamon buns since I was a kid. My nana would make them every year during the holidays." The memory made him smile. "When Stella and I got old enough, she wanted to teach us but we both said no, that it was her special treat. Sadly, she never wrote the recipe down, so it's gone forever."

The oven timer buzzed, and Mom said, "I hope these live up to your nana's."

"Can I help?" he offered.

"Just relax. We want to hear all about your meeting with Charles yesterday."

Dad leaned forward. "I know you said it went well, but tell us more."

Tessa gave a small laugh. "I'm not going to bore you with the mundane details, but he was gracious and charming as always. I'm pretty sure we surprised him with our wines." She flashed Max a huge grin. "And we walked away with a six-month exclusive contract and with a commitment of a sizeable initial order. It was well worth the trip." She touched the slightly reduced deep-purple egg on her forehead. "Despite the accident."

Dad looked at Max. "Thankfully you're both okay."

With a flourish, Mom set the plate of cinnamon buns in the middle of the table along with a bowl of extra icing. Tessa reached out and wiped a goop of icing from the edge and popped her finger into her mouth.

"So delicious." She picked up a spatula and put a generous-sized bun on the plate and then passed it to Max. "Wait, you need more icing!" She drizzled the spoon over the top. "Your taste buds are going to weep after your first bite." She watched as he pulled out the soft center and seemed to savor the smell of sweet goodness before popping it in his mouth. This was so comfortable, having breakfast together. It was like they had done this many times before. She pointed to his chin. "Icing."

He wiped it with a paper napkin and gave her a wink. "You're right; they are delicious." He looked at Sherry. "These taste just like Nana's."

"I'm glad you like them." Mom perked up at the compliment. "Now tell me. Have you talked with your sister about Thanksgiving?"

"I did, last night. She wanted me to ask what we can bring."

"Was there something special your family always had for the holiday?" Mom asked.

"Stella makes a great apple pie."

"That's perfect. Can you bring two?" She sipped her coffee. "I like to have duplicates of all desserts. With this size crowd, just one doesn't cut it."

"Consider it done." He looked at Sam. "May I bring some wine too?"

Sam sat back in his chair. Tessa knew the stern look was his cover for attempting to be funny. "The other night, I snuck a taste of Fuse." He held up his hand. "I couldn't resist."

She covered her hand with her mouth to keep from laughing. Just like her father to be sneaky.

"And, sir, what did you think?"

She was happy to see Max holding his own against Dad.

Max continued. "It's a small batch blend that I played around with. I think it aged quite well."

Dad raised his eyebrows. "Well..." Her father drew out the word and was letting Max dangle in the wind. "How'd you feel about bringing over a case?"

Max put on a poker face. "Will that be enough?"

"There will be twenty-two adults, and it will be the featured wine of the day." He stopped and looked at the ceiling. "You're right. Make that two cases."

Max looked at Tessa. She knew what he was thinking.

"Dad, we'll do you one better. We'll bring some white too. We will only serve Sand Creek this year."

Dad beamed at them both. "Good. Now that that's settled, I have work to do." He picked up his coffee mug and plate, then kissed Tessa's cheek. "Your mom and I are headed over to the winery. Call if you need anything."

"I'll be fine. I'm going to hitch a ride with Max to Creek and spend a few hours working, and then I'll drive my car home."

Mom frowned. "Neither of you should work today. It might be better to hang out and play an old-fashioned board game."

"Stop worrying."

Max glanced at her parents. "It might not be a bad idea to take the day off. We've both been working pretty hard and that was before all we've been through in the last twenty-four hours."

She caved. It did sound good to be lazy. "I guess we're going to take the day." She was happy to spend the day with Max. "Besides, we're going to be really busy this weekend at the tasting room. So we need to rest and recover."

He said to Tessa, "I'll drive you home."

"And we can relax and hang out."

He flashed her a huge smile. "Do you have games or cards?"

She looked at her mom. "Can I raid the game closet?"

"Sure, take whatever you want, but you can hang out here too." Mom looked at Dad. "Right, Sam?"

"Sherry, they'll be fine, but we need to get going. Stop worrying. Max will be with her."

"Absolutely, sir."

"You can stop calling me sir. I'm just Sam." He patted Tessa's shoulder. "Check in later, kid."

Mom pecked Max's cheek and smiled at Tessa. "Don't overdo it, young lady."

Tessa waved. "We'll clean up before we leave." After the back door closed with a thud, she felt herself relax in the chair.

"I'm sorry about all of that." She drizzled more icing over her now cold bun. "Sometimes they still treat me like I'm twelve."

He cut into his bun. "You shouldn't apologize for being a part of a close-knit family. Today is the first time I've really missed having a family breakfast."

"It must be hard with just you and Stella." She toyed with her coffee cup, wanting to know more but not wanting to bring up sad memories for him.

Softly he said, "It is."

*

*W*atching Tessa enjoy time with her parents gave Max a sharp reminder of how much he missed his parents. Stella would be here soon, and he was going to talk with her about moving to Crescent Lake. She could work from here and he'd be happy to take her back to the city for any appointments or tests. When he thought about what he wanted, it was to be here with Tessa and his sister. He'd call the real estate agent and end the search for a winery.

"Earth to Max." Tessa leaned over and tapped his arm.

"Sorry. Guess I went into a minor cinnamon coma."

With her waves of auburn hair in an uncontrolled riot around her face, his heart flipped. She was so beautiful.

"Yeah, I get it. Mom's a good cook. Just wait until all of us are together for turkey day. If you think this put you in a coma, you are definitely going to be in one by the end of that dinner."

"You know, if it's too much, Stella and I can have dinner at my place. I don't want to intrude on family time."

"First of all, if you even tried to skip it now, Mom would drive to your place and drag you here, and second, you'd hurt her feelings." She drained the last of her coffee and carefully stood up.

Was she feeling dizzy? He was ready to catch her if she started to waver.

"Holidays are important to my mom and she loves the house busting at the seams. It comes from her and Dad growing up as only kids. We tried to have dinner at the winery a couple of years ago. It was nice, but it just wasn't the same." Tessa placed her cup and plate in the dishwasher.

"I'm going to run upstairs and get my bag, and then we can head to my place after I grab a couple of board games." She leaned against the counter and crossed her arms over her midsection. With a mischievous grin, she said, "After, maybe we can run by the office, but we won't tell Mom."

"So, are you trying to pull me into a plot to deceive your mom?" He shook a finger at her. "If we get caught, I'm blaming you."

"Then we'd better not get caught 'cause I'll throw you under the bus, and who do you think she'll believe, her daughter or the charming man?"

He didn't need to answer the question. Instead, he latched on to the last few words of her comment. "You think I'm charming?"

She eased away from the counter. "Don't let it go to your

head." She pointed to the plate. "Can you put a piece of foil on that? We're taking them with us." She handed him a box from the counter.

She was funny and tough as nails, already itching to get to the office. "I've got this covered, and I'll need to swing by the winery and check messages on the office phone in case the insurance company calls."

"Good. Give me five minutes." She gave him a smile that was a shot straight to his heart.

He was a goner.

⚜

*M*ax was content with Tessa curled up next to him on the couch. He didn't care what they were doing as long as he could be close to her.

She looked up. His heartbeat stuttered and he lowered his mouth to hers, their lips barely touching. Her eyes widened and then closed. He kissed her again. She tipped her head back, encouraging him to kiss her a third time. He took his time placing small kisses on her mouth and trailed over her jaw and behind her ear. Her breath came out in a rush as he waited to see if she wanted him to stop.

*K*issing Max was unexpected but felt natural. He cupped her cheek, and the gentle touch took her breath away, leaving her wanting more. He stopped and looked deep into her molten chocolate eyes. She could see the desire hovering there. As much as she wanted to continue to linger in his arms, she needed to slow things down. What were they doing? Was this a residual reaction to yesterday?

"Max?"

His mouth paused its exploration. "Do you want me to stop?"

"No. Yes." She sat up. "Are you kissing me because of yesterday?"

He brushed her hair off her face. "In part, but not the way you think."

She tipped her head to the side. "I don't understand."

"The accident reminded me life is fleeting, and when I was holding your hand while the firefighters were working to get you out of the car, it hit me that I'm falling for you."

Her mouth formed a large O.

He tapped her chin and she closed it. He pecked her lips. "Is there a chance we could keep work and our personal lives separate and maybe you'd like to date me?"

"Yes." She lifted her lips to his and murmured, "And right now, let's consider this a date."

18

*T*essa hung her down jacket on the peg just inside the office as Max had done. She shuddered in spite of the warmth of the building. Not that it was really cold, but she kept thinking about the storm two days ago. Max was at the conference table, reading the newspaper. He looked up as she walked in, greeting her with a smile that warmed his eyes. Was he going to kiss her hello?

"Good morning. You look great." His eyes took in her simple outfit of green slacks and a cable knit sweater. He crossed the room.

She ran a nervous hand over her floral scarf. "Thanks. Dressing for comfort today."

He leaned in and kissed her lips. "Yesterday was nice. Kinda felt like we were playing hooky from school."

She liked the spicy cologne he was wearing. "Best day I've had in a long time." It had been nice to just hang out and get to know each other better, and it turned out they liked the same quirky movies and, in an even better surprise, that they liked each other. A lot.

"How do you feel today?" He tucked a lock of hair behind

her ear, and it set her heart racing. She definitely liked how he looked at her.

"I slept like a rock. I'm still a little sore today, but nothing like yesterday. How about you? Are your wrist and back feeling better?"

"I'm fine."

She sat in her chair.

"Coffee?" he asked.

"You read my mind." It was totally comfortable between them. Other than the way he looked at her with that soft smile that lit up his eyes, everything was the same. Ha, who was she trying to kid? Since they were in this room the last time, so much had changed.

"About the last couple of days," she began. "I was serious yesterday about us."

He pointed to her and then him. "Us?" In a few steps, he swept her from the chair and into his arms. He looked into her eyes. "This has been the single best week of my life." He kissed her. "Even the accident—not the part where we got hurt—but it opened my eyes to so many possibilities for the future."

She was at a loss for words but she knew what he meant. "It has been a great week." She thought she'd throw in, "Remember it's not typical, so don't start thinking it will be like this all the time."

"I don't care if we stay on this trajectory professionally. And personally, I'm a happy man."

Her coffee finished brewing. Max released her to get it for her. "Can you believe our sales this week alone?"

"Just an observation," she drawled.

He stopped midpour of the cream. "What's that?"

"When we first met, you gave me one-word answers." She crossed her legs and looked at him. "And now you talk almost more than I do."

"I don't talk around people I don't know."

"A shy guy," she mused.

"Reticent may be a better description." He stood next to her chair. "Can you forget how surly I was the first time we met? I wasn't in a good place."

"Consider it forgotten." She stood up to hug him, but the room swam in front of her eyes. She gripped the back of the chair.

His arm slid around her waist. She could feel his breath on her cheek. "What's going on?"

"I stood up too fast."

"Should we call the doctor?" He held her close to his side.

"No, I'll be fine." She blinked hard to force the fuzzy feeling away, and when she opened her eyes, she could see the concern in his and she felt safe in his arms. "I want to have some coffee, but I'll settle for herbal tea," she said. "But if I think we should call the doctor, I'll tell you." She made the cross sign over her heart. "Promise."

He wrapped his arms around her and held her close. "I'm gonna hold you to that." He kissed her temple, then walked her to the armchairs, where she could put up her feet.

"Stop fussing over me and let's talk about the delivery for Edwards."

He got her coffee mug and set it on the table next to her before sitting down. "I'll set it up for tomorrow. Brad will finish the local orders today and then in the morning head to Buffalo."

"He'll have to be at Edwards by ten." Tessa took her phone out of her pocket. "I'll text Gordon to confirm when he'll be at the restaurant."

"While you do that, I'll enter the orders into the system and print the delivery slips. Do you plan to use snail mail for invoices or email?"

"Shouldn't the accountant do that?" She sipped her coffee. It helped clear her head.

He looked at the floor. "I scaled him back to handle the quarterly stuff. I've been doing the rest myself."

"I'll print them." She made a mental note to have a meeting with the accountant to see what else she could turn back to the professionals.

Max stretched his legs out. "When did you say the photographer is coming to take photos?"

"That's a good question. I expected to hear from Pad before now, but I'll give Ellie a call." She picked up her phone. "You're going to really like them. They're nice people, and Pad is an amazing photographer." She held up her finger when she heard, "Hello. The Looking Glass; this is Ellie."

She smiled into the phone. "Hi, Ellie. It's Tessa."

"Hey, you must have ESP or something. Pad and I were just talking about you over breakfast."

"I hope only good things," she joked.

"Of course. How does this weekend look for us to come up? We'd drive out Friday night and be ready for the photo shoot on Saturday."

She moved the phone away from her mouth. "Any plans for the weekend, other than the tasting room?"

"We'll be open from noon to four but otherwise I'm free."

Strange how that comment filled her with happiness. She turned her attention to Ellie. "You're welcome to stay at my place. I have plenty of room."

"Thank you, but we're going to stay with Kate and Don. You know my big sister loves to play hostess, and I'm pretty sure she wants tons of access to the baby."

"If you change your mind, it's a standing offer." Not that she would. Ellie and Kate were very close. She gave Max an eyebrow wiggle and mouthed, *We're good to go.*

"Kate said she'd keep the baby and Pad and I will meet you midmorning at the winery."

"We'll have dinner with Don and Kate." Max pointed to his chest. "And Max too."

"Interesting." She could hear the teasing in Ellie's voice and was glad he couldn't.

"Drive safe and we'll see you Saturday."

She put her feet on the floor and decided to try the whole standing thing again. Max held out his hand to steady her.

With a stubborn shake of her head, she said, "I'm okay."

He watched her intently. Her head was clear, other than a dull ache behind her eyes. "Now, about dinner."

"Tonight? My place or yours?"

She chuckled. "I wasn't talking about tonight, but that sounds nice. I was referring to Saturday. I'm going to ask Kate if she'll host. If not, we'll make reservations at Sawyers. I'd cook, but I don't feel up to it."

"Do you want me to cook at my place?"

She arched a brow. "No, we both got knocked around. The last thing either of us should do is pull together a dinner party."

Max waved a dismissive hand. "It's not that big of a deal. Steaks on the grill, salad, and wine."

She took his hand and squeezed. "Next time we can show off your grilling prowess."

He touched her cheek. "I'm going to work on putting the orders together, and the invoices."

"I'll call Kate and meet you downstairs in the warehouse in"—she glanced at her watch—"fifteen minutes."

He picked up the clipboard with the printed orders. "Take your time."

She eased into the chair and waited for her head to stop pounding. With Max downstairs, she didn't need to fake that she was okay. Today was going to be long. She texted Kate. *Any chance you want to host a dinner Saturday at your place? Ellie and Pad, me and Max, something simple? Let me know. If not, Sawyers?*

She tossed her phone aside, leaned back, and closed her eyes. So much had happened over the last few days. She needed to have a few quiet minutes to absorb it all. Sales had gone up significantly. She couldn't really say they had skyrocketed, but they were moving in the right direction. She still needed a sound marketing plan to promote Fuse. Should they change the flow of the tasting room? She needed to take a few minutes and meditate. It would clear her mind and plan for the next steps. Her thoughts turned to Max and everything else faded away.

*M*ax and Brad reviewed the last order and he placed a double check mark in the top right corner.

Brad taped the printout to the top case. "I'll load the van in the morning and start deliveries."

"What about getting some local deliveries done today, then start tomorrow by driving to Buffalo?"

Brad nodded and shifted from one foot to the other.

"What's on your mind?"

"I was wondering if you knew when I'd be laid off." He shoved his hands into the front pockets of his jeans. "With things looking up, I'm hoping you'll need me through the new year."

Max understood where he was coming from. Brad was a hard worker and during those few months when things had historically gotten slow, he battled with depression. Long, cold winter days and no job to go to were a double whammy.

"I can't make any promises, but if we have strong reorders and the Buffalo restaurant keeps reordering, there's a good possibility you'll be working." He clapped a hand on Brad's shoulder. "You're a good man and I appreciate the direct question."

"Thanks, Max. If there's anything else I can do, just ask. I'm happy to paint or whatever."

"Good to know."

"Well, I'm gonna take off." Brad grabbed the dolly and made short work of loading it.

Max stacked cases on the push cart. "Want help loading the van?"

"No, I've got it. I'll be back to reload the van tonight so I'm ready tomorrow."

"Park the van inside the bay tonight so the wines stay at a steady temp." Max wanted to reiterate the protocol since Brad had never had so many deliveries stacked up before now.

He waited until the door closed before he went looking for Tessa. He thought she would have come down by now. He bounded up the stairs two at a time and stopped short. She was leaned back in the chair, her coat draped over her, sound asleep. He leaned against the doorjamb, his arms folded over his chest. He was torn between letting her sleep and waking her. He tiptoed in the direction of the stairs.

"Max?"

Was she calling to him? He waited, hovering out of view.

"Are you there?"

The soft sound of her voice caressed his ears. He came back to the doorway.

"Hey there. Good nap?"

She sat up in the chair and brushed the hair from her eyes. Under each eye was a smudge of dark makeup. "I'm so sorry. I was going to meditate for a few minutes and you caught me sleeping on the job."

He put a finger to his lips. "Not to worry. My lips are sealed."

"I appreciate that." She flashed him one of her dazzling smiles. "Tell me, how did it go?"

"Brad's making the local deliveries now and tomorrow morning, he'll go to Buffalo." He placed the clipboard on the desk. "He did ask if there'd be layoffs after the holidays."

"What did you tell him?" She tossed her coat to the vacant chair.

"I didn't commit, but if our sales stay high, we'll need to keep him on." Max watched as the soft side of Tessa was replaced by the businesswoman he had come to respect.

"I want to keep Brad and Mrs. Hanley on for the winter. The tasting room needs more publicity and if we run specials, we should be able to get some decent foot traffic."

He perched on the edge of the table. "She usually goes south to spend time with family."

Tessa tapped the pencil on the pad in front of her.

Max said, "I can handle the tasting room."

She cocked her head to the side and tipped her chin up. "Then we'll do it together."

"We seem to be spending a lot of time with each other."

"Is that a problem?"

He leaned in and kissed her cheek. "I consider it a perk of the job."

19

*M*ax wasn't used to hanging out with groups of people. Usually it was just him and Stella or a friend or two, and dinner parties were definitely out of his comfort zone. But Tessa had pulled him into her family like it was the most natural thing to do. He hoped he didn't get hives just thinking about tonight. A knock on the front door interrupted his thoughts.

He called out, "Come in."

The doorbell rang several times.

He strode down the hallway and flung open the door. Tessa had a bag hanging off one arm and a large platter in the other.

She blew the hair out of her eyes. "Surprise!" Her eyes sparkled and she held out the bag for him to take.

"What's all this?" He looked inside.

"I got ingredients to make appetizers for tonight. I thought it would be nice if we contributed to Kate's dinner party." She walked through the door, stepped out of her clogs, and padded to the kitchen in hot-pink striped socks. "Since she agreed to cook."

He watched her tight-fitting jeans and waist-skimming

pink sweater. Mesmerized by her heart-skipping presence, he was slow to close the door.

"Are you coming?" she called over her shoulder. She was in high spirits.

"I thought we were going to meet Pad at the winery in an hour?"

"Nope, he called and got all the pictures he wanted, which means we're free for a couple of hours." With hands perched on her hips, she said, "Besides, you've met my family and know we like to eat." With a laugh, she said, "If we get started, we'll have time to relax before dinner."

He had to agree with her. The prospect of working together would be fun, especially when they got to the relaxation portion. He put the bags on the counter. "Tell me what you'd like me to do."

"Oh, good." She emptied all the bags and folded the canvas totes and set them on the side counter. She pushed up her sleeves and with a cheeky grin said, "All we need are knives and a cutting board, and then we can commence chopping."

⚘

*A*fter a busy hour of prepping fancy appetizers, Tessa filled two glasses with club soda and a splash of cranberry juice and added a slice of lime. "Ready to sit? We don't need to leave for another hour."

Max liked how it was easy with her here and was glad she felt comfortable enough to drop over. He ushered her into the living room and flicked the switch on the fireplace. He waited while she stretched out her legs on the coffee table. Then she patted the cushion next to her.

He sat and pulled her close to his side.

After handing him a glass, she took a long drink. Looking

at the fireplace, she asked, "Are you happy with the direction we're going?"

"Why? Aren't you?" he stammered.

"Over the last few weeks, things have changed rapidly and I'm just wondering if you think we're on the right path?"

"I… I think we are." As he echoed her words, he acknowledged it was how he felt. It was good to be happy again.

"It's been a while since I've dated, and if you had changed your mind or wanted to slow things down, well, I thought it was best to be honest with each other." She wiggled her sock-covered toes and rested in the crook of his arm. "I can't wait to get the pictures from Pad. I'd like to update the website."

"Oh." He felt as if he had all the air taken out of a balloon. She changed topics fast. "The website?"

"Of course. Otherwise, new images wouldn't be needed." She gave him a quizzical look. "What did you think I was talking about?"

He nuzzled the sensitive spot behind her ear. "What if we make a deal? We can spend the next fifteen minutes talking business and then get to know each other better. This way, you avoid confusing me by your rapid-fire switch of topics."

Her eyes twinkled. "Oh, we could play twenty questions."

"Uh, no. Just talk." Their lips brushed.

Tessa tilted her head back and the kiss deepened. When they eased apart, she said, "I like this kind of getting to know you."

He nuzzled her neck. "Me too."

"Max, I have an idea I wanted to talk about before tonight."

He paused midkiss. "You're killing the mood."

"Give me ten minutes and we can get back to where we were."

He had offered her fifteen, so ten was a cakewalk except for how he was enjoying exploring the curve of her neck. "So far your ideas have been top-notch, so whatcha got?"

"With the holidays coming, most restaurants won't have time for meetings, but we can certainly pick up sales calls after the new year. I made a list of shops for us to attack on Monday, since we may get some shelf space, but that's a long-shot since they'll be going into a slow-down mode after the new year. Which brings me to my latest idea."

She scooted around to face him. "Valentine's Day is on a Saturday. What if we could hook up with CLW and cohost a limited ticket event? Kate and her staff could cater it. We'll hold it at Creek and for each course, we'll pair it with different wines from us and CLW." She held up her hand as he began to speak. "We'll serve five courses. Appetizer, soup, salad, entrée, and dessert. We don't have a sparkling wine but CLW does, which is perfect for dessert. Each course will be holiday-inspired."

He didn't say anything immediately, instead watching the flames in the fireplace and mulling it over. CLW's customer base was extensive and would draw people to their doors, along with Kate's menu. It would give Creek the exposure they sorely needed in the local community.

"Do you think Don and Kate would be interested?" he asked.

"If you agree with the concept, I'll broach the idea tonight over dinner." She sipped her club soda. "If Don says yes, I'll get in touch with the rest of the family. We'll need all hands on deck to pull it off."

Max stood up and grabbed a pad and pen from the counter. "I think we could fit maybe thirty-five tables in the tasting room." Then an idea took shape. "What if we took the warehouse, put flowers everywhere, created dining sections, and we could set up about one hundred tables for two? Especially if we stagger the dinner seatings. We could do the first one at five for early birds and eight for the next seating. It would give us time to clear and reset."

Tessa laughed. "Now that is ambitious."

"I'm thinking about the bottom line. We'll need to host a larger event to cover the cost of rentals and staff. No reason we shouldn't turn a profit too."

"Any ideas off the top of your head for a menu?"

"No, other than chocolate and strawberries for dessert with a sparkling wine?"

Her brow shot up. "Have you had the CLW sparkling rose?"

"Yeah. It's good. Slightly sweet and very light. It would pair perfectly with any dessert, in my opinion."

They continued to write down ideas for flowers, linen colors, how many servers they might need, and what family member could do what job. "You are always surprising me." She looked at the clock and finished the last of her drink. "We need to leave soon. Can I freshen up?"

"Sure, use the master bath." Would she think that was odd to use his room and not the main bath?

"I'll grab my bag from the car."

Her voice was steady and relaxed. Apparently not.

"I'll get it," he told her. "You can plate the appetizers."

The cold air hit him as he stepped out and closed the front door behind him with a thud. It felt so good to let go and see what might happen. It had been a long time since he had been in a relationship. This woman had wormed into his heart without him noticing it was happening. He crossed the driveway and pulled a small tote bag from the passenger seat of her car.

His cell phone pinged. It was the real estate agent with another property. He glanced at the house and figured he had a few minutes to make a quick call.

He walked to the mailbox to keep his distance from the house just in case Tessa came looking for him. His real estate agent answered.

"Did you get the information I sent over about the winery in Michigan?"

"About that. I've decided to put the search on hold indefinitely."

"Okay. Can I ask why?"

He looked at Tessa's car and his home, where she was inside, waiting for him. "My situation has changed and for now, I'm not thinking of relocating."

"Well, if you change your mind, give me a call. Happy Thanksgiving, Kevin."

"You too, Robert."

⁂

*T*he large oversized mirror was well lit as Tessa applied pale-pink lipstick. She wiped a small smudge from the edge of her lip and fluffed her waves. Why did she feel so comfortable in this man's home? Each detail of the bath was suited perfectly for a woman. He didn't seem to have any major flaws, so why wasn't he involved with someone before she came along?

His voice from the hallway interrupted her train of thought.

"Tessa, almost ready?"

"Coming." She slid her makeup into her tote and zipped it up and then stepped into the hallway.

A low whistle greeted her. "You look terrific."

She felt her face grow warm at his compliment. He leaned forward and adjusted her collar—a simple gesture, but intimate at the same time. His cologne teased her nose, spicy and woodsy. She savored the scent as she would the bouquet of a fine aged cabernet.

"You look nice too." She was tempted to stand on tiptoes to kiss him. She gave in and did.

He wrapped his arms around her waist and held her close.

"We're going to be late." Her voice was husky.

He slowly released her and took her hand. "We can pick up from here later."

"That's your best idea today."

❦

*M*ax drove Tessa to Don's house after they swung by her place to drop off her car. He was surprised to discover that Don's house wasn't a mini mansion but instead an understated two-story set back from the road, surrounded by extensive lawns and dormant flower beds. A swing set could be seen in the side yard. The house was lit up and seemed to welcome them.

An SUV was parked in front of the garage. That must be Kate's sister.

They stepped into the foyer without knocking. Tessa took his coat and hung it in the closet. Laughter drifted in their direction.

"Come on; let's go see what's going on." Tessa took his hand. "You're going to like Ellie and Pad; they're really nice."

Kate was in front of the stove with the oven door open and was talking to Don. "The lasagna should rest for about fifteen minutes."

Don took the potholders. "You got it, hon." He flashed a grin in their direction. "Hey, you two. Welcome. There's wine open or, if you prefer, beer in the fridge, or we have soft drinks too."

Kate gave Tessa and then Max a warm hug. "Make yourself at home. We're working on dinner."

Tessa set the platter on the counter. "We brought appetizers."

"You didn't need to go to the trouble." Kate gave Max a smile. "I told you she could cook, but did she guilt you into helping?"

He slipped his arm around Tessa's waist. "Not at all. We had fun cooking together."

Tessa's gaze slid to the other side of the room. "Come with me. I'll introduce you to Ellie and Pad."

They crossed the spacious room to join the couple, who were peering into a stroller.

Ellie said, "Do you think he's warm enough?"

To Pad's credit, he tenderly kissed his wife's cheek. "He's sleeping. You know our son. If he was wet, hungry, or chilly, your mom back in Loudon could hear him cry."

"Ellie, Pad?" Tessa said.

The petite blonde threw her arms around Tessa and carefully hugged her. "Hi. Kate told us about the accident. Are you alright?"

"We're both much better." Tessa extracted herself from Ellie's hug.

"Hi, I'm Max. Sorry I missed you today; I was holding down the tasting room." He shook her hand and then Pad's. Ellie ran an appreciative eye over him. "It is very nice to meet you." She nodded at Tessa and then winked. It was a good thing he was the kind of guy who didn't blush. He was pretty sure he just got a thumbs-up from Kate's sister.

Pad gestured to the sofa. "Why don't we sit down and talk about the photos I took today? There are some spectacular views at your winery."

Max motioned Tessa to sit, but once she did, he sat closer to her.

The conversation flowed, as did the wine and appetizers. Pad pulled out his camera to give them a preview. He was being modest. The photos, even on that tiny screen, were incredible. Once again, Tessa had been spot-on with hiring him.

Don looked at the pictures and joked, "I wish I had thought to hire you first. Now I can't, since it'll seem like I'm following in Creek's shadow."

"There are worse things, big brother." Tessa said, "Speaking of following my lead, we have an idea we'd like to run by you. But it can wait until after dinner."

Kate sat on the couch and Don perched on the arm. "You can't dangle something and then make us wait."

"It's about Valentine's Day." She took Max's hand. "You tell them."

He announced, "We'd like to discuss the possibility of a joint Valentine's Day event with Crescent Lake and Sand Creek."

*S*ilence. Tessa gave Max an encouraging smile and he plunged ahead. "Our idea is to open the warehouse at Creek for an evening of romance and dinner just for couples. We'll serve five courses"—he smiled at the group— "to be determined, and with each course, serve either a CLW or a Creek wine."

Tessa looked at Don. "What's your initial reaction?"

Don watched Ben dropping toys from his toy box. "Are you proposing the two wineries join together and host the event?"

Tessa couldn't tell if Don was interested or thought they were nuts. "Yes. It would be an excellent opportunity to highlight the collaborative efforts of our wineries, and it's something that hasn't been done in The Valley before. Who knows? It might end up becoming an annual event if it goes well."

Don looked at his wife. "I'm assuming Kate would be in charge of the meal."

Kate nodded. "It could be done. The pairings will be critical but if we select the wines first, it would be easy to match the food." She brightened. "We just need to confirm how many times we'd have to turn the tables to be profitable."

Max said, "Tessa and I thought two separate seatings for one hundred tables of two; one for the early birds without dancing and another for a later group who may want to linger and dance. Total of four hundred meals."

Don said, "Ambitious, but that should turn a profit."

Tessa could see Kate's wheels turning. She pushed forward. "I was going to ask Liza to handle the band and decor. Jack could handle the bar, and Anna and Leo could pitch in wherever was needed."

Ellie and Pad put their hands up like schoolkids volunteering. "You can count on us. We'll take pictures. As long as Mom and Ray will keep the baby."

Tessa beamed. She knew it was going to work, and it would be a huge success. The only sticking point was her dad. She needed him on board too. "Don, I'm going to call Mom and Dad later, if you and Kate agree."

He gave her a thoughtful look. "You have always had the best ideas. I say we do it."

Kate asked. "Is this event going to be semi-formal?"

"Yes, we'll advertise it that way. It may appeal to a wider group." Max glanced at Tessa.

"Since we have a consensus, I'll talk to the rest of the family tomorrow and Kate, what do you think about brainstorming the menu tonight?" She looked at her brother. "Can you select two wines, a white and a red? We've already chosen the sparkling blush as our dessert selection."

Kate said, "We have a busy night ahead of us. Let's have dinner and we can continue the conversation." Don followed Kate into the kitchen.

At that moment, Ellie's baby wailed. "That is definitely a *feed me* cry." She hopped up and Pad gave them a smile. "We'll be back."

Tessa grasped Max's hand and squeezed. "Told you they'd jump on board."

"That you did."

"Do you think Stella would be interested in helping? We could use a hostess."

He caressed her hand. "She'll jump at the chance."

Tonight couldn't have gone any better. Tessa's heart softened. He fit in with her family. "Good. Then we have our hostess."

⁂

$\mathcal{M}$ ax pulled into Creek and veered down his driveway. Thankfully it was an early night. Tessa looked tired. She leaned back in the passenger seat. "Did you enjoy yourself at dinner?"

He kept his eyes on the road. "To be honest, more than I thought I would. Everyone is really nice." He wasn't ready to call it a day. "Care for a nightcap? If you're feeling up to it. It's been quite a week."

"I feel good, and a nightcap sounds nice."

He parked the car and they walked to the house. The glow from the lamp on the table in the foyer softly illuminated the space. He took her coat and laid it across the bench.

"I have a bottle of ice wine I picked up when I was downstate the last time."

"Sure." She moved with ease to the sofa and sat down with a sigh. "Tell me, have you ever thought about making ice wine? We have the climate for it."

"It's crossed my mind. It's quite a process. After the frozen grapes are harvested from the vine, they're pressed frozen. The yield is low but the concentrated juice does make the sweetest wine." He pulled a bottle from the wine fridge and selected two petite glasses from the cabinet. After pouring, he carried them to Tessa and handed her one. "I hope you like it." He eased into an overstuffed chair across from her.

She inhaled the bouquet. "It does smell sweet, a bit like

honey." She took a small sip. He watched as her eyes grew wider. "This is from a New York vineyard?"

"It is." A hint of a smile played across his lips and he leaned closer to her. "What do you think?"

"It's really good." She took another taste. "We should talk about doing a trial next fall if the weather cooperates." She set the glass on the coffee table.

"I've toyed with the idea, but conditions need to be just right, and then the yield on the grapes is low and the price of the finished product will be high." He studied the pale-yellow color. "But most of the wineries in the region aren't doing it, so it could give us a distinct advantage." The words slipped off this tongue.

"That's what I was thinking. A few years ago, Jack wanted to let the Riesling go, but Dad preferred a high yield of the wine."

"I'm surprised. I got the impression your dad was on the forefront of taking risks."

"Nah. He's more conservative. Don, on the other hand, likes to make bold moves, but he carefully considers the risks." She gave him a long look. "That is another reason I wanted to step out on my own. Be a risk taker, make my mark on the industry."

"You're certainly making an impact on Creek. In a short time, you've increased sales, had one widely successful event, and now we're on the verge of another."

He couldn't help but wonder what it would have been like to have retained ownership of Creek with someone like Tessa on his team. Correct that. Not someone like her, but to have Tessa on his team. It would have made all the difference for his business and his personal life. If only he hadn't been so damn stubborn and arrogantly thought he could overlook a well-developed marketing plan. He was starting to realize that having a partner didn't mean you would be abandoned at some point.

"Not to be boastful, but I know how to market wine." Her brow wrinkled. She leaned forward. "I'll confess I am a little nervous about the event in February. Will we get enough reservations to break even?"

"I thought the goal was to get more exposure for the wines, not to make money off the event." She groaned and he knew what was coming next. Ever the businesswoman.

"We don't need to make a profit, but we will have to cover all the expenses and you did suggest two seatings which will make a difference in our return on the investment. Kate's menu will be a draw, but we're looking for two hundred couples to venture out to what they might think is a huge, drafty warehouse to have dinner. But we'll create a romantic, elegant setting. I'm going to need to carefully craft the messaging."

He saw the look come over her face, the one he had come to realize meant she had another idea. "What are you thinking?"

"I know this will be a lot of work, but what if we take one small section of the warehouse and stage it for pictures? You know, set the scene, so to speak. I can use that to promote the event."

"Let me guess"—he gave her a grin—"you'd like to be able to do this before Ellie and Pad leave so he can take the pictures. Am I right?"

"You're starting to understand me. What's it going to be like a year from now? I'll never be able to spring a brilliant idea on you."

"I'm sure you'll always have something up your sleeve to surprise me." He rose and placed a hand against the mantle. "Describe your vision?" He watched the flames reflect in her eyes. He didn't want to influence her ideas but let them build organically.

"We can take a couple of tables and chairs, set them with linens and china, which I can bring from my place. I'll run to the discount store and pick up some long white sheers, the kind people use on patio doors, and drape a small area in the warehouse so it will give the impression of an intimate dining experience."

"Don't forget flowers and a bottle of wine."

She snapped her fingers. "Actually, five bottles. I'll use this as the time to feature the wines." She hopped up from the couch. "Hold on. I need to send a few texts."

"Can't it wait until morning?" He glanced at the clock. "It's getting late."

"I need to strike while the iron is hot, and we'll need Liza and Leo's help tomorrow. I'm going to ask everyone to meet us at noon. That should give us enough time to go shopping and get supplies."

Her enthusiasm was contagious. Max said, "I like it."

She danced a jig in the space between Max and the coffee table, but then she whacked her toe against the leg of the chair and cried out. Tears sprang to her eyes and he pulled her into his arms. She lifted her face.

Max brushed her hair back; his lips grazed her oh-so-kiss-able mouth. Tessa melted into his body. Her kiss tasted like honey. For a long moment, he clung to her like a man drowning and she was his lifeline.

Her heart pounded under his. She brushed his cheek with the back of her hand, and he realized his heart was in step with hers. He'd never kissed a woman with such tenderness and passion, and he wondered what she saw as she searched his eyes.

"Tessa." He whispered her name and claimed her mouth again. Max longed to touch her.

He walked them to the couch and eased her down without breaking their connection. His finger grazed her jawline and then caressed her throat.

· · ·

*T*essa wanted more. She had never, ever felt this intensity. Was it because of all they had been through in such a short time? Throwing caution to the wind, she allowed herself to be swept away in a mind-blowing, never-ending kiss. In his arms was where she wanted to be.

*T*essa never had a more romantic night. Of that, she was sure. It wasn't fine dining and candlelight, and it suited her perfectly. Time spent alone, dinner with family, and then a nightcap and more alone time. She finally knew what people meant when they said their toes curled when they were kissed. "It's getting late." She could see the question in his eyes and she placed a hand on his chest. It was too soon to spend the night. "I need to go home."

He took her hand and pulled her to a standing position. His hand cupped her cheek and his thumb ran over her lips. "Today was amazing. Let's do this again."

She tipped her head. "Is tomorrow too soon?"

"Can't wait."

*M*ax walked through the darkened house and locked up for the night. He had taken Tessa home but wished the night had ended with her lying next to him. The winery was taking off; their working relationship flowed nicely, and for the first time in a long time, he felt a part of something bigger than just a family of two. There were so many in her family but with her standing next to him, he could adjust.

He entered his dark bedroom. Tessa's perfume lingered: hints of jasmine, rose, and sandalwood, a classic. Just like Tessa. He pulled his shirtsleeves down and opened the glass door, stepping onto the deck. His feet crunched the heavy layer of frost on the wood planks. He leaned on the railing and looked into the inky black surrounding his house.

She had kissed him without hesitation. Her lips and body had melded with his. His blood hummed at the memory. The connection he had felt was new to him. The intensity stunned and scared him, but he wanted more of her. How did he go from trying to convince himself he was not going to fall in love to kissing her lipstick off? And he couldn't wait to do it again. Pleased with the way his life had changed, Max looked to his left and smiled. Nestled in the corner was a small dark-green wrought iron table and two chairs.

*

essa arrived at the office early the next morning. Expecting to see an empty office, she was surprised to discover Max leaned back in his chair, headphones on and eyes closed.

She poked the toe of his cowboy boot. "What are you doing here?"

He pulled the headphones off and gave her a sheepish smile. "Hey, sorry. Didn't hear you."

"You typically roll in around nine." This was her quiet time, almost an unspoken understanding that she was in the office by seven. "I'm the early bird."

He sat upright and tossed the headphones on the tabletop.

Interlacing his fingers, he rested them on a stack of papers and waited as she hung up her coat. "You look terrific today."

She dropped her bag on the table. "Thanks. You don't look so bad yourself. Nice boots." She gestured to the pot. "Coffee?"

He gave her a half nod. "Thanks." His eyes were bright and a smile graced his mouth. "Tessa. Can we talk about last night?"

His voice was soft, almost a caress against her skin.

"It was successful, with the family agreeing to the event." She looked him in the eyes. "If you're referring to the personal interaction, it was nice. Very nice."

"I need to explain a few things."

She looked at him. "Are you having regrets?" Why had she said that? By his facial expression, he looked happy to see her.

He crossed the space between them. "We're blurring the lines between our business and personal relationship and I like where we're headed."

"I do too, but whatever happens between us can't affect the winery." She wanted to kiss him, but in the office, she wanted to preserve their working relationship.

"We're in a good place and I don't want to mess anything up. In the past, I haven't been very good at relationships."

She could hear the tentativeness in his voice. He cared for her! Her elation soared. At least how she was feeling wasn't one-sided. His concern was valid; she didn't want to mess this up either.

"We won't. I've never dated someone I closely work with." She tore her eyes from his mouth. The memory of how it felt last night to be lips on lips, bodies pressed together, hearts hammering, made her sigh. "We need to be careful that one part of our relationship doesn't change the other. If we have a disagreement at the office when we leave, it stays here. And vice versa."

Relief flashed over his face. "That is exactly what I was thinking. We're going to butt heads, but that's healthy in any relationship." He cupped her cheek and bent his head and then checked himself. "What are the rules for kissing in the workplace?"

She took a step deeper into his arms. "I'll need to consult with our human resources department and get back to you." She pecked his cheek.

One look in his eyes let her see what smoldered underneath: desire. He wanted her just as much as she wanted him. It was almost enough to forget about the plans they had and run off with him for the day, but she was still the owner of a winery and today, there was work to do. "Wanna play hooky some afternoon and go for a hike or something? A Sunday do-over?"

"Count me in. Just say when and where."

Playfully, she said, "Today we work and tomorrow we make plans." She crossed to the table. "I've made a shopping list." With a quick look at her wrist to confirm the time, she said, "We should hit the road and head to Rochester. They have that big craft store, and there is also a home goods store where we can get everything else."

He helped with her coat and picked up their coffee cups. "Ready to roll." He winked. "But I'll remember where we left off."

With a laugh, she said, "I wouldn't let you forget."

*

*M*ax wasn't sure if he was annoyed that she changed the subject so quickly or if he appreciated her focus. The way she kissed him showed a woman who knew how to make a man want more. This was the first time since before his sister got cancer that he had real hope for a future. His thoughts had returned to yesterday when she said, "Hey, are you listening?"

"I am. Two different stores."

"Here's the list." She thrust it at him. "We'll take my car." She grabbed her car keys from the table.

"Good idea." He scanned the paper. "From the looks of your list, we'll need more space than I have in the pickup."

They descended the stairs. "You never did say, what's the status of your SUV? Can it be fixed?"

"Nope. I'm waiting for the insurance check, and then I'll replace it."

"I'm sorry to hear that." Tessa looked genuinely sorry.

"It's okay. The vehicle did what it was designed to do. It protected its occupants. I'd say we were lucky due to excellent German engineering." He pushed open the door.

He didn't want to continue to talk about the accident. But he had to remind himself again that it could have been so much worse.

Tessa settled in the driver's seat and turned up the heat. "Stella's coming for Thanksgiving, right? No changes there?"

"She is, and you'll love her. She's funny and outgoing and loves everything about the holidays. The food, decorations, and being with people."

"I can't wait to meet her."

He buckled his seat belt. "I know she's going to like everyone. It's been a long time since we've spent the holidays with more than just the two of us."

"I hope we don't overwhelm her." She whipped the car out of the parking spot, and he pretended to hold on to the dashboard for dear life.

He chuckled. "Maybe I should drive."

She grinned. "There is shopping to do and an event setup to rock. No time for Sunday drivers." She picked up speed outside of town. "I'll use Pad's photos to promote the Valentine's event in print and online ads. I was thinking we should have an event page on the website too. We can open up if someone wants to get married or have other kinds of parties on the property. Another idea I'm exploring is small, intimate events in the tasting room."

"Does your brain ever stop?"

Tessa pulled her cell phone from her jacket pocket. "I need to text Kate and ask her to grab wine from CLW. Since she's got a good idea on what she plans on serving, it makes sense. It'll enhance the pictures, right?"

He took her cell phone. "You drive. I'll text." He tapped in a message, then read it back. *Tessa wants you to bring wine for photos, including the sparkling rose. Thanks.*

"Send it."

He put his phone in his pocket and Tessa's on the console. "Do you think, depending on when you start running the ads, we could pick up some holiday sales?"

She nodded, her fingers tapping the top of the steering wheel. "We could drop it on social media right after Thanksgiving and do a post once a week until New Year's Eve and then go wide."

He gave her a smile. "Pure genius."

She flicked back her hair and laughed. "But of course, in case you missed the memo, I'm an award-winning VP of marketing."

He clapped his hands together one time and said, "I saw the awards you have displayed in our joint office. Impressive."

A crooked smile splashed over her face in a self-depre-cating way. "Don't tell anyone, but it's not that big of a deal. I really like those different campaigns, and I got lucky."

"Tee, don't be so modest. It's a talent to select imagery and a tag line for any product. And we both know it's not in my wheelhouse."

She glanced at him. "That's why we make a great team, and even though I don't put a lot of stock in awards, one of these days, there will be awards that feature Sand Creek wines and our marketing campaigns cluttering up our walls."

"I don't have any doubt about your skills." She took the on-ramp at a higher rate of speed than he would have liked. "Well, except maybe your driving."

22

Bang. Bang. Bang.

Max stumbled down the hallway in bare feet, wearing flannel pajama bottoms. He pulled a t-shirt over his head. Who could possibly be at his front door before the sun was up, especially the day before Thanksgiving, when people should be home enjoying family time? He flung open the door and, standing there, rain soaked, was the one person on this earth who could always put a smile on his face.

"Stella." He pulled her into his arms, uncaring that his shirt would be soaked. "What are you doing here?"

His sister looked amazing. She rocked brown cowboy boots with her jeans tucked in, a down jacket open to a black turtleneck sweater, and her signature floral scarf. Her blue eyes sparkled and her face wore a healthy glow of color that he knew wasn't makeup. She was tall and still very thin but looked fit. Her blond hair had grown in and she was wearing it in a short, stylish cut.

She pecked his cheek and pushed him into the house. "Can I come in? I'm freezing."

He shut the door and took a large, overstuffed floral duffel bag from her hand. "I thought you'd be here around noon?"

"Change of plans." She draped her wet coat on the hook inside the closet. "I woke up around two and decided I was going to hit the road. Less holiday traffic and all." She held up the palms of her hands. "And here I am."

She walked toward the semi-darkened kitchen. "No coffee?"

"Sis, you woke me up. I don't often get a chance to sleep in."

She scrutinized his face and reached out a hand to his brow. "Are you sick?"

"No, just, well, we've been really busy for the last few weeks and I haven't been sleeping that great."

"Is Tessa here?"

He could hear the teasing in her voice and, without answering, pointed to the kitchen. "You make coffee. I'll get dressed and drop your bag upstairs in your room."

She brightened. "My room. I do like the sound of that. You always make me feel like I'm home when I get here."

"Wherever we're together, we are home."

"That's an odd statement." She folded her arms across her chest and gave him a side-eye. "Is there something we need to talk about?"

"Not at all." He gave her a playful push to the kitchen. There was no need to broach the idea of moving, not now. "You're on KP duty." He took her laptop bag from her hand before starting up the stairs. "You need to tell me about the book you're editing."

Her laughter echoed after him. "What else is new, and we'll talk about work later."

After a hot shower, Max pulled on well-worn jeans and a blue plaid flannel shirt and scuffed into slippers before following the aroma of coffee and food. It was good to have Stella here. Hopefully he could convince her to stay through the Christmas holidays—unless, of course, she had a doctor's appointment. As a freelance editor, she could work here just as easily as in the city.

He rounded the corner as Stella poured a mug of steaming coffee. She handed it to him. "Drink. It'll loosen your tongue."

He scanned the counters. "What are you baking?"

"Scones, and I'm going to scramble a few eggs." She pointed to a stool across from her. "Spill your guts."

He sat down, but he really didn't want to talk about Tessa. He wasn't quite ready.

"There's not much to say." He lifted the mug to his lips. The coffee was strong, just the way he liked it.

"Tell me about Tessa Price. Is she as bad of a boss as you thought she'd be, or a better girlfriend?" She stayed busy cracking eggs and setting out plates and forks.

"Honestly, she's not at all what I had expected." He set the mug down. Keeping his voice even to avoid betraying his true emotions, he continued. "She's brilliant, which I had surmised. But she listens to ideas and she's very logical. Sales have shot up."

"Really?"

The word hung in the air and made him chuckle. "I know you told me I needed help with marketing and I didn't listen."

"Yeah, why listen to your little sister? Did you think I had chemo brain?"

He frowned. "Hey, you shouldn't be joking about your cancer."

"Chill, big brother. Sometimes the best way to deal with the big C is to crack jokes. Otherwise, I'd spend all my time depressed and crying. That's not good for recovery."

"I guess. It's just a little too close to reality." A cold chill raced down his back. She was all the family he had left.

Stella reached across the countertop. She placed her warm hand on his ice-cold one. "I will fight like hell to be a very old lady." A tear glistened in her eye. "I have big plans for an amazing life."

He clapped his other hand over hers. "I'll be by your side."

"You have been, and being in remission is an amazing gift. I'm starting to live again. Which leads me to an important question." She pulled away and opened the oven door. He waited while she pulled the pan of scones out and placed it on the granite counter.

When he couldn't wait any longer, he said, "Any reason you want to keep me in suspense?"

"I'd like to move out of the city."

His heart skipped a beat. "And move where?"

"Here, to Crescent Lake." The words came out in a soft rush. "That is, if you don't mind."

He could feel his grin go from ear to ear. "I've got plenty of room. It'll be great."

She held up her hand. "Hold on there. I didn't say I wanted to move in. I want my own place. I might need to stay here while I'm looking, but only if you don't mind me knocking around."

He went around the peninsula and wrapped his arms around her. "That's the best news I've heard in a long time."

She squeaked. "You're crushing me."

His arms loosened. "Do you need to go back next week, or can you stay a while? Not that you need to find a place because you can live with me indefinitely."

"You're an amazing brother, but we need our space. However, I might just take you up on staying a little longer this trip, and when I go back to the city, I'll pack up the few things I have. Then when I come back at Christmas, if it's okay with you, I'll stay. Permanently."

"That's great, and it's one benefit of renting a furnished apartment. But why the change? I thought you loved city life."

"I've been thinking about it for a while, but seeing you reminded me of what I'm missing, and life is too short to not be with family." She pointed to the stool. "Let me scramble up the eggs, and then we can get back to talking about your personal life." Within minutes, Stella set a plate of eggs with cheese and sliced tomato, and a fresh scone, in front of him and then sat down next to him.

"Tell me about the Price family. I'm looking forward to meeting everyone tomorrow. You've said they're nice but there's a lot of them." She popped a fork full of eggs into her mouth. "Eat while they're hot."

"Make up your mind." He waved his fork in the air. "First you say talk, then eat."

She pointed her fork at his plate. "Do both."

He told her about each family member and that they worked together at the winery, with the exception of Leo. He skipped over Tessa. His sister had enough details about her. "But you can judge for yourself when you meet everyone."

She finished her breakfast and lingered over coffee. "So basically, you've spent all these years mistrusting them, and now they've welcomed you into their home for the holiday *and* been supportive of Creek?"

"Weird, right?" The irony wasn't lost on him. If he had embraced the growers' community, he might never have lost the winery. Now one of the most successful vineyards in The Valley had embraced him and his sister and his life's passion was thriving.

"Everything has a way of working out as it's supposed to." She rose to get another cup of coffee. Max held out his mug for a refill.

"You mean like fate?" He didn't believe there was such a thing as destiny.

"You're always given choices but depending on if you zig or zag, you'll end up where you were meant to be." She poured his coffee.

"Are you saying I was meant to lose my dream?" He could feel his stomach clench.

"What happened with Sand Creek was a direct result of me getting sick and you doing the only thing you could. You sacrificed your dream to save my life. Not all brothers would go to such extreme lengths."

"Of course they would." How could Stella think there might have been another choice?

"Think about it. Mom had breast cancer and we lost her, and then Dad died in the accident. It put a different perspective on everything when I was diagnosed. Without insurance, I wouldn't have been able to see the best doctors. *You* made that happen."

He could hear how she put the emphasis on *you*.

"*You* saved my life."

A lump rose in his throat. "We shouldn't dwell on what was. You're in remission and that's where you'll stay."

"I don't plan on dying. But if I hadn't gotten sick, you wouldn't have paid most of my medical bills; you would never have discovered new friends, and you definitely wouldn't have met Tessa. Wherever you go from here, you've learned so much more than you realize. I'm proud of you."

"You're the one who fought the tough battle."

Slowly, she nodded. "I did. I've discovered that I have very little control over some things and because of that, I've developed a deep faith that things will work out in the end."

"Are you telling me I should trust in something I can't see?"

"That's right." She socked him in the arm. "And you have to listen to me. I'm super smart!"

"Ha." He drained the last of his coffee and placed the mug on the counter. "If you're so smart, we should get down to the market and lay in some major groceries for the next week or so."

She snapped her fingers. "That reminds me. I need to get

ingredients if I'm going to bake pies for tomorrow. I'm sure you don't have anything that I need."

"I'll clean up the kitchen and you can pull your car into the garage." He pulled open a drawer near the sink. "Here's an opener you can put on your visor."

"You know, if you make it too comfy, I won't leave." She laughed as she caught the gray plastic rectangle midair.

"You found me out." He gave her a long look. "In all seriousness, I could add a wing on and we could share the common spaces. Family homes are becoming more popular."

"That's really sweet, but I think it's more about you wanting to keep an eye on me."

He leaned against the counter. "Just give it some thought, okay?"

She flashed him a megawatt smile. "I promise." She pointed to his feet. "You might want to change your shoes to something waterproof."

He watched Stella literally sashay out of the room just like she had done countless times as a kid with braids swaying across her back. Even if she got her own place, it was going to be great having her close by. Maybe there was something to fate. It brought his sister home and he had Tessa in his life. *It's going to be the best Thanksgiving we've had in a long time.*

23

*S*tella carried two pie plates, and Max had a case of wine. As they threaded through all the cars, she ogled them. "Just how many siblings does Tessa have?" She was beaming.

"Five, and then there are some nephews. This isn't going to be our usual holiday. But I'm glad you're excited, sis."

Socializing had always been much easier for her. He had managed a short knock on the front door when it swung open halfway and three little boys were looking up at them.

In unison, they yelled, "Happy Thanksgiving," and promptly ran down the hallway.

The hum of voices and a mixture of traditional Thanksgiving aromas teased Max's senses.

Don pulled the door wide. "Come in."

Stella crossed the threshold with a huge grin on her face. "Is it always like this?"

He took a pie plate from her hand. "Welcome to Thanksgiving, Price style, and yes, every family dinner is like this. Insane, and my mom wouldn't have it any other way. She thrives on family, and lots of it." He stuck out a free hand. "I'm Don and I'm guessing you're the famous Stella." He closed the door, shutting out the crisp November air. "I've heard a lot about you."

She gave Max a sharp look as if questioning what he had told everyone. "It's nice to meet you, but I'm not sure what's been said about me."

"It's all good and that you're a hotshot editor for a couple of my favorite suspense authors. Be warned, later I'm going to corner you and ask lots of questions." He gave her a wink. "I've often wondered what their process is like."

Max could see her shoulders relax and he let go of the breath he was holding.

"Well, I can't give you email addresses or anything confidential about works in process, but I love talking books."

Kate rushed down the hallway. "Don, let Stella get inside before you start pumping her for inside details on those books you like to read." She gave them a welcoming smile. "Hi, I'm Kate, Don's wife and mother to Ben, the smallest little towheaded boy who greeted you."

She took Stella's coat and hung it on an empty hook. "Come inside and I'll introduce you to everyone. Don't worry if you forget names; there're a lot of us." She held out a hand to Max for his coat.

"I have to run back to the car," Max said.

"We'll see you inside then." Kate took the pies from Don and Stella and ushered her down the hall. They were talking like old friends and Max thought it was good to see his sister pulled into the group. He was grateful to see how smoothly it had gone and asked himself why he had worried at all. He was surprised to admit but the Price family were some of the nicest people he had met in a long time, even if they seemed to come out of every corner of the house. He gave Don a smile and held out the carton. "I brought some Fuse and I have another in the car, along with some white."

"I hear it's my sister's favorite." Don took the box and set it on the floor. "Should we get the rest now?"

"I'll be right back."

Don grabbed his coat. "I'll help."

He followed Max outside and they each took one case. Max said, "I hope it's okay we brought the wine. Your dad said it was fine when Tessa offered it."

"Of course. I'm looking forward to trying the Fuse too. Come on; let's get back inside."

Max hung his coat up and Don led the way down the hall. "Tessa's in the kitchen, putting the finishing touches on her Brussels sprouts." Over his shoulder, he said with a chuckle, "They're smothered with bacon and maple syrup, so they're more decadent than healthy."

The oversized kitchen and great room buzzed with activity, and family members were setting the table. Max and Stella seemed to be the last to arrive. His eyes sought Tessa and there she was, just as Don said, sliding a pan into a wall oven. He hadn't noticed it the last time, but this kitchen was designed with multiple ovens and tons of counter space, all currently laden with various items for the feast ahead. The longest table he had ever seen ran right down the middle of the great room. He looked around for the kids' table but didn't see one, so he surmised it must be on the other side of the kitchen.

Tessa's smile spread from her lips to her eyes. There was too much chatter to hear her say the words, but she mouthed, *Hi, I'm happy you're here.*

He pointed to Kate and Stella and motioned for her to join him. Tessa lightly kissed him. "Hi again."

He caught the scent that was distinctly her. "Tee. Happy Thanksgiving. I had no idea what a family dinner would look like; this is bedlam."

Taking his hand, she said, "It'll calm down once we have dinner and the kids are watching a movie later." She tugged on his hand. "Introduce me to your sister."

He couldn't wait to see Stella's reaction when she met

Tessa. Would they have that instant friendship that Stella seemed to have a knack for?

"Stella, this is Tessa." To his surprise, Tessa hugged her first.

"I'm so happy to meet you. I've heard a lot about you." Stella's smile broadened, and that said it all. The two women in his life would be friends.

"Stella, I've been looking forward to meeting you. I hoped you'd swing by yesterday so we could get to know each other before"—she gave a sweep of her arm—"chaos ensued."

"Max and I had some catching up to do and, of course, pie baking."

Stella watched them intently. It wouldn't be long before she figured out exactly how Max felt about Tessa, that it was more than he had let on. To divert her attention, he said, "Stella's decided to move to Crescent Lake."

A smile returned to Tessa's lips. "That's great news. Do you know where you want to live yet?"

"I'm going to stay with Max while I'm looking, but I'd like to find a nice apartment, preferably a two-bedroom so I could set up a home office. I need to be careful with rent costs. Just getting back on my feet and all."

"Max told me that you had a difficult time." She placed a hand on Stella's arm. "But if you'd like a friend to go with you while you look, just ask. I'm happy to show you around the area."

"Tessa." Stella's voice softened. "You can say cancer. I'm a survivor. Besides, a six-letter word can't hurt me."

Max liked how Stella put everyone at ease regarding the disease she had battled like a warrior princess. Even when she started to lose her hair, which he knew had devastated her on many levels, she had said it was just another part of her journey. Her survival was more important than temporary hair loss and if it didn't grow back, she'd wear a wig.

The women looped arms and Tessa drew her deeper into

the mayhem. Over her shoulder, she winked. "I'm kidnapping your sister to make the rounds so she can meet everyone."

Before he could say anything, Tessa whisked Stella across the room to Anna, Liza, and Sherry, who were filling platters and bowls. She was greeted with more welcoming hugs. It was as if Stella was a long-lost friend.

Jack came up beside Max and clapped him on the back. "They're pretty amazing, aren't they?"

"They have got to be the most welcoming group of women I've ever met."

"Mom loves her sons, but I swear the women in her life, family and friends alike, it's like they're all connected by some secret society." He gave a chuckle. "Which I'm okay with."

Max wasn't sure what to say.

"Come on. Looks like they could use a few more hands to get dinner on the table and if you think things were nuts when you got here, you haven't seen anything until we all sit down."

*

*M*ax enjoyed coffee and pie while sandwiched between Stella and Tessa. This was the first time he had small kids at the holiday dinner table, and he liked it. Not a kid table in sight. Wine flowed freely and bowls and platters were still pretty full. If anyone was leaving the table hungry, it was definitely their own fault.

Tessa eased her chair away from the table and sipped her coffee. Her eyes twinkled with merriment. "So, what do you think of us now? Ready to decline all future invites?"

"Not by a long shot." Stella gave her brother's shoulder a playful poke. "This has been the best holiday we've had in years." She then excused herself, leaving the couple to talk.

"I'm sorry." She rested her hand gently on his arm. "It's been just the two of you for so long."

He felt the old sadness tighten in his chest. "We did okay."

Her smile slipped and Tessa looked around the room at her relaxing family. "I couldn't imagine what it would be like if I didn't spend the holidays with the people I love."

He regretted letting his sorrowful past intrude on the day. "I tend to get a little melancholy on holidays. I try to hide it from Stella; she doesn't need to worry about me." His sister was chatting and sharing a laugh with Liza and Leo. "I've always done my best for her."

"It shows." She set her cup down. "Does she know what happened with the winery? Why I was able to purchase it?"

"We've never explicitly talked about it, but she's smart and she knows I paid her medical bills and others as needed." He swirled the wine in his glass, his coffee forgotten. "I'm not going to tell her, either."

"No. I would agree." Her voice trailed off.

"What?" He touched her hand. She tilted her face up and he looked into her soft-brown eyes.

"Nothing."

"Say what's on your mind."

"Maybe you should explain our relationship. I wouldn't want her to get the wrong idea since we spend so much time together. She's bound to notice now that she'll be living here."

Over the last few weeks, Max had fallen in love with her.

His voice was gruff as he caressed her cheek. "She'll be happy for us." His fingers were warmed by her skin. It felt good to be connected to her, even in such a small way.

"I'm going to put the leftovers away. Want to give me a hand? Also, we've got containers so you can take some home too."

With a shake of his head, he said, "Thanks, Tee. We're all set. I'm sure your family will want them."

Her eyes sparkled with amusement and she pointed to a

stack of containers. "Oh, you are so going to be in trouble with Mom. She has expectations that everyone takes to-go containers. Heck, I swear that's why we have so much food for dinner." She interlaced their fingers and tugged him with her. "Either you can pack your own or I'll do it for you."

He happily followed her to the kitchen. "If you insist, then."

She laughed. "Now you're starting to see things my way. Maybe I should bring up rearranging our office space."

He twirled her around, enjoying the moment. "Why change what isn't broken?"

She gave him a sly look. "I think the coffee pot is too far away."

"Getting up is good for both of us. Gets the blood moving."

"Well then, maybe we can get new chairs?"

His lips twitched with a grin. "We'll need to check with the accountant. Make sure it's in the budget."

With a laugh, she pulled her hand free in one smooth motion, grabbed a potholder off the counter, and whipped it at him.

"Hey." He swept her into his arms and she landed against his chest.

He heard her breath catch and she said, "I'm sure we can buy chairs."

His breathing slowed. Forgetting they had an audience, he lowered his mouth and kissed her. Her breath caught and her lips parted, her eyes half closed.

Before he could fall completely under the spell, their knees buckled. Her nephew Johnny came running through the kitchen and tripped into them. Thankfully, they broke his fall; he might have gone face-first into the counter.

"Hey, kiddo." Tessa steadied the boy. "No running in the house."

"Auntie Tee, I was just gettin' a drink."

He looked so angelic, Max smothered a laugh. Tessa said, "You need to be more careful, okay?"

"I will. Now can I have a drink?" Johnny looked between her and Max. "Please?"

She gave him a cup of water and said to Max, "Now, about those leftovers."

*M*ax pointed to a bowl. "I have to have some of Kate's sausage stuffing and your Brussels sprouts."

Tessa took a large container and made quick work of filling it with a little bit of everything, enough for several generous servings. She handed the top to him and then the container. "If you'd like something else, feel free to add it." She nodded in the direction of the hall. "I'm not a football fan but the game is on in the living room."

He got the distinct impression he had been encouraged to wander. "Yeah, that sounds good."

Before leaving the kitchen area, he walked over to Stella. "Let me know when you're ready to leave."

She gave him a stern look. "Go help her." She looked over his shoulder.

"She suggested I watch the game." He shrugged. "I took the hint she wants me to bond with her brothers."

"Idiot," she hissed. "Go back in there."

"You really think I should?"

She turned him one-eighty and gave him a gentle shove.

"The way that woman looks at you, yeah, I do. You can bond with the brothers another time."

*T*essa could still feel Max's hand in hers and how her fingers tingled when they touched. Distracted, she dropped a bowl into the soapy water in the sink.

Max was at her elbow. Quietly he said, "I'll wash and you can dry."

They worked side by side. Anna had come in and put food in containers, and the rest of the family drifted in to help —except for the little boys, who were conked out in front of the television with *The Santa Clause* movie playing.

It didn't take long to clean up the kitchen. She wiped the last dish, disappointed it went so quickly. She would have liked a little longer with him. She wiped her hands and handed a dry towel to him. "Are you taking tomorrow off?"

"I think Stella wants to get a wreath and a Christmas tree this weekend. She loves the holidays."

"Do you go all out?"

He gave a chuckle. "She will." He hesitated. "Do you want to come over and help? She always makes it fun and I swear she has a magic wand."

"I'd like that, and you love every minute of it." Tessa laughed softly.

He grew quiet. "There was a time I wasn't sure we'd have more holidays. It's good to have her here."

"You mean in remission and embracing life?" She leaned against the counter and touched his hand. She couldn't imagine what it had been like for them.

"She's not the same carefree woman. There's a quiet strength and patience I didn't see before she was diagnosed." He seemed to shake off where he was going. "We have much to be thankful for. Her health and what lies ahead."

Did that include something long-term between them? "I agree." Tessa glanced at her dad. "The future looks like a perfectly ripe grape, ready for harvest."

"Wine analogy again?"

"I guess it's just a part of me." She filled the tea kettle and set it on the stove. "Tea?"

"No. I think we'll head out after I see Sherry and Sam."

"Are you sure you want me to intrude on your holiday preparations?"

He shifted from one foot to the other. "You're not intruding. I want you with us. You'll get to know Stella better and I'd love to see you."

She didn't want to seem eager, but to spend time with Max was always fun, and she did want to learn more about what kind of apartment Stella was looking to rent.

The tea kettle whistled and he moved away. Tessa watched as Max approached her parents. They were relaxing on the sofa in the family room with the little guys snuggled up close to them. She couldn't hear what he said but Mom beamed and Dad chuckled. Max held up his hand as if telling them not to get up.

Stella approached her. "Tessa, thank you for inviting us today. I had a blast."

"I'm glad you came. Max invited me to hang out with you tomorrow and decorate. I hope that's okay."

Stella's smile grew. "It's more than okay. Come early. We have to find a tree farm for the wreath and tree, and it has to be huge; his front room screams for at least a ten-footer."

"I know just the place and I'll bring the snacks. We'll call for takeout later."

Stella gave her a hard hug. "This is going to be fun. It's been a few years since we've had an old-fashioned Christmas."

Tessa caught Max's eye. He arched a brow. She could feel her cheeks flush. His lips twitched to a smile and he winked.

She read his lips. *Care to walk us out?* She nodded. If she hurried, before Stella was done making the rounds, she just might be able to steal a goodnight kiss or two.

‡

"*M*ax!" Stella yelled from the front entrance. "Tee's here. Come on! We need to go."

He strolled into the hall and chuckled. She was wearing the ugliest Christmas sweater he had ever seen. "The trees will be there if it takes us an extra half hour to leave."

"I'm excited." She wagged her finger in his direction and tossed a sweater to him. "This one's yours."

He grabbed it and held it up. "No. I don't think so."

She pulled open the door as Tessa approached and then tossed a look over her shoulder. "Don't worry. I made sure there's one for your girlfriend too."

Max could feel heat rush to his face. He liked how that sounded, but they hadn't formally said they were exclusive. Did people their age even do that, or was it assumed?

Stella gave Tessa a quick hug and pulled her inside the foyer. "Good morning."

"Hey, you two. What's going on in here?" She looked at Stella's sweater and the one he was holding. "Do I sense a theme for today?" She flashed a lopsided grin.

"You do, and I have a sweater for you."

Tessa unzipped her parka and held it open. "Look!"

Max started to laugh. She was wearing a sweater with a snowman covered in sparkles. "Sis, she's one step ahead of you."

Dressed in jeans tucked into knee-high black winter boots, with her sweater and a white parka, she was beautiful. She pushed her sunglasses to the top of her head, revealing her brown eyes had just a hint of eye makeup to make them pop. When they said eyes were the window to the soul, Max knew it to be true. Tessa's eyes welcomed him into her life and heart.

$\mathcal{T}$essa zipped up her coat and said, "We need to get going before all the good trees are gone."

He looked between the women. "Are you both going to gang up on me all day?"

They both shrugged at the same time and laughed. "Maybe."

He slung his arm around Tessa's shoulders and kissed her. "Be prepared. Stella has to look at every tree in the lot before we'll actually be able to cut one down."

Tessa squeezed her arm around Max's waist. "Oh good. Me too."

He dropped his head back and groaned. "Heaven help me."

$\mathcal{T}$he tip of a ten-foot Christmas tree was partially through the front door. A flash of frustration drifted across Stella's face. "Max, don't just stand there," she groaned. "Pick up your end."

He wasn't sure what struck him as funny, but a big belly laugh rose up. "Stella, we didn't have to buy the biggest tree on the lot."

Tessa was holding the door. Deadpan, she said, "It wasn't. Just in the top ten." She grabbed the top and tugged. "If you want to do Christmas right, the tree sets the tone."

Max gave a shove and the tree slid part way in the door. "We might have the tree, but I'm not sure if I have enough lights and decorations. The last couple of years, we've had Christmas in New York."

Stella beamed. "Not to worry. I bought boxes of lights and craft supplies. We'll make ornaments to hang on the tree."

He squeezed between the door and the casing. "I'm not artistic."

"They don't need to be perfect. It's about having fun," Tessa said. "I haven't done that in years."

Stella puffed up her chest. "Tessa agrees with me and whatever we need after that, I'll buy." She picked up the top of the tree and grinned. "Maybe this can be the start of a new tradition."

Max smiled to himself. So far, today had been the best holiday since his parents had died. Stella glowed with good health, and Tessa was here and having a good time. He was a lucky guy. With a good shove, the tree slid across the tiles. He closed the door behind them.

"Stella, before we go any further, by any chance did you think about a tree stand?"

She snapped her fingers. "I did and it's in the backseat of your new SUV. It's the mammoth green wrought iron thingy I bought at the tree farm."

"I didn't see you do that."

She popped a hand on her hip. "You were picking out wreaths with Tee."

"Right. Will it hold up this small portion of the forest?" He grinned.

"As a matter of fact, mister smarty pants, it weighs at least twenty pounds on its own." She stepped around the front of the tree. Needles fell on the tile. "I'll get it."

"No, I'll get the stand and I'm guessing you have bags of other supplies that need to come in." He carefully set the trunk down, hoping sap wasn't going to get all over the floor before they got it set up.

"I do. They're in my car."

"I'll help him." Tessa slipped her hand into his. Her eyes

sparkled as Stella closed the door, saying something about moving furniture. "I like her. She's fun."

Max opened the back of Stella's car and handed Tessa a large shopping bag. "She got the funny gene." He looked toward the house. "She's a lot like our mom in many ways." This was their first Christmas season without radiation and chemotherapy and now with remission. This really was going to be the best holiday season.

He kissed her cheek. "I'm glad you're here to share in the chaos."

"Me too."

A mischievous gleam came into her eye as, in one smooth motion, she dropped the bag and grabbed a small handful of snow and tossed it at him. Laughing, he ducked and a snowball fight ensued.

After the meager snow supply had been exhausted, they retrieved all the bags and the tree stand from his vehicle. Before they could get up the walkway, Stella opened the door.

"If you two are done playing in the snow, *now* can we decorate the tree?"

He held up the box with the stand. "Where are we putting it?"

The trio stood in the living room. Tessa pointed to the triple window overlooking the front yard and driveway. "If you want my opinion, that's the perfect spot. The tree will fill the angle of the ceiling and it'll be stunning from outside too."

Max set the box in the middle of the floor in front of the window. "It's official. Our tree has found the perfect spot."

essa couldn't remember the last time she had such fun doing crafts. It had never been her thing, but here she was covered in glitter and glue. Stella had gone outside in search of some small twigs and from what she'd collected, Tessa held up the pine cone she had crafted into an angel and dusted in gold. After it dried, it was going to be really pretty on the tree. There was holiday music playing softly in the background and a fire flickering in the hearth. She rested her hand on Max's back.

"What are you working on?"

He held up fishing line and a needle. "I'm going to make a popcorn garland. Want to help?" He dropped his voice. "I'm not very good at crafts. I'm better with food or wine, so I figured I had a fighting chance with a garland since I'm starting with food."

She held up her mug. "Cider?"

"I'll get us some, and cookies too." He took her mug and stepped over to the Crock-Pot, where the cider was being kept warm. "Do you want something stronger?"

She shook her head. "No, that's good."

He handed her a mug filled to the brim and then set a

plate of cookies between them. He then topped off his coffee and sat next to her.

"Have you done this before?"

Tessa soaked in his nearness. She could feel the warmth of his body with his arm so close to hers. Here was a man who knew how to dress for any occasion and look damn good. He had taken off the sweater and was now wearing a dark-green plaid flannel shirt that looked touchably soft, and his faded Levi's molded to his lower half.

She pulled the bowl of popped corn close and then threaded the needle. "It's all in where you poke the kernel."

He kept a close eye on the process, watching her every move as she strung the kernels together. She looked at him through her lowered lashes. "Are you ready to give it a try?"

He picked up his needle, which he had threaded before she sat down, and a piece of popped corn. "Like this?" He carefully stuck the needle in the center of the corn and cautiously pulled the fishing line through.

"That's perfect." Tessa watched as he did a few more. "Did Stella get any cranberries to string too?"

She came through the door. "Did I hear my name?"

Max didn't look up as he continued to string the popcorn. "Tessa asked if we have any cranberries for the garland."

"Actually, we do. When we're done, we'll have to give it a couple of coats of shellac before we can hang it on the tree."

Max glanced at Stella. "Why?"

"You have to, since the cranberries are fresh. They'd be gross if they got all moldy and rotted on the tree. Don't you think?"

"I guess I hadn't thought of that." He kept stringing popcorn, each kernel carefully sliding onto the fishing line.

Tessa slid from her stool and got the berries from the refrigerator. She came back with the bag and sat back down. "Do you have a pattern in mind or just winging it?" She liked the idea of haphazard.

Max suggested, "You do one strand and I'll do another and we'll see what we get."

Stella looked between them and said, "You two don't need my help. I'm going to hang some ornaments."

Tessa picked out a few berries and asked, "Did you do this as a kid?"

"Yeah. Mom was big on handmade everything, right down to having us make a gift for each other."

"What a nice idea. Is Stella artistic?"

He jabbed his thumb with the needle and swore softly. She looked over at the dot of blood on his finger, chuckled, and handed him a paper napkin from the end of the counter. He wiped off the droplets and balled it up.

"All good." He began to string a berry on the fishing line. "To answer your question, she is more so than me. Each year, I used to paint a winter scene for my parents and one year, for Stella, I made a dollhouse. You know the kind that looks like a Victorian home. It was ambitious and I didn't get the furniture done in time."

Her eyes grew wide. "For someone who says they're not crafty, you can paint and you built a dollhouse, so I say you're more than talented." She touched his arm. "And sweet." She glanced at him.

"It was a lifetime ago, Tee."

Stella strolled back to see the strands had grown into long lengths of garland. "Looking good, you two." She squeezed her brother's shoulder. "Takes me back to when we were kids."

Max tied off the end of the garland. "I was just telling Tessa that when we were kids, we made gifts for each other."

Tessa watched as Stella's eyes lit up. "Do you remember the dollhouse you made? It was my favorite gift ever." She gave her brother a sweet smile and patted his cheek. "For over a year, it was your sole mission. You used to sneak around, but I knew you were working on something." She perched on the edge of a stool. "You should have seen it. The first year, it was just a shell of a house, but then he made beds and chairs and even kitchen cabinets. Then he added electricity. It was amazing."

"What happened to it?"

Stella's face dropped. "I'm not sure. Last I knew, it was in a storage building you rented in town along with a bunch of our parents' stuff. Max, do you know if it's still there?"

"I don't remember seeing it, but after the holidays, we can look." He got up from the counter and picked up the strands of finished garland. Without looking at either woman, he announced, "I'm going to spray these in the garage so they can dry." He hurried from the room.

"Is he okay?" Tessa asked after the door leading to the garage was closed.

"He has a good heart and when we talk about our parents, well, let's just say he took their deaths really hard, and then I got sick and he lost the winery. That's a lot of hard knocks and loss in thirty-five years. He had a lot to shoulder on his own."

"My life has been a picnic by comparison." How could she have felt sorry for herself when she had both her parents and her siblings, and their family had gone through life pretty much unscathed? Except for Liza losing her husband in the accident and their dad's heart attack, they were blessed.

"Tessa?" Stella brought her back to the moment. "Can I talk to you about your relationship with Max?"

Tessa hoped she had masked her surprise. "Yes, of course."

"You really care for him."

Nothing like cutting straight to the chase. "I do." She leaned back on the stool and put the popcorn aside. "When we first met, I thought he was cold." She smiled, remembering his one-word answers on that first day. "But over time, I've learned there's so much he keeps hidden." She could feel her cheeks grow warm. "We talked about keeping our relationship strictly professional, not blurring the lines."

Stella let out a low chuckle. "Girl, that didn't work out as you planned. You and my brother have definitely"—she did air quotes—"blurred lines. I'm happy you both could see what was in front of you and have thrown caution to the wind. Max is a great guy." In a quiet voice, she said, "He never gave up on me. He's the guy who'll always have your back." Stella stood up and placed her hand on Tessa's arm. "Do me one favor. Don't break his heart."

*

*M*ax lingered in the garage for longer than he had intended. Perched on a cold metal stool, he treasured the day spent making memories with Tessa. She fit perfectly into his life.

Stella came out. "Are you coming in soon? I was just getting ready to set out chili and cornbread."

"I was thinking about things."

She cocked her head. "About a very pretty brunette hanging pine cone angels on our tree?"

"Yeah." He picked up the can of shellac and put the top on it. "I'm glad she's here. It's the second time this house has felt like a home."

"You've been living like a recluse for too long. With Tessa in your life and me moving to town, those days are over." She gave him a playful shove.

He sent a look toward the kitchen door. "I still can't believe we're seeing each other."

Stella continued. "I've never seen you look at any girl the way you look at her. You know better than anyone that tossing away a chance for happiness is stupid. If I were you and had someone I cared about sitting in my house, I sure as hell wouldn't be hiding in the garage."

His eyes narrowed. "Stella, did you just have a similar conversation with Tessa?"

She thrust her chin out. Her eyes glinted with a challenge. "If I did?"

"I would politely ask you to stay out of my love life."

"Kevin Maxwell. Don't be an ass. In life, we don't know what is around the next corner. Stop being a coward and tell her you love her. The rest will fall into place."

"I don't want to mess this up. But what if after a few months, she walks away?"

"Is that why you're holding back?"

He wouldn't look at her. That cut close to the core. He was afraid she'd change her mind and break things off just as he opened his heart. "Maybe."

"Mom and Dad didn't leave us because they wanted to, but if you hide from sharing your life with someone, you'll regret it for the rest of your life." She looked at the door. "She's good for you."

"You think I should jump in with both feet and throw all caution to the wind?"

Instead of answering him, she pointed to the door. "We've been out here five minutes too long."

He slid the stool under the bench. She was right. Why was he hiding out here when he could be inside with the two women who meant the world to him? One who would never leave and the other who might just decide he was worth sticking around for.

$\mathcal{M}$ax leaned back in his office chair and propped his feet on the desk, a calendar in his hand. Christmas was less than a week away and he still needed to shop for Tessa. From Thanksgiving until now, he and Tessa had gotten shelf space in half a dozen stores—they had hoped for at least twice that—and he'd driven to New York City and packed up Stella's apartment. Stacked neatly in his garage was the evidence that his sister had much more than either of them had thought. His new SUV was parked in the driveway but once she found an apartment, he would reclaim the garage. Not that he minded. The holidays were best spent with family, and this year was a new beginning for the Maxwells.

He closed his eyes, slumped in the chair, and tried to come up with a gift idea for Tessa. He wanted something special but not over the top. What did that mean in context of gift giving? Cashmere scarf or leather gloves? Earrings? She loved to read but never made time to get immersed in the latest novel. What about a nice watch or maybe handbag? They all were impersonal, in his mind.

"Hello there."

Her voice broke through his contemplation. He dropped his feet and sat up. "Tessa. I wasn't expecting to see you today. I thought you had some shopping to do."

She dropped her bag and gloves on the table and shrugged out of her charcoal-gray wool coat. He couldn't help but notice her gloves were mismatched. Curious, he asked, "What's with the gloves?" She was always meticulous with her appearance.

She scooped them up and shoved them into her bag, color flushing her cheeks. "I was in a rush and couldn't find two that matched. Matching gloves and me aren't compatible; I'm always leaving one someplace."

He left gloves on the potential gift list.

"To get back to your question, I finished my to-do list and wanted to get a few things done before our date tonight. We're still planning on eating at my place, right?"

"We can go out if you'd like." Max was intrigued about her cooking skills. She downplayed them, but having seen her in action at Thanksgiving, he was sure she was an accomplished cook, just like everything she did.

"No, I'll cook. But what about you? Working on something interesting?"

"Just thinking about Christmas and how I've already received the two best gifts: having you in my life and my sister moving here."

She automatically poured two cups of coffee. "Family is everything at any time of year." She added cream and handed him a cup and brushed his lips with hers before sitting down.

He would have preferred that her mouth lingered on his. But she was in work mode, which was okay with him. They'd have time later to be close. "Did you see the ticket sales for Valentine's? At this rate, we're going to sell out before the end of the year. It was a brilliant idea to advertise with the pictures Pad took." He took a sip of the coffee.

"They did turn out nice. He has an excellent eye." She

197

opened her laptop. "Are you up for a little brainstorming session? We should discuss the plan for spring to keep sales growing."

He stretched his arms overhead. "In past years, I've opened the tasting room April first. Friday through Sunday."

"Since we plan on staying open weekends through the winter, adding Friday in early April will be good. We can open on Thursdays if it looks like we'll be busy. But how do we bring in the foot traffic. Advertising? Some other kind of special?"

He took a sip of coffee. "Spring is busy in the fields. My time will be divided between the office and working the vines."

She nodded thoughtfully. "I hadn't really thought of that. When do we start bottling?"

"The day after the Valentine's event. I'm planning now, and then the big push will be on to get the wines bottled and ready to sell. Once you announce the extended hours for the tasting room, we'll need to be able to devote most of our spare time there. Have the new labels been ordered?" He shifted in his seat, thinking about the next round of changes.

"I printed the samples." She crossed the room and pulled out a folder from her bag. She shuffled the pages and handed one to Max. "Here are the proofs. Do you have a preference between the two?"

Damn, they were good. She was brilliant. He did have a preference, but he wasn't going to sway her. This was Tessa's decision.

"Which one do you like?" he asked.

Without hesitation, she pointed to the second label. "I like how the S and C intertwine and the rich silver-gray color will pop on any background."

That had been his first choice too. "I agree. Classic and elegant. What's the lead time?"

"They'll be in at the end of January." She took the folder

and set it next to her computer. "Have you completed inventory for bottles and cork?"

"Done and done. Orders are placed. I expect everything to be in by the second week of January. I'll store everything in the outer warehouse so we don't trip over boxes during the event."

She made a note on her ever-present legal pad. "I have a meeting with the accountant tomorrow. Do you have time to go with me?"

He was curious as to how much had changed in the last few months, but he didn't think it was his place. "Not to sound like a jerk, but this is your business. Would you like to keep your finances personal?"

In a clipped voice, she said, "I thought you'd like to hear how we've improved, as it directly affects your bonus." She didn't look up.

"Tessa. I didn't mean to—" He searched for the right thing to say instead of having to pull his foot from his mouth.

She gave a dismissive wave of her hand. "It's not a big deal." She tapped on the laptop keys. "So what else can we do this spring?"

"Can we talk about this?"

"Max, I shouldn't have asked you to come."

"I'm straddling the line between wanting to know how things are going and giving you the respect you deserve as the owner of Creek." He was at a loss for how to adequately explain that it was hard for him to go to meetings like that and not be actively involved. It reminded him all over again that he had failed.

Tessa's phone pinged and she glanced at the screen. "Can we get back to our strategy session? I have to leave in about an hour." She gave him a half-smile. "Forget I asked."

He decided to let it go for now and refocus on what was important to their plan. "For opening weekend, what if we did an early May Day event?"

Her eyes sparked with merriment. "You're gonna need a big pole or a huge bottle so we can wrap it with ribbons."

He exhaled. It was a good sign she wasn't annoyed about the accountant.

fter she and Max finished their meeting, she had made up an excuse that she needed printer ink but really, she needed time to think. Tessa shut her car door but didn't pull out of her parking place. She didn't need Max to go with her to the accountant. He was right. It was her business and she could handle it. But deep down, she knew the reason she wanted his support. What if things hadn't improved as much as she hoped? Would she fail at running Sand Creek? She shuddered, trying to imagine going to her father to ask for her job back at CLW. Would he even give it back to her? The humiliation was unfathomable. She had to make this business not just show a profit but thrive and be ready to take a prominent place on the wine trail. Damn it. Max was a significant part of the future. He wasn't just an employee. He really was her business partner.

A sharp rap on her driver's side window made her jump. She put a hand over her hammering heart and turned to see Max standing in the frosty cold. She slid the window down.

"What are you doing out here?" There was an edge to her voice.

"If the offer still stands, I'd like to go with you tomorrow. You might have questions on how I did things before you bought the business."

The viselike grip around her chest lessened. She wasn't in this venture alone. "Go inside. I'll come up." Should she explain herself to him?

He stepped back and opened her door, waiting while she gathered her bag and gloves. He took her hand as they crossed the gravel parking area and walked through the large double doors together. Side by side, they climbed the stairs. Tessa was formulating what she wanted to say and she appreciated that Max knew to give her time.

Once in the office, she dropped her coat on the chair. He didn't mention it or the uncharacteristic untidiness.

"Max, I owe you an apology. I walked into this building with a chip on my shoulder. I've got a lot to prove running a successful winery." Before he could speak, she held up her palm to him. "Let me finish."

She paced off the length of the room, clasping her hands in front of her. "I've been in this business since I started to work. Trailing around after Dad and Don, absorbing all I could. When Don moved to Loudon, I worked my ass off, thinking I would get the chance to shine, so to speak. I wanted to be president of Crescent Lake Winery, and I would have done a great job. And then Don and Kate moved back after Dad had a heart attack. My parents even dangled the bistro in front of Kate to sweeten the pot."

He kept a steady gaze on her without speaking.

"It worked, but not after a lot of persuasion on my parents' part. For the first time, I knew without a doubt I had gone as far as I could in the family business. I wanted more. When I heard the rumor about Sand Creek going on the market, I took it as a sign. This was my chance to step out of the long shadow Sam Price cast."

She sat in a chair next to Max. "Part of owning a successful business is knowing where your strengths lay. For a while now, I've known I'd be in the dark on certain aspects of Creek if you weren't working with me. It would have taken me a lot longer to get up to speed. So, I'd like to proposition you."

His eyebrows shot up and his lips tipped into a slow and easy grin. "I'm intrigued."

She gave a nervous laugh. "Behave."

"Can't blame a guy's brain for going in several different

directions when a beautiful woman says she's going to proposition him."

With a laugh, she said, "Focus."

He pretended to zip his lips together.

"I would like to offer you a partnership in Sand Creek Winery. The way it should have been from the start."

"Tessa, you don't need to do that. I'm fine the way things are."

With a shake of her head, she said, "I'm not. Tomorrow I'm going to see my lawyer and accountant to have the papers drawn up—if you agree, we'll be business partners." She stuck out her hand. "Are you in?"

He took her hand and the electricity jolted her. "If that is what you want, I'm all in."

27

Stella was cleaning up the kitchen when Max strolled in and perched on the edge of a stool as he watched her. "Need any help?"

"I'm finished. How was your date with Tessa?"

"Good. For inquiring minds, she can cook."

She tossed the wet dishtowel at him and chuckled. "What made you doubt it?"

"When I first met her, she made it seem like she wasn't any good, especially compared to others in her family." He patted his full belly. "She's wrong. I ate enough for three days."

"Tessa and you complement each other."

Max came around the island. "Wine or something stronger?"

"I'll make tea." She gave him a sideways look. "Something on your mind?"

"It's just nice having you here. I know you're itching to get your own place, so I'm going to enjoy our time together while we're under the same roof." He ruffled her hair as he walked by, leaving it a spiky mess.

"I'll only let you get away with that if you tell me what you got Tessa for Christmas."

Maybe Stella would have some ideas if he confessed he was stuck. At least her gift was done and he was looking forward to seeing her face on Christmas morning.

"I haven't bought anything yet."

"Max." His name came out like he was a schoolkid being admonished by a teacher. "You have less than a week."

"I know. It can't be just any old gift. It has to be the right gift." He poured some whiskey in a glass and added ice before taking a sip.

"Tell me what you're thinking, although you have a knack for choosing the perfect gift." The tea kettle whistled and Stella poured hot water over a tea bag.

"I was thinking of a cashmere scarf or maybe a pair of earrings. Maybe a handbag. I noticed she has a favorite designer."

Stella shook her head, a frown on her lips. "Anyone could buy her those things, and stay away from jewelry. Save that for Valentine's or something special." She crossed to the sofa and sat down. "Max, come over here. Maybe we can come up with a better idea."

He flicked on the fireplace as he walked by and sat on the sofa, sipping his whiskey.

"What about a weekend getaway?"

"We have to cover the tasting room on weekends from January through March. Things are too lean to hire more people to work when we can do it."

"What about a midweek overnight at a charming inn? You do take a couple of days off, don't you?"

"It's an idea." But that didn't strike him either. He went to thinking of her mismatched gloves. It was a charming flaw in her façade. He could buy her new gloves, but unless he intended to tie a string on each end and then slide it through the sleeves of her jacket, they'd have the same fate as her current pair. Still, it was an option. "I'll give it more thought and if I need to bounce ideas off of you, I'll ask." He stretched his legs out in front of him and sighed in contentment.

Stella matched him, getting comfy. "What should we have for breakfast on Christmas morning?"

"Are you cooking?" He flashed her a sly grin.

With a lighthearted laugh, she said, "I'll fix eggs Benedict if you clean up."

"You've got yourself a deal." He extended his hand and they shook on it. "And mimosas too."

"Are you going to invite Tessa to join us?"

That was a very interesting idea. "I'll ask her tomorrow." He wouldn't mind waking up with her in his arms and then celebrating the holiday, but they weren't at that point in their romance, at least not yet. Maybe next year. A few short months ago, he thought he'd be long gone from Crescent Lake and Tessa, but now there was no place he wanted to be more than right where he was.

꙳

*S*nowflakes were drifting to the ground when Max opened the door. It was only eight o'clock, but Tessa and Stella had wanted to get a jump on breakfast so when it was time for dinner at Sam and Sherry's, they might be hungry.

"Merry Christmas, beautiful." He slipped his arms around Tessa's waist and kissed her.

"Merry Christmas and good morning to you."

Max took the bags from her hands and they looked up. The flakes landed on their faces. "The snow makes it feel like it's Christmas."

She gave him a brilliant smile that included faint dimples. "It does."

Stella was standing in the open door and called to them, "Come on, you guys. Santa came."

Max slid an arm around her waist. "Fair warning when it comes to Christmas morning. My sister reverts back to a ten-year-old. You'd swear she drank liquid sugar the way she's bouncing off the walls."

"Maybe it's the excitement of being with you. I know I couldn't wait for eight this morning."

He stopped and stood in front of her. Her head tilted back as if offering her lips up in surrender to a kiss, but he'd get to that in a moment. "I wanted to ask you to stay last night, but I didn't want to put any pressure on you, like we were rushing something."

Standing on tiptoes, she pecked his lips. Her voice was soft and husky. "Next time, ask." She walked around him, leaving him standing on the walkway, momentarily speechless.

His long legs closed the distance between them and for her ears only, he said, "I will."

*T*essa, Max, and Stella sat in the living room with a large pile of discarded wrapping paper and bows off to one side. Tessa held Max's hand. "Stella, breakfast was delicious. I never make hollandaise sauce; too time consuming."

"Can you keep a secret? I use a package and just add the butter and fresh lemon juice. Comes out perfect every time." Stella's eyes slid to the table next to the tree. Perched on top was her old dollhouse with a fresh coat of paint. "Max, I still can't believe you found my dollhouse and had time to clean it up. It is the best gift of my life, again."

He said, "Even better than the first time I gave it to you?"

She blinked away the tears that hovered on her eyelashes.

"Yes. This time, I understand how much work you put into this and I'll treasure it always."

He pretended to wipe a bead of sweat from his brow. "Thank heavens. But there's no pressure for next year."

Stella stood up. "I'm going to go call a couple of friends. Will you two be able to handle being alone?"

Max looked at Tessa "We'll manage."

Stella said, "Have fun."

Max nuzzled Tessa's neck. "Alone at last." Her body gave a shiver of delight as his lips trailed down her neck and back up to her mouth. "Wait. I have one more gift for you."

She put a hand on his chest. "You've given me more than enough." He had been generous with his gifts to her and she was glad he seemed to like the book on wine history she had given him and the new briefcase backpack and a bottle of his favorite ice wine.

Max pulled out a slim box wrapped in red polka dot paper and a white ribbon and bow.

She ripped off the paper and grinned. "I know I'm like a kid." She took off the top of the box and gave a small laugh. "You bought me gloves." Her eyes twinkled when she looked at him. "And they match."

He pointed to the box. "Look under the tissue."

She unfolded the pale-red paper, and nestled there was a gold dragonfly clip attached to a ring. Confused, she picked it up and turned it over.

"What's this?"

"An ingenious little item known as a glove holder. Ladies attach it to their handbag and then slip their gloves through the ring. This way, their gloves never get lost."

She gave him a sheepish grin. "You hope." She clutched them to her chest. "I love them. Thank you." She leaned forward and brushed her lips to his. Time stood still. Her heart pounded and in a split second, he pulled her into his arms and kissed her with all the desire that had built up inside. Her body melded into his without hesitation.

"Tessa," he breathed.

She placed a finger across his lips. "Thank you for another Christmas present. It's very thoughtful." She replaced her finger with her lips. Her eyes were shining. "We're going to have to leave soon for my parents' house."

"I know. But don't you wish we could stay here just like this for hours?"

With a soft laugh she said, "Until Stella decides to make her reappearance."

He groaned. "We could go to your place."

She sealed her lips to his in a passion-filled kiss. "Later."

"I'm going to hold you to that." He hadn't released her from his arms.

"I'm counting on it." Tessa kissed him again, hoping it left no doubt in his mind what her intentions were. She wanted him.

*

*T*essa floated on a cloud as she helped her mom serve dessert and coffee. She glanced at Max when he wasn't looking, smiling to herself about his very sweet gift and that toe-curling kiss.

"Tessa." Mom's voice interrupted her wandering thoughts. "Can you get the whipped cream from the refrigerator?"

"Sure, Mom." She grabbed the bowl and dropped a serving spoon in it before setting it among the pie plates, tubs of ice cream, and trays of cookies.

"Talk about a sugar rush," she muttered.

"What's your favorite?" Stella appeared at her elbow. "I can't decide."

With a laugh, Tessa swept the full array with her arm. "A

taste of everything is what I strive for, but if that fails or doesn't strike your fancy, the pecan pie with a dollop of cream is always an excellent choice."

Stella handed her a plate. "Care to join me?"

"Sounds nice. Would you like a cup of tea or coffee?"

"Coffee's good." Stella sliced two slivers of pecan and added whipped cream to their plates and, as an afterthought, added mini slices of chocolate cream pie too. "I know. After all the amazing food today, the fact I still have room for dessert is shocking."

Tessa poured coffee and pointed to the table in the corner of the kitchen which overlooked the side yard, out of the path of the insanity. Christmas lights twinkled in the growing dusk.

"Have a seat."

Stella crossed the room, avoiding little ones who snuck back into the kitchen. They grabbed a cookie in each hand before going back to the family room where Mimi and Poppi were working on building a large Lego structure.

Stella's face was serene as she took it all in. Max and Leo were chatting on the other side of the room. Probably about Leo's latest car restoration project.

"You're very lucky."

Tessa set the mugs down. "I know, to have a large family is a blessing. But don't let the holiday glow fool you. We bicker and argue just like all siblings do."

Wistfully, she said, "Still, your family continues to grow."

Tessa scooped up a bit of whipped cream and dropped it in her coffee. "If we keep having kids, we're going to run out of room at the dinner table."

"It's nice that Max and I are included. It's been the two of us for so long, we've forgotten what it's like to have more than one person to talk to after the holiday meal is forgotten."

"What was it like after you lost your parents? Did you have aunts, uncles, or cousins?"

"A few, but no one we were really close to. Max did his best for us." She toyed with her pie. "You should have tasted the first Christmas dinner he cooked." She laughed at the memory. "The only thing edible was the rolls, and they were from the bakery."

Tessa's hand covered her laugh. "Oh, no. Really?"

"He roasted a goose, and he didn't know he should have boiled it to get rid of some of the fat before roasting. He has a heart of gold." Stella glanced at her brother and then at Tessa. "Did you like your gifts?"

She bowed her head and smiled at the thoughtfulness of his last gift to her. "Did he tell you how I'm always losing my gloves?" Without giving Stella an opportunity to answer, she continued. "And that vintage glove holder. Just beautiful. I wonder where he found the idea."

"I didn't know about the glove accessory. Sounds handy."

"It's beautiful, and the dragonfly on it is so intricate and unique."

Stella sipped her coffee. "He does have a way of finding the perfect gift."

Tessa couldn't help but wonder if she sounded like she was gushing. "The dollhouse was a very thoughtful gesture."

Stella ate a bite of the pecan pie and wiped the corners of her mouth. "There are many layers to Kevin Maxwell. He's like an onion—some make you cry, like today, but it's always worth it to find the core."

Tessa didn't want to talk about the many layers to Max, at least not right now. She maneuvered the conversation to apartment hunting for the coming week. Stella promised she'd check some online listings tonight and see if she could make any appointments.

They were enjoying the last of their dessert when Max joined them. "What are you two plotting?"

Smiling brightly, Stella said, "Tessa and I are going apartment hunting."

"Sis, I told you there is no rush at all."

"Maybe not for you, but did you stop to think you might cramp my style? What if by some miracle I meet someone and get asked out on a date? I don't really want to say, *Hey, can you pick me up at my brother's place?*" Stella pretended to shudder. "That would just be weird."

Tessa couldn't help but laugh as she watched them banter back and forth. "Max, it'll be fun. In fact, there might be a sublet in my complex and I think it's vacant. I'll check tomorrow."

Stella brightened. "On the way home, can we drive by Tessa's place so I can see what it looks like from the outside?"

"I can do you one better," Tessa interjected. "I'll give you the grand tour of my place. The units are not identical, but it'd give you an idea and let you see if you like the overall vibe."

"Perfect."

Max said, "It's Christmas, Stella. We shouldn't expect Tessa to leave her family tonight just to accommodate your burning desire to look at her place."

"Max, I offered."

His sister's smile was victorious. It was as if she had just won a small skirmish.

He threw up his hands. "I'm outnumbered." He leaned in to Tessa and kissed her cheek. "You'll soon discover that when my sister puts her mind to something, nothing can stop her from achieving her goal."

"Well, I can relate to that." Tessa high-fived Stella while they grinned at Max.

He sank into the chair and chuckled. "Oh, jeez. It's two against one. I give up."

"I didn't get a chance to ask you yesterday, but what did Max give you for Christmas?" Anna reclined in her office chair with her feet propped on the desk. Tessa had claimed the side chair.

"A box of my favorite truffles, a travel book on Italy, some perfume and—" She withdrew the lambskin leather gloves from her bag, attached with the dragonfly clip.

"He gave me cashmere-lined gloves and this holder, which I can use to secure the gloves in my handbag. Isn't that the cleverest thing you've seen?"

Anna gave an appreciative whistle. "That's definitely vintage. I've seen something like this in an antique shop." She turned the piece over and studied the workmanship of the dragonfly. "Circa nineteen forty would be my guess." Anna handed it back to Tessa. "You know these aren't easy to find."

"I figure he bought it online." She slipped the holder back into her bag.

"Definitely not." Anna's eyes widened in mild surprise. "Do you have any idea what the dragonfly symbolizes?"

"It's just a pretty little clip. Why are you making this a

bigger deal than it is?" A small frown tugged the corner of her lips.

"Since you don't seem to be a bit curious, I'll enlighten you. First off, it is obvious to everyone that he's crazy about you. To go to the effort of finding something so exquisite and perfect should tell you something."

"I never said it wasn't sweet." She tried to act nonchalant, as she wasn't ready to share that she had fallen in love with Max. Not just with Anna, but with anyone.

"Do you know a dragonfly lives its entire life in seven short months, which is a good reminder to live life fully in the present."

"Anna"—Tessa squirmed in her chair—"you always have interesting trivia about things no one else would think of."

With a sniff, Anna said, "I think about more than business on a regular basis. You might want to try it."

Chastised by her older sister, Tessa asked, "What else is important about it?"

Anna's face softened. "I'm glad you asked. It represents a change in perspective or a change to your life. Adaptability, joy, and lightness, with the emotional depth of wisdom. A dragonfly is very symbolic."

"I had no idea. Do you think Max knew all of that too?"

"Well, think about that question. If he put so much thought into finding this for you, I'm sure he chose this one specifically."

She grew thoughtful and twirled a lock of her hair around her finger. "Well, that does put a different spin on things."

"Tessa, what are you going to do now?"

She pulled on her down coat and a black beret. "I'm off to help Stella look for an apartment. She's meeting me at my place since the first one on the list is a unit in my complex."

"Are you going to work today?"

"No. I'm going to check some financials and then run over

to the house later. I promised Mom I'd help her make soup for dinner; we'll have pots of turkey and ham."

"Save me some." Anna dropped her feet to the floor.

"Dinner will be around six." She gave her sister a quick hug and hurried down the stairs and through the tasting room. She looked around, thinking of how far she had come. Her life was different than working at CLW, but she was happy, sales were up—not as high as she had planned, but moving in the right direction—and plans for the upcoming year were underway. They had even booked a couple of small private parties.

Although she stood in the shadows, her sigh was audible.

"Tessa, is that you?"

She peeked around the corner of the stairs. Her dad was sitting at a table in the tasting room. She walked over to him.

"Hey, Dad, are you doing okay?"

"I'm fine. Sometimes I like to sit here when it's quiet and think about how much has changed since I took over from your grandfather. Your mom and I worked hard in the early years to build the business, but somehow everything remains the same."

Tessa hesitated. She needed to meet Stella, but Dad was in a rare nostalgic mood. Maybe he would clarify a few lingering questions. "Mind if I join you?"

His face brightened. "You're not in a hurry to get someplace?"

She pulled out a metal chair and sat down. "I have some time to spare."

"How are things at Creek?"

Even though Dad hadn't been happy when she left the family business, he was the consummate professional and, more important, he loved her. "I'm starting to see repeat orders from the new customers we picked up after the cocktail party."

He nodded slowly, his finger tapping on the tabletop.

"Good. And what about the contract with Edwards? Is that bearing fruit?" He gave her a smile. "Did you see what I did there?"

"Dad, your puns never get old." She crossed her legs and relaxed. Talking with a veteran in the business was nice. "Charles is pushing all the varieties and sales are brisk. I think our wines are becoming a primary seller for him."

"That's good news."

A companionable silence fell between them.

"Dad, can I ask you a question and would you give me an honest answer?"

"Of course."

She inhaled and exhaled a deep calming breath. "Why wasn't I good enough to run Crescent Lake Winery? I worked my ass off for this business and you never saw me as anything more than the vice president of marketing." She swallowed the lump in her throat. "You sold me short." She hated the way her voice cracked.

Dad's mouth gaped open. "Tessa, is that really why you left? Because Don came home and assumed control?"

"You know it is. It was a direct result of Don's return." That didn't sound good, but she plowed ahead. "You were never going to recognize my contribution. You gave me credit for marketing, but I was doing a helluva lot more. I was running the winery and was damn good at it. I wanted more and frankly, I deserved to get the opportunity at the big chair." She swallowed hot tears. "But I need to know why."

"Oh, Tessa. It wasn't about whether or not you were capable." He looked away from her and ran his hand over his graying blond hair. "When I had my heart attack, I got scared. I wanted all of my children, Don and Kate included, to be here, working our family business." He lifted his eyes to hers; they were filled with regret. "I'm embarrassed to admit I bribed Kate with her own kitchen and shamelessly reminded Don he had spent years planning to take over when it was time for me to retire. I used my heart issues to control my children, and I'm ashamed of what I did." He cringed and dropped his chin to his chest.

Tessa sat in the chair, shocked. "I never had a chance to run the company, did I?"

His voice was gruff and he avoided her eyes. "I'm sorry, Tee. It was definitely not one of my finer moments to pass over you to get Don back home."

Her voice was thick with a multitude of emotions. "But did you think I was capable?"

"Honestly, if you had a couple more years working with me, you would have been unstoppable."

"Huh." She was dumbfounded. So, it was less about her and more about surrounding himself with those he loved.

Dad slid his hand across the table and waited for her to take it. He was never one to give in to emotion, but he was visibly shaken. "I was shocked when you announced you purchased Sand Creek. I didn't think you were ready. But watching you the last few months, I have to admit I've been impressed." He patted her hand. "I was wrong. You could have taken over for me and done a solid job."

She blinked away fresh tears. All these years, all she wanted was her dad's approval, and it took striking out on her own to get it. "Are you serious?"

"Like a heart attack." His deep-brown eyes grew misty. "I'm proud of you."

She squeezed his hand, unable to speak. This was the first time that, without a doubt, she knew the decision to buy Creek was the right path. She was making her mark outside the family. Change and wisdom. That's what Anna had said about the dragonfly. Maybe Max was perceptive about life.

"Thanks, Dad. That means a lot to me."

"I am in your corner all the way. Whatever you think you might need to continue your trajectory up, just ask. The entire family is your cheering section." He glanced around. "Don't tell your brothers and sisters I said this, but I think there are times when they're a tad envious of you."

"Why on earth would they be envious? I've used all my savings; I'm in debt up to my eyeballs; cash flow is tight, and I have no idea what the growing season is going to be like." She grinned. "But I'm having the time of my life."

"Exactly my point. You're living your dream."

"I am." She sat taller in her chair.

"Could I give you one piece of advice about Max?"

Hesitantly, she said, "Sure."

"He's poured all of his heart and sweat into that winery and when you can, make him a partner. Not fifty-fifty, but something. He's given you a good foundation. I've never seen anyone with his talent or instinct for growing and making wine, with the exception of Anna. Together you can exceed beyond your wildest dreams."

With a small laugh, she said, "I did right before Christmas. We're a sixty–forty operation."

"Good for you. And Tessa, one last thing."

"What's that?"

"Open your eyes and really see the life you could have. I'm not talking about the business. But to be loved and love someone in return is the best kind of partnership you'll ever embark on. I almost walked away from your mother, but your Grandfather Donald encouraged me to follow my heart. You know, I see parallels between your mom and me and you with Max. Right after we got married, the winery struggled. Together we worked hard to build the business. With her talent for finances and my love of the product, we were unbeatable." He gave her an appreciative look. "You get your attention to detail from her. The first time I brought her to the tasting room, she suggested we paint the door a bright color. That's how it ended up burgundy. She said it would be easier for the customers to know which door to come in." Dad pushed the chair back. The legs screeched against the cement floor. "I'd better get home before your mom starts wondering where I've wandered off to." He kissed the top of her head. "And you said you had someplace to be."

"Thanks, Dad. For everything."

He gave her a wink and walked in the opposite direction. "See you at dinner, and make sure you bring Max and Stella. You know how much your mom loves the house filled wall to wall with people."

Tessa didn't answer him but instead she kept replaying the words she had longed to hear for years. Dad was proud of her.

***

$\mathcal{T}$essa zipped down the winding drive to her condo. Stella's car was in the visitor parking area and she got out of her car when she saw Tessa.

"Hey, sorry I'm running a bit late. I ran into Dad at the winery, we got talking, and I lost track of time."

"Never apologize for spending time with your dad. If I could have just five more minutes with either of my parents, I would take them in a heartbeat."

Tessa looped arms with Stella. "What do you say we go see a condo?"

The two girls fell into step together. "If it's as nice as yours, I'm going to cancel all other appointments and sign on the dotted line."

"It would be fun having you as a neighbor." They approached the office door and Tessa said, "Don't worry. I'll give you a glowing reference."

Straight-faced, Stella said, "I was worried."

"Ha. I just have one very important question. Can you cook as well as your brother?"

"I can make a wicked good breakfast and I'm exceptional at calling for takeout. Does that qualify?"

"It does, and when we need home cooking, we can always stop by my parents'."

With an easy smile, Stella said, "It sounds like we're going to be roommates, not neighbors."

"Better than either of those." Tessa couldn't help but grin. "We're going to be great friends."

Stella pulled open the door to the office. Max was waiting for them. "Well, this is a surprise. What are you doing here?" She gave him a wide smile.

Tessa's heart fluttered. He looked handsome in his leather coat and well-worn jeans.

"Ladies"—his gaze slid over Tessa with a smile—"I happen to know if Stella signs the sublet agreement this morning, which is a foregone conclusion since she loved your condo, moving will commence ASAP. Checking it out gives me time to plan how to move boxes and furniture."

"Max, you do know me so well."

Tessa said, "You'll have help moving her. My family will pitch in too."

"Is there anything they won't do for you?"

"Oh," Tessa protested, "it's not about me. Your sister has charmed my entire family. I think if they could, they'd adopt her."

"Excuse me. I'm standing right here." Stella waved her mitten-covered hands. "And for the record, I don't have that much stuff to move."

"Tell my aching back." He winked at Tessa. "There's at least one box truck or a bunch of van trips."

Tessa looked between the Maxwells. It warmed her heart to be a part of their inner circle. "We'll borrow the CLW box truck and get it done in one trip. But let's not count our chickens. Stella has to see the place first."

He dangled a key from his finger. "The manager had to step out but gave me the key. Stella"—he handed it to her—"lead the way."

Stella flung open the door and skipped down the ramp. "Come on, you two. Time's a-wasting."

He gestured for Tessa to go ahead of him. "With Stella in your life, it'll never be the same."

Tessa flashed him a broad smile. "I think that could be said for both the Maxwells."

29

*T*he silence at Max's home was deafening. It had been six days since Stella signed for the condo. She had gotten lucky that the owners were in Europe for a year, so they had let her take it over as soon as they checked her references and credit. She had officially moved in twenty-four hours ago; now she was getting settled. Tessa was with her sisters. Unable to get her off his mind, he decided to layer up and walk the vineyard. It always soothed his soul to wander through the vines, especially on New Year's Day, a fresh start for so many things. His cell rang and he grinned when he saw the caller ID. "Hi, Tessa."

"Hi." She sounded slightly breathless. "I was wondering what you're doing?"

"I was just going for a walk through the vineyard."

"Want some company?"

He was surprised she asked. "I thought you were going to hang out with your sisters. But I can swing by and pick you up."

"No need to backtrack. In fact, I'll pick you up. What time will you be ready?"

"Ten minutes?"

She gave a quiet laugh. "Make it twenty."

"Alright then. See you soon." He disconnected the phone. *So much for spending the day alone.*

Exactly nineteen minutes later, he heard a quick *toot toot* from his driveway. He stuck two bottles of water in his jacket pocket and pulled his knitted cap down over his ears. He started out the door and turned around. "Gloves." They were on the bench.

Tessa waved at him, a huge grin gracing her face. He got in and brushed her lips with his. After he buckled up, he asked, "Are you sure you're up for this? It's cold out."

She showed him she had three layers on under her coat. "I love walking through the vines this time of year, and I'm dressed for it. Besides, I find it to be very cathartic. You know, all the quiet. The only sound you hear is your boots crunching over the ground and the occasional bird."

He dipped his head, acknowledging another similarity. "That's exactly how I feel too. I get some of the best ideas when I'm out there wandering around."

She dropped the car into gear. "Well, today, I'm hoping we can just relax and enjoy the fresh air and the company." She eased the car down the road for the short drive to the main entrance of the winery. "I saw Stella earlier. She is all unpacked and is working."

"Want to join us for dinner tonight? We usually do Chinese food to kick off the new year."

"Sounds like a nice tradition. I'd love to join you."

They drove past row after row of vines. He pointed out the window. "See all these vines?"

"Impressive, and they're all ours."

"I planted them the first spring I was here. The land had been prepped but the previous owner didn't have the funds to take the next step. When I came to look at it, there was just a huge vacant field as far as I could see."

"Now look at it. Nothing but vines."

He could hear the distinct note of pride in her voice. Of course she was happy they were good producers. And he was happy he'd let go of his fears. It wasn't productive and he was happy where they were now.

"When it's time to start pruning, would you mind if I helped?" She slowed the car and turned left, so she missed the shocked look on his face.

"You want to prune vines. Have you done it before?"

"I've spent time in the vineyard at CLW. I'd like to be hands-on here too. Also, it will help me build a rapport with the seasonal field workers."

"Yeah, sure. I guess." He was having a hard time picturing her working in the field. But he'd be by her side, just in case she needed help.

She pulled up behind the warehouse, turned the car off, and stashed her keys in the console. Then she pulled on her mittens and hat. "Ready?" She pulled the collar of her down jacket close and snapped it. "I'm ready. Lead the way."

They walked hand in hand around the main warehouse and toward the stark fields of grape canes standing like twigs with tentacles stretched across their trellis.

"There's nothing like walking the land in winter where you can absorb the vibe."

He gave her a sidelong glance. "You really do love the entire process, don't you?"

Her free hand swung by her side as they strolled down the first row. After a few moments of quietly walking, she said, "I love getting my hands dirty. I believe to be successful, you have to immerse yourself in the enterprise one hundred and ten percent."

"That's where we're different. I love the growing and harvest and of course making the wines. But as far as office stuff, sales and marketing, to me, that was a chore."

"You did it though. If it hadn't been for circumstances beyond your control, I predict you would have been very successful." She gave his hand a quick tug and pulled him close.

He tipped her chin up. "That means a lot. Thanks." She tasted like vanilla. "I like your lip gloss."

"I have other flavors too." She tilted her head to the side and looked at him through her lowered lashes. "Just in case you're curious."

Max paused to inspect a vine before they continued to the end of the long row and turned to walk up the next. After a few more rows, Tessa softly hummed off-key as they continued to walk hand in hand. It was as if they had been doing this every winter together for years.

"This is nice." He held up their clasped hands.

She took a step closer to him and slid her arm around his waist. "We should make it our tradition."

He lowered his mouth and tenderly kissed her lips. "You're cold." It wasn't a question but a statement. "We should head back."

She didn't move. "The temperature is definitely dropping." Just as the words left her mouth, tiny snowflakes drifted down.

"Look up." He gestured to the ominous clouds. "We're in for a bad storm and if we don't put a wiggle on it, we'll look like Frosty." He wanted to linger in the middle of the vineyard with Tessa, but common sense urged him in the direction of the warehouse. They hadn't had the best of luck with snowstorms. Apparently they had walked quite a distance from the office because the building looked like the size of a Monopoly house.

"How long will it take us to get back?" The corner of her mouth twitched. "Just an idea, but what if we continued our day in front of a warm fire?"

He focused his gaze on her mouth. "Shortly, and the idea of you and me in front of a cozy fire sounds perfect."

. . .

*A*s they walked through the fast-falling snow, the silence of the world around them was calming. Tessa peeked at Max to see how he looked, worried or relaxed.

"Are you freezing?"

"Not at all. Walking is keeping me warm. I was remembering how fast the weather can change and our accident." Her glove-covered hand grazed the scar on his forehead.

"Not one of our best adventures, but thankfully we both walked away in relatively good shape."

Tessa slipped her arm through his. But it had changed her life. She had started to fall in love with Max while they were in the hospital. "Can I ask you a question?"

"Sure." His quick response surprised her.

"Why me?"

He looked straight ahead and his steps matched hers. "I'm pretty picky about the woman I wanted to get involved with. I never met a woman who intrigued me enough to even consider the possibility of falling in love."

Her steps slowed. Did he just say the word *love*?

She stumbled over a clump of frozen dirt. He pulled her against his chest and she looked into his eyes. Her heart slowed. She wanted him to say those three words. If he didn't, she would.

"Tessa"—his voice was soft and husky—"I have fallen in love with you."

"You have?" The words came out in a whisper. "I've fallen for you too."

"Good to know." He tapped the side of his temple.

She playfully slapped his jacket. "Is that all you can say?"

He picked her up and twirled her in his arms. "I love you, and today is the perfect day in the middle of the vineyard to tell you exactly how I feel."

She slipped her arms around his neck and kissed him

deeply. Her emotional slide into loving Max had been easy and that kiss was core melting.

He caressed her cheek. "The snow is coming down harder and we have another twenty minutes or so before we get back." They had taken a few steps when he stopped and put pressure on her hand. "Look." He gestured up ahead. Standing between them and the warehouse was a small moose. "It must be a yearling."

If there was a baby, there had to be a mother nearby. Her mouth went dry and her voice was hoarse as she said, "What are we going to do?"

"It will get tired of just standing there and wander away."

The snow continued to fall and the minutes seemed like hours. She would have liked to pull out her phone and take a picture to commemorate her first moose encounter, but didn't dare. She heard a low grunt and glanced around nervously. Max smiled without looking at her.

From the left side of the field, a large moose lumbered to the baby, either completely unaware or not caring who or what might be around, as if they had more right to be there than anyone else. Tessa watched as the momma strolled past the smaller one, turning her head forward and back as if beckoning it to follow her. Tessa's breath caught as the wind shifted from the side to their backs. Would the wind carry their scent? The momma moose lifted her head and sniffed the wind. Still unhurried, she did another short grumble and walked away. The smaller moose followed her.

When they were completely out of sight in the scrub, Max gave her a one-armed hug. "What did you think of our company?"

"That was incredible, but weren't you scared?" Her heartbeat was still hammering in her chest.

"Nervous, yes. Scared, no." He urged her forward.

"Why not?"

"Mama moose was pretty relaxed and we didn't do anything to give her a reason to charge."

She could feel her eyes pop at his blasé attitude. "But they could have trampled us. That momma was huge!"

He slipped his arm around her waist and held her close. "Probably around eight hundred pounds, but we left them alone and I always carry a pistol when I'm out here, just to pop a warning shot in the air to scare something away."

They crossed the gravel road and grew closer to the back entrance. She glanced over her shoulder. "You could have told me that when we were out there."

"Tee, I wanted us to watch the moose, and talking might have spooked them. I would never allow anything or anyone to hurt you."

"You wouldn't?"

"Of course not." He reached out and brushed her hair from her forehead.

She couldn't tear her eyes from his. "I won't let anything hurt you either."

30

"What do you think of this outfit?" Tessa looked at Stella, who lounged on a living room chair. She was excited to be going out with Max tonight, and nervous. Chinese last night with Stella was fun, but she was looking to kick things up in her relationship with a very handsome man and she had decided tonight was the night.

Stella studied the forest-green silk blouse, black jeans, leather ankle boots, and a dark-green and black waist-skimming jacket. She twirled her finger so Tessa would do a three-sixty turn.

"The stacked heels are sensible, but you need a scarf. Something fashionable but warm; the temperature will dip into the teens tonight."

Tessa snapped her fingers. "Good point. I've got a black cashmere scarf I can wear."

As she hurried from the room, Stella called after her, "What's with the dark colors? It's a romantic date after all."

Tessa popped her head around the doorjamb. "I don't want to look like I'm trying too hard. You know, put the right amount of effort in to look nice but be understated."

"If Max only knew you've tried on most of the clothes in

your closet, he'd know how hard you're trying to make a good impression." Stella laughed. "Without trying too hard."

Tessa came back into the room holding two different scarfs. Stella pointed to the pale-green one in her left hand and Tessa looped it around her neck.

"You look beautiful, Tee."

"I'm so nervous." She adjusted the scarf and checked her lipstick for a smudge.

"You could wear old jeans and a ratty shirt and he wouldn't care."

The doorbell rang and Tessa's smile grew. "He's here."

"Answer the door before he's an ice sculpture on your doorstep."

Tessa swung the door wide and the first thing she saw was an enormous bouquet of flowers. Max lowered the vase. His expression said more than words ever could. She had chosen the right outfit.

"Hi. You look beautiful."

"Come in."

Max stepped inside and handed her the clear glass-cut vase with wildflowers, roses, and lilies. The scent was sweet and spicy.

"Thank you for the flowers. They're beautiful." She buried her nose in a pink sweetheart rose.

Stella popped out from the living room. "Hey." She had her coat on. "I'm going to take off." To neither of them in particular, she said, "Talk to you tomorrow." She softly closed the door after her.

Max followed Tessa into the living room. She placed the vase on a table. "Do you want to have a glass of wine here before we leave?"

"No, we have reservations at Sawyers."

"Let me just get my coat."

He picked up her long dark wool coat off the sofa and held it while she slipped it on. Tessa pulled on the gloves he had given her for Christmas and picked up her handbag. "I'm ready." She flipped the switch on the living room light, leaving the room in a soft, cozy glow.

He held the front door for her as they stepped into the biting cold. He cleared his throat. "I'm glad we're going out tonight. I asked Alan Waters if we could have a table near the fireplace. Being funny, he asked if we wanted to sit on the patio."

Any nerves Tessa might have had disappeared. "I hope you said for tonight, maybe inside would be a better choice."

"Actually, quite the opposite. I asked if we could have the patio to ourselves."

Standing on tiptoes, she slid her arms around his neck and pulled him close. She gave him a slow and lingering kiss. "We might need something to keep us warm."

He held her close to his chest. "I like how you think." He returned the kiss with a demand and promise for more.

❦

From his seat across from Tessa, Max studied the way the firelight cast a soft glow over her heart-shaped face. He was filled with a sense of feeling whole. Their conversation flowed over salads and they were waiting for their main course to arrive when Tessa pointed at the bottle of red they were enjoying.

"I'm a little surprised you didn't order one of ours."

He liked how that sounded when she referred to Creek. "Don't tell your dad, but I've been a fan of the CLW cabernet for quite some time. Besides, it's good to drink wines from other vineyards. Sometimes there's a note of something I may want to see if we can enhance with our wines."

"Who knew?" She glanced around the sparsely filled room. "I guess the cold is keeping people home tonight."

"Are you warm enough?" His heart tripped in his chest.

He longed to finish dinner and warm her up in a different way.

"The fire is nice." Her eyes sparkled with mischief. "Do you want to catch a movie tonight?"

What? She wanted to see a film? Oh, wait. He noticed she was holding back a grin. Two could play this game. "There are several good choices. The kids' movie about falling into a video game, an action-packed thriller, or a classic Scrooge from the nineteen fifties is playing." He toyed with his fork. "Lady's choice."

She wrinkled her nose. "Nothing sounds interesting."

He could think of two ideas. His place or hers.

She rubbed her thumb across his palm. "We could bring dessert back to my place, kick back with a glass of wine, and continue our date in private."

He turned her palm up. Pressing a tender kiss to the very center, he said in a low and husky voice, "I have a fireplace and my sister doesn't live a couple of doors down."

"All true statements."

They were interrupted by Alan delivering their dinner. Tessa reluctantly withdrew her hand.

It was hard for Max to focus on his meal when he was looking forward to what was to come. "You never said. My place or yours?"

"My place is closer." She gave him a seductive wink.

He almost dropped his fork on the plate. Her sexy laugh caused his blood to go from warm to hot. "Then let's finish our dinner and we can brave the cold."

"Take your time. We've got all night."

He loved the way she was looking at him, and what she said made his pulse race.

*M*ax held her hand on the drive back to her place. Tessa's heart pounded in her chest. Maybe they should go to his house. Had she left her bedroom a mess, with clothes strewn everywhere? Did it matter? She glanced at him from the corner of her eye. Despite not being one to rush a romance, she was exactly where she wanted to be. It was time to seize the moment and savor it.

He released her hand as he parked the car and hurried around to open her door. She took his hand, and with one fluid motion, he pulled her into his arms, waiting a fraction of a second before lowering his lips. She molded to his body, kissing his cool, full mouth and wanting more.

"Let's go inside."

He nuzzled her neck. "Yes."

Tessa eased back and hoped her laugh sounded more seductive than nervous. "Come."

Without releasing his hand, they hurried up the walkway. She withdrew her keys from her bag. Max took them and eased open the door. Habit kicked in and she shrugged her coat off and threw it on the chair, all the while maintaining physical contact with him. They crossed the front entrance and he swept her into his arms. The room was bathed in a warm, soft glow from the solitary lamp Tessa had left on.

She took the lead. This was her decision and she didn't want Max to have any doubt about it.

"Let's relax in the living room." Her voice was soft. She didn't want to break the spell which had enveloped them.

He willingly followed her lead.

She pulled him down next to her on the sofa and wound her arms around his neck.

"Kiss me." It wasn't a demand or a plea but her desire.

He cupped his hands on each side of her face but hesitated. "Are you sure this is what you want?"

"Yes," she breathed.

He kissed her tenderly. Passion fed her need for him. His body pressed firmly against hers, a perfect fit. Lost in the sensations that washed over her, Tessa allowed her fingers to slide down the length of his arm, over his broad shoulders and upper back. She wanted to memorize every square inch she could touch.

He pulled back and dropped his chin. "We should slow this down."

Confused, she struggled to sit up. "Why?"

"For the first time in my life, I don't want to rush."

A flash of hurt flared inside her. "You don't want to be here with me? Like this?"

"The exact opposite. I'd love to sweep you from this couch and take you to bed and make love to you until the sun comes up. But before we take that step, I want you to understand how I really feel about you."

She sat back on the sofa and studied him. Was he just giving her a line? She looked at him closely. "What do you mean?"

He held her hands in between his and brought them to his lips. He searched her eyes, the blue in his more vivid and intense. "I've never felt about a woman the way I feel about you. This is new territory for me and I feel vulnerable. I'm scared I'll screw up and lose you."

"How could you possibly screw it up if it's what we both want?" She gestured toward the hallway.

"I want more than just one night with you." He tipped her chin up and looked her in the eyes. "I love you."

"My darling Max, just breathe. You're not alone in this relationship."

*T*essa's heart pounded in her chest. After that declaration, she rose and walked down the hall, leaving a trail of clothes like breadcrumbs for Max to follow.

He'd get the message loud and clear and there would be no doubt she had said yes without being asked the question. But she wanted Max next to her, touching and caressing her body.

He stood in the bedroom doorway.

"Clothing is not optional."

He shrugged his clothes off and she flicked the covers back and invited him in.

His hands were gentle as they slid over her skin, leaving a trail of goose bumps in their wake. Each caress caused her to crave more. She slid her hands around his neck and pulled him to her.

His mouth came crushing down, devouring her as if he were a man starving. His hands rested on her hips. Tessa had never felt more alive.

With her lips, she followed his jawline to the hollow at the base of his neck. His head arched back, giving her access. He groaned softly.

She eased him back and continued her exploration. He was lean and muscular, and she enjoyed the journey. Her hands ran lightly from his shoulder to biceps to forearm, ending at his fingertips. She sighed.

It was his turn. He stroked and caressed each curve, taking his time as she had done. She wanted more of him.

The only indication of time going by was that the moon moved across the room, fading as it withdrew its light.

"I want more of you." She gave him a saucy smile.

"We have all night." He chuckled and buried his head in her neck, his body lying half on her. She wanted to memorize every part of him. He slowed his fingers, sliding them over her skin while her heart raced.

She whispered, "Do you?" Her voice trailed off.

"Yes." He moved away from her, leaving her exposed to cool air for a moment.

She urged him to touch her in all the right places. They came together without haste; their breathing came in short gasps until it culminated in one final rush. It was loving and tender and perfect.

Max covered her face with feather-like kisses.

"That was amazing." Her fingers traced the outline of his lips.

He kissed her again. "It was."

He kept one arm around Tessa and picked up two glasses of wine, which she hadn't realized he had brought with him. She sat up and rearranged the covers over them before accepting a glass.

He raised his glass to his lips, but she stopped him. "Let's toast." Her smile was intense.

"What should we toast to?"

She tipped her head. "To a promising new year together."

Their glasses clinked and she sipped. She felt dizzy as if the wine went right to her head with the first taste.

He cupped her cheek. "Tessa, I'm probably rushing things, but after living through the last ten years of my life, I know every day is precious. To not tell the people who mean the most to you how you feel can be an opportunity you'll never get back."

She felt happy tears prick her eyes.

"You don't have to say a word. I just wanted you to know where I stand."

She snuggled close to him, wanting to pour out her heart, but held back. "I'm right where I want to be."

"That's all I need to know." He kissed her temple and held her close.

31

*T*essa floated on air as she ascended the stairs to her shared office with Max. She could still feel his good morning kiss on her lips. She entered the spacious office and flicked on the overhead lights but even the illumination didn't hide the blinking light on the office phone, signaling a voicemail. She dropped her briefcase on the table and punched in the code.

"Kevin, this is Robert Haskins. I have great news. I just came across a listing for a winery, roughly the same size as Sand Creek, in Michigan. The owners are highly motivated and it's in excellent shape, so you'll need to act fast if you want to scoop this one up. Give me a call."

Shock washed over her. What was going on? After how far they had come in their personal relationship, Max was planning to leave? She sank onto a chair. Was he going to expect her to pay him for the forty percent share he had in Creek? She clutched a hand to her heart. How could he think of leaving now? The winery was doing well, and their personal relationship had gone in a new direction. She blinked the tears from her eyes, pacing the room. Or worse, was he going to ask her to leave The Valley and her family and start over with him? A clean slate. What could she do? Her thoughts spun without a coherent thought beyond the hurt and fury she was feeling.

"Tessa."

She crossed the office and looked over the banister. "Don, what are you doing here?"

He walked up the stairs. "I wanted to walk through the plans for Valentine's."

The last thing she needed was to think about the most romantic night of the year. "Sure. We can go over the plans. Come on up."

Don sat at the wooden table.

"Can I get you a coffee?" She moved to the machine and inserted a pod.

"Thanks."

She could feel his eyes follow her. She avoided his when she handed him a mug, and continued to do so when she sat down. "For the event, we have a couple of tables open." She handed him a folder from the stack in the middle of the table. "The details are in there."

He tapped the closed folder and regarded her carefully. "Do you want to talk about whatever has you so upset?"

"It's nothing." She toyed with her coffee mug but didn't pick it up.

"You might be able to avoid talking to some, but I know you as well as I know myself. Spill it. Are you having a problem with Max?"

"Not in the way you might think."

"Talk to me. Maybe I can help."

"Please don't say I told you so." Her voice cracked.

Don's forehead creased. "It can't be that bad. Where is he today?"

"Meetings in Rochester. He'll be back tomorrow." Her finger hovered over the voicemail button on the phone. "Listen to this."

The message played through without Don's face changing expression. When it was done, Tessa said, "This isn't good."

"Sis, that isn't what I heard. It was a real estate agent calling to pass along some information. Max could have been working with this guy for a year or more. I don't think you should jump to conclusions."

Her temper was going from simmer to hot. "Are you taking his side?"

"Of course not. But I've seen how he looks at you when you're not watching. That guy has got it bad for you. Before you change the locks, give him a chance to explain, and if I turn out to be wrong, I'll change the locks for you."

Could he be right? It gave her something to think about. She gave him a tentative smile. "You're a pretty good brother. Now, let's talk about our event. It's going to be a smashing success."

<hr>

*M*ax saw the lights on upstairs when he came in from the parking lot. He couldn't wait to tell her about the sales he had closed yesterday and had picked up a bag of her favorite muffins and a coffee to celebrate. He had left her a voicemail, but she must have had dinner with her family since she hadn't called him back.

When he got to the top of the stairs, he noticed a light was on in the small office next to the space he shared with Tessa. She was nowhere to be seen, but he could hear her talking. Curious, he walked down the hall and stopped short at the door.

"I'll need to look over the reservations, and I wonder if we got enough place settings. Liza ordered two hundred and fifty of everything, thinking we can wash them in time, but I'm not sure." She glanced at him and gestured to the chair across from the desk.

She had family pictures on the desk and if he didn't know better— No, she wouldn't have moved into this office to get away from him. Everything was going great. Max set the cardboard tray with two coffees and a bag at the edge of the desk.

"Alright, Kate, I'll defer to you and Liza." She laughed. "I can't help it." She doodled on the pad in front of her. "Okay, I'll check that off my list and move on to something more exciting, like ordering single red roses for us to give to each couple when they arrive."

She paused. "Hold on. I'll ask Max; he just came in." She gave him a polite smile. "Do you know how many tables we have free for the seatings at five and eight?"

He kicked back in the chair, attempting to look casual, and rested his ankle on the opposite knee. "We're booked solid as of two days ago." He wasn't going to get all uptight until he knew what the hell was going on.

"For both?"

He gave a short nod. "Yup."

"Great news, Kate. We're sold out!" The smile that filled her face about the event would have been better if it was about their personal relationship. But what was he thinking? Her comfort zone was business.

After she hung up the phone, he looked around the space. "New office?"

"I thought it would be best to give us some personal space."

He jutted his chin toward the desktop. "I brought breakfast to celebrate. I got three texts this morning and all the restaurants want to carry us."

She was silent. His heart constricted like it was in a vise. "Hey, are you alright?" He dropped to one knee.

She pointed to the office phone. "You have a saved message."

"Who?"

"Maybe you should listen to it."

He could hear the biting tone in her voice. He played it on speakerphone and his face paled. "Tessa, it's not what you think. It was from before."

"Before what?" She pushed back from the desk and glared at him. "What's to explain? You're thinking of leaving. That's clear." She paced to the window and hugged her arms around her body. "You say you love me but this whole time, you've been looking for a new winery." She swept her arm in the direction of the vines. "Do you think I can't handle running this winery without my family's help? Maybe it's crossed your mind that I'll never be more than a marketing director, always in Don's shadow as second best. Is that what you think?" She spun around. "Or you've been looking at new locations and you're planning to convince me to leave The Valley." She shook her head. "As much as I love you, don't ask me to choose between my family and you." She stifled a sob. "Stella and my family are all we have in this world that really matters."

Just when he had started to believe in a happily ever after for them, everything was spinning out of control. The ideas she was sputtering were crazy. He crossed the room and stood beside her and his fingers trailed down her arm. "Tessa, I haven't been looking for months. I told Robert that I was happy and staying here at Creek."

"Then why did he call? Obviously, he didn't think you were serious." She was tapping a pen against her leg, a sure sign she was stressed.

"You shouldn't be surprised I had thoughts of leaving. Losing my dream and seeing someone new follow theirs was excruciating. I'm not going to apologize for considering my limited options. Nothing might have panned out, but I had to try."

She glared at him. "What changed?"

"You. Me. Us." He placed his hands on her arms and turned her so they were face-to-face.

She sniffed in disbelief and averted her eyes. "You've been stringing me along."

"No. Tessa, please look at me. Look in my eyes and listen to my words. I am not planning on going anywhere without you." She didn't ask a question but didn't move away from him either. "After the accident, I knew I had feelings for you. I was confused. You were a woman I'd vowed to respect but not get close to, as I was going to leave town once our one-year agreement expired."

"Then what changed your mind?"

"My feelings for you have grown every day, but I've been alone except for Stella for a long time. Then I realized I didn't want to leave The Valley because this is where you are, everything clicked. After you offered me the share in the winery, I came to understand and respect you even more. You trusted me with your dream and I still have a future on this land. Would it be different, yes, but I have a new dream. Surely you can understand that?"

She winced. "You're only staying for the potential of money?"

"No." His hand slid down her arm to take her hand and his voice softened. "Money has nothing to do with my decision to stay. I want to be here." He pounded his chest and swallowed the lump that rose in his throat. "My heart is here, with you and this winery. I want us to have a future, creating new wines, selling our new blends. We can build something special together. And those forty acres that I own, *we* can decide what *we* want to plant there. It's our future; let's nurture the tender roots and grow it together."

She pulled her hand from his gentle hold. "I have to go."

"Wait. Please. Do you remember that first day when we talked? I thought you'd value your family over me. That's why I called the real estate agent, not because I didn't have faith in you, but I didn't want to lose the winery again—and now you. I never thought I'd be the family you put first."

She pulled on her coat. His heart broke as tears cascaded down her cheeks. He dropped his hands to his sides, shoulders slumped. "We're like two canes that have been grafted together. Maybe we didn't want to become a new version of what we were, but we're at the critical stage of coming together, stronger, with the potential for roots to take hold and branches to soar."

"You should have told me you had contacted a real estate agent. I would have understood if you'd been honest." She couldn't hide the pain in her large brown eyes; tears clung to her lashes and she wiped her cheeks with the back of her hand. With a shake of her head, she said, "And you're using a grape vine metaphor to explain how you feel about us?"

His shoulders hunched over. "I'm not good with explaining my emotions but like you, vines are my comfort zone."

Fresh tears flowed freely down her cheeks. Her black mascara smudged under her eyes. "I have to go," she said.

His eyes followed her to the stairs, willing her to turn back, but she didn't.

*

*M*ax watched Tessa race down the stairs. Away from him.

"What the hell?" He kicked a chair, the sound echoing in the empty room. Deciding to take care of business, he called Robert, who answered on the second ring.

"Kevin, good to hear from you. I take it you got my message."

Max said, "I did and as I said before, I'm not interested. I plan on staying here at Sand Creek." That was, if Tessa didn't kick him to the curb. He wanted to go after her, but she needed time. Hopefully she'd understand what had happened and why.

"If you change your mind, give me a call."

"Thanks, but I won't." Max hung up the phone. He prowled the room, at a loss for what he could do. Stella would have good advice.

She answered on the fourth ring. Her voice was breathless. "Hello."

"Sis, are you okay?" A familiar flash of worry washed over him.

She gave a short laugh. "You need to chill. I'm fine."

"It's hard for me to get used to the new normal for us."

"I get it. The knee-jerk reaction of waiting for the next shoe to drop. But we're going to have smooth sailing from here on out."

Max ran his hand through his hair. "Well, that's why I'm calling. A high heel dropped. Do you have a minute to talk?"

"What's going on?"

The concern in her voice comforted him. "I've made a mess of things with Tessa and I need your advice on how to fix it."

"I happen to be a genius with other people's relationships, so let's hear it."

He took a ragged breath. "After Tessa bought the winery, I thought we could move. Buy a new winery and make a fresh start for both you and me. I did some research, just speculative, as I had agreed to stay on for a year."

"I can see where you're coming from. You do like a backup plan."

"After the car accident, I realized I was in love with her. I told the real estate agent I had been working with I changed my mind."

"So what happened?"

Her voice was comforting, and it encouraged him to keep

talking. "The real estate agent left a message yesterday to say he had come across an opportunity in Michigan."

"I see." Those two words held a sharp rebuke.

"No, you don't. Nothing has changed, but I'm afraid Tessa thinks I'm going to pressure her to buy back the forty percent share in the company she gave me before Christmas."

"Why would she give you a forty percent stake in the winery?"

He could picture her shaking her head in disbelief. "She said that without my efforts, the winery wouldn't have been worth buying."

"Or you could have sold the forty percent to an investor, giving you the cash to buy a new winery. She's been in this business a long time and her mind would have gone there. You can understand why she jumped to that conclusion."

He smacked his forehead with the palm of his hand. He groaned. "I get it, but after the other night, she should know I wouldn't want to be anywhere but here. She does it for me, and someday I want to marry her."

"Does she know that?"

"Not the marrying part but the rest. At least, I thought so." Now he was questioning if she did understand how deep his feelings were for her.

With a snort, Stella said, "You're not going to like this, but a woman wants to hear how the man she loves feels about her. She wants to see your heart beating just for her. No wonder she thinks you're going to bolt."

"How can I convince Tessa she's the only one for me?"

"You need to sit her down and be totally honest, about everything. That includes how you're still dealing with the ripples of losing our parents and me getting sick. You thought I was going to die and leave you alone like they did. Hell, I had a few of those days myself. Don't gloss over the painful stuff. Tessa can handle it."

"What if I can't? I've been trying to, but in the back of my mind it feels like when I let myself love someone, they leave."

"If my hunch is right, she's the woman who can help you chase that monster away and let go of the past. Look at the way the entire Price family has welcomed us into their lives. We've made friends who treat us like we're family and I don't think it is entirely to do with Tessa's relationship with you. They're genuinely good people who care."

He looked around the office that, up until two days ago, they had shared. "What if I'm too late?"

"How will you know unless you try? Tell her everything. You'll feel better when you share the burden you've carried all these years. Now it's time for you to have a happy life."

He stood up and grabbed his coat. "Thanks, sis. You're the best."

*a*fter driving around town, checking the diner and the park, Max had no luck finding Tessa. He swung by her condo. She wasn't there; her parents' place was the next logical stop.

He cruised back through town to make sure he hadn't missed her. At the end of Main Street, he drove in the direction of CLW. He picked up speed while still keeping an eye open for her car. The words he wanted to say were jumbled in his head. Stella was right; it had to come from the heart if he wanted Tessa in his life.

His hands clenched the steering wheel. How should he begin, with an apology? No. He didn't do anything wrong in planning for his future. When he started down this path, he had believed he wouldn't be able to work for her. When she walked through the front door, he hadn't been prepared for the woman he met: genuine, intelligent, and with a sense of humor. He had planned his exit on his terms. She would understand that was exactly what she had done when she left CLW.

He drove up the long tree-lined driveway at her parents'

home. If her car wasn't there, he could take the back drive down to the winery. If he still couldn't locate her, he'd go back to the office and wait.

No car at the house. He eased left and headed down the wide gravel road. At the bottom, the heart of Crescent Lake Winery rolled out before him: the vineyard. He slowed to a crawl and drank in the sight. It was inspiring. He understood the decades-long sacrifices Sam and Sherry had made to enjoy this success; a winery like this didn't sprout up overnight. With Tessa at the helm, Creek could mirror this success. But is that what she wanted, to be just like CLW, or was it possible to move forward to do and create something independent of the Price family?

He rounded the corner to the tasting room entrance and there it was. Her car was parked next to the bright-burgundy door. He steeled himself for what came next. If she chose not to believe him about leaving, he'd relinquish his shares in the business and fulfill the original contract. He hung his head. *That is the last thing I want to do.* But this wasn't about him. It was about Tessa.

He pulled the door open into a dimly lit space. Across the room, the stairs to the offices were in front of him and he took them two at a time, then paused at the top. He looked right and left, unsure where she might be. He heard female voices to the right, so he hurried in that direction. His gut tightened. There was so much riding on this conversation. Their entire future.

His soft-soled shoes didn't make a sound as he hurried down the long sunny hallway. A few office doors stood open, but the rooms were empty. He reached the end of the hall and stuck his head in the last door, Anna's office. Tessa wasn't with her; it was Peyton talking to Anna who he'd heard.

"Hi, ladies." He looked from Peyton to Anna. "Have either of you seen Tessa?"

Anna's brow arched. "She's talking with Dad and Don." She pointed in the direction he just came from. "At the opposite end of the hall."

He forced a strained smile. "Thanks." He had stepped into the hallway when Anna called out. "Max."

He backtracked and looked her directly in the eye. Without a hint of a smile, Anna said, "Good luck."

He couldn't mistake the tone in her voice as anything but protective. With a slow shake of his head, he said, "Thanks." He wondered if she was being sincere. It was hard to tell because Anna had a good poker face.

Reaching the midpoint of the hall, he took a deep breath and rolled his shoulders up and back. He strode toward the door and stopped to rap on the casing. He could hear them talking about Creek. Was his original suspicion accurate? Was she planning on folding it into CLW? He needed to let that go once and for all, and he certainly wasn't going to bring it up again. She had made it clear that Creek was her business, not part of the Price family winery. But Tessa needed to believe in herself; she didn't need to rely on Don or the family to be a success. Without waiting for Don to respond to his knock, he walked in.

Tessa's head swiveled around. Shock filled her face.

"Max, what are you doing here?" She got up, her back to Don.

"Looking for you. I'm not leaving you, but we need to talk."

Her eyes grew wide, her lips thinned. "Why? We don't have anything more to talk about." She crossed her arms over her chest. Her brown eyes, like her voice, were chilly. "I'm not walking away from what we've already worked so hard to accomplish just to start all over again in Michigan just because you don't believe in me and want to be where the name Price won't matter."

Don stood up behind her, his voice controlled with a

protective undertone. "Max, maybe you should have waited for her at the office."

Max's gaze swung from Tessa to Sam, who simply sat there, and back to Don.

He threw his hands up. "Give me ten minutes, and then I'll leave."

"So you can call your real estate agent? Maybe he's found another winery you can check out, one that is even better than Creek." Her gaze didn't flinch.

He took a step closer and softened his voice. "That is not my plan. It was, but not now."

Sam heaved himself from the chair. "Don, we should give them some privacy."

She touched her father's arm. "Thanks."

Sam and Don left the room.

Max stepped closer to her. He wanted to take her hand but instead jammed his into his jacket. "I'm sorry. I didn't mean to hurt you."

"Who says you did?"

"Tee. I told the agent I was done looking for a property right after the accident. I knew then and now this is where I want to live and work, with you." He glanced out the window before he continued. "When you first bought the winery, I thought you did it to prove to your father you were an astute businesswoman."

She sat down. "Go on."

"I was wrong. You didn't have anything to prove to anyone. You saw an opportunity and you seized it. You had a dream and you found a way to see it realized. I know your family has your back and they support you, but you need to realize you have the skills it takes to be successful as Tessa and not because of your last name." He looked around the room. "After you left, I talked to Stella. She encouraged me to share everything with you. Bare my soul."

She gestured to a chair. "Have a seat."

He crossed the room and sat next to her. Was he ready to peel away the protective layers he had spent years building?

*S*he watched the color drain from Max's face. She had no idea what he was about to tell her. She said, "Go on. I'm listening."

"Some of this, you already know. It started when my father died."

She couldn't begin to imagine what it would have been like to lose both her parents so young and to take care of a younger sibling.

He wrung his hands, his knuckles white. "At the end of my senior year in college, Stella was still in high school. Dad took our boat out on a river near our home, and it capsized. It was the second worst day of my life." He blinked away the tears that filled his eyes. "As kids, we spent countless hours on that river, swimming and boating. He was an excellent swimmer, but when he was found, Dad didn't have a life vest on."

"I'm so sorry." She wanted to take his hand and provide some small measure of comfort, but he stared at the floor.

"He always said he felt close to Mom on the boat." His voice cracked. "My graduation was in a few weeks. I knew that in order to take care of Stella, my degree was essential. She stayed with her best friend's family. Then as soon as finals were over, I went home and got a job so she could finish high school."

"That was a selfless thing to do."

He lifted his eyes to meet hers. "She was all the family I had in the world. I'd do anything for her."

He sagged against the chair, head tilted back and eyes closed. "She went to the University of Buffalo, and I wanted to be nearby. I found this place. Stella had her independence but I was close in case she needed me. Our lives were going great until she found the cancer. It was like a rerun of our mother and I was helpless to protect her."

"You were there when it counted most." Tessa hoped her words offered some kind of comfort.

His eyes flew open. They were filled with a fierceness she hadn't seen before. "I'd do anything to protect my family."

"And I bought the one stable thing in your life. The winery." She rose from the chair.

"You didn't take anything away. It was sinking." He held out his hand, and she took it.

"You took care of Stella, which was incredibly selfless."

"Her cancer almost destroyed me. It didn't matter I was pulling all the profits from the business. I had to do everything possible. I couldn't lose her too."

"Why did you think I was going to hand over the winery to my family?" She cocked her head. "Despite me telling you that was never on the table."

"It's hard for me to trust that I won't lose someone or something I love again."

"I never thought when I walked into the winery how you would deal with the changes. I jumped in with both feet, full steam ahead."

"It was your right."

She bobbed her head from side to side. "Yes. I could have been more sensitive, but I appreciate you telling me." For the business, she could put this aside, but there would be changes at the winery. "I'm going to work from home for the rest of the day. If you need something, send me an email." She hoped it was clear from a business perspective that they were fine. Personally was a different story. She needed time to process what he had said.

He dropped her hand and stood up. "Oh, well, I have stuff to do. See you tomorrow?"

"Sure." Tessa remained standing next to the table and watched Max turn and leave the room without a backward glance.

33

_T_essa watched her father leave the tasting room and her makeshift office. After the first day, she hated the new office and now two weeks later, this was a better compromise. She told herself working in the tasting room was a good way to figure out how she wanted to organize the space, but the truth was that she wanted to be in the same office with Max. Even though she'd settled in to her new, familiar routine of work and meals alone, she missed him, missed having dinner with him every night or sharing a laugh or a brush of his hand on hers. It was better to keep things professional. With her eyes closed, she thought back to the night they had shared. Waking in his arms and beginning a new day was something she thought they'd do often. She could even see herself living with Max. He was that special.

Max walked into the tasting room through the back door. "What was that all about?" He pointed to her dad crossing the parking area.

"We've been the topic of conversation with my parents and they've decided to stick their noses into our personal lives by inviting us for dinner."

He gave her a thoughtful look. "Does this mean there might be hope of a reconciliation?"

"Max." She shook her head.

He sighed. "Just friends. I get it. I'll meet you there."

She softened. "We can drive together since we'll be coming from work." Her fingertips lightly touched his arm. Electricity jolted through her.

He reached out but then pulled back.

⁂

Tessa glanced at Max as he drove. "You didn't need to buy Mom flowers."

"My mother drilled into me to never show up empty-handed. It's rude."

"It's just my parents."

He flashed a frown in her direction. "Every other time, I've brought wine. This time, I had to do something different." He groaned. "Is your mom allergic to flowers?"

"Relax. She loves them." She patted his arm in an attempt to reassure him. "I'm sorry for making you nuts about tonight. They knew we were dating and now we're not and even though things changed, we can certainly have a meal with others."

He slowed the car on the last turn. The house was ablaze with lights, and Christmas lights still twinkled along the porch. "My feelings for you haven't changed."

Tessa looked out the windshield. "I miss being with you." She turned in the seat. "I understand why you hesitated about us working together, but when we acknowledged our feelings, why didn't you tell me that you had looked at other properties? I don't understand the secrecy."

"That's just it—it wasn't a secret. Once I made my decision and I knew there wasn't anyplace else I wanted to be, it was a non-issue for me. Why bring it up and dissect it? What would it have accomplished?"

"I don't know." She chewed on her lower lip. "I'm scared."

"Of what?" His voice was gentle and he held out his hand.

She laced her fingers with his. The warmth of his touch made her long for more.

"I took a huge leap in my career, and falling in love with you wasn't part of the plan. I want to have the kind of relationship my parents have. Based on friendship, honesty, trust, and love."

Up ahead, the porch light flicked on.

"We need to go inside." She tugged her hand away. "Remember, it's just dinner with Sam and Sherry."

"Tee, we want the same things. Can we finish this conversation later?"

"No promises." Her voice was cautious but optimistic.

He took his foot off the brake and rolled to park in front of the garage. "I'll take it."

The front door was flung open before they even made it to the bottom step. Dad filled the doorway.

"Come on in. Your mom has been cooking up a storm and she just took the roast out of the oven." He left the door open so Max and Tessa could follow him inside. "She said it's got to rest or something."

Tessa laughed. "Hi, Dad." She kissed his cheek and hung her coat on the hook.

Mom came around the corner, wiping her hands on a towel. "Tessa, Max, I'm so glad you're here."

He held out the bouquet of flowers to her. "Sherry, these are for you."

She beamed. "You shouldn't have, but they're lovely. Thank you." She lightly kissed his cheek.

Tessa took his coat and hung it next to hers. "Dinner smells good, Mom."

"We have a pot roast, veggies, and I whipped up a gingerbread for dessert."

"Sherry, it sounds like you've been in the kitchen all day."

She waved a hand. "Nonsense. I love cooking for my family. I'm going to put these in water. Dad will open the wine. Go sit and I'll join you momentarily."

"Mom, do you need help?"

"All set." She effectively dismissed Tessa with a wave of the flowers.

They walked to the opposite end of the kitchen. The dining table was set for four and Tessa gave a soft sigh of relief. She had thought they'd be ambushed with other family members showing up. But what were her parents up to? Why the dinner?

The evening passed with a delicious meal, dessert, and coffee without so much of a peep about her personal relationship with Max. But they had discussed the Valentine's Day event in great detail.

Mom said, "Sam, events like the cocktail reception and Valentine's dinner would have been helpful when we took over the winery from Donald." She tented her fingers, elbows propped on the table. "The wine trail was just starting up, and it wasn't like it is now. We worked more on distributing the wine to stores than selling direct to our ideal customer."

Dad got up to add a log to the fire. Sparks danced behind the screen. "It was Sherry's idea to hold events on the property. We even built a gazebo for small weddings. That was long before Kate opened the bistro. Have you thought about event space at Creek?"

Max said, "When I had the new building put up, I did keep that in mind. Off the back of the tasting room, we could expand the patio and create a larger event space."

That was exactly what she wanted to do. They did make good partners; it was too bad the way things were headed.

"Good. Planning for the future is important." He leaned against the mantle. "Speaking of the future—"

Oh no, Dad was not going to use that as a segue to poke his nose in. Tessa got up. "Can I see you in your office for a minute?"

Dad looked at Mom. "Now?"

"Yes." She led the way down the hall. When they got to the office, Tessa closed the door firmly behind them.

"What do you think you're doing?" she fumed.

He gave her his *I'm innocent* look. "I'm talking business with Max."

"I think you're sidestepping the truth. It seems to me you were getting ready to poke your nose into our private life."

"Honey, I want you to be happy." He sat down on the edge of his desk. "Is that so wrong?"

"I'm a grown woman and you need to trust me to make my own decisions. I appreciate you wanting to look out for me, but I'm fine the way things are."

"Do you love him?"

She shuffled from foot to foot. "It's complicated."

"Did you ever hear the story about when your mother and I first started dating?"

"We all know the story, Dad." She placed her hands over her heart and sighed. "A perfect romance."

With a snort, he said, "Hardly. I almost blew it with her. Around the time Grandpa Donald had his first heart attack, I showed up at her apartment and saw her with some guy. I jumped to a wrong conclusion and got mad. I took off instead of talking to her. It wasn't until my dad told me about falling in love with your grandmother and that it was love at first sight for them that I started to listen to my heart. Your grandmother told Grandpa Don their hearts knew from the minute they laid eyes on each other. She believed in fate." He looked at Tessa as if he were seeing her for the first time as a grown woman. "He asked me how many chances did I think we got in life to find love and challenged me to think about what I was running away from. I was scared of how deep my feelings were for her and that it happened so fast. My mother had died a few years earlier and I saw firsthand how hard my dad grieved for her. I wasn't sure if I was strong enough for heartache."

"I thought Mom worked in the flower gardens and Grandpa offered her a job and the rest was fate." Tessa wondered what other family stories might have alternate versions. "What brought you back together?"

"I chose to face my fear and take the chance. There are no rules with love. You can fall in love with the person you want to spend a lifetime with in as little as one day. Then, for the rest of your lives, you fight like hell to hold on. With love and a bit of luck, you can have an amazing life."

"It worked out well for the two of you. Here you are, what? Forty-plus years later." This was something to think about.

"Max is a good guy, and maybe he was scared. I see a bit of myself in him." He hugged her. "Don't get upset with your meddling old man. All I want is the best for you."

"I love you, Dad."

Mom and Max were sitting in front of the fire when she and her dad joined them.

Tessa asked, "What have the two of you been talking about?"

He smiled. "Sherry told me what the winery was like in the early days."

She sat next to him.

Mom said, "It was hard work." Her cheeks flushed and Dad's color deepened too. "I wouldn't have missed a single moment of our life together."

"You two are an inspiration to all us kids." Tessa touched Max's hand, not sure what else to say. "Max, are you ready to go?"

*T*essa pulled her collar around her neck. She and Max stood in the driveway. "It's cold." Her breath made puffs of frosty air when she exhaled. "Have you seen the gazebo at night? Dad had it strung with lights. We could walk down and take a look. Maybe we should build something like it at Creek." Well, that was stupid. Here she was trying to find a way to talk to Max about rekindling their romance and she brought up business.

He pulled a knit cap from his coat pocket and put it on, then took her mitten-covered hand. "Let's have a look."

Now Tessa was at a loss for words. Where should she start? "Did you get enough to eat at dinner?" Inwardly, she groaned. That was lame.

He hugged her arm to his side. "Everything was great, but being with you was the best part." The gravel crunched under their feet as they walked a few hundred yards down the driveway. As they grew closer, the colored Christmas lights shone like gemstones on the snow.

"About ten years ago, Mom mentioned she'd like a gazebo where she could sit and enjoy a glass of wine," Tessa began. "Dad is a softie when it comes to her, so he had a small gazebo built in the backyard, complete with screens and a door so she has a respite from the sun and bugs whenever she wants." She steered Max to the left of the main road, to the stone path leading to the doorway.

"Sam is not a guy who I'd think had a soft side."

"You'd be right—except for his bride." She pulled her arm away as she stepped inside. "When Dad saw how much she loved it, all she had to do was mention it would be a beautiful place to hold a wedding. It lit a fire under Dad to have a big one built here, so the next spring, this was constructed. It's really a cross between a pavilion and a gazebo, but don't tell Mom."

He steered her to a bench against the wall. "As much as I enjoy the lowdown on the history of the gazebo, can we talk about us?"

She gave a nervous laugh. "Instead of me chattering like a magpie?"

"I could listen to you talk for hours about nothing, but we left a lot unsaid earlier." He put his arm around her and held her close. They sat quietly for a few minutes. "My parents had a marriage like yours do."

She looked at his face. His crystal-blue eyes pierced her heart and she softened. "You said if you could change things, you wouldn't have looked for a winery?"

He tightened his arm around her. "It was an impulse that I reached out to a real estate agent. I was angry at myself, and it wasn't about you. I've thought about it a lot over the last couple of weeks. I should have told you, and I'm sorry. I never want you to doubt me or my commitment to us. I'm giving you back the forty percent of the winery; I'll call the lawyer and have him revert it back to you, and if someday we say I do, there will be a pre-nup stating that I relinquish all rights to Sand Creek Winery."

"Max, no." She turned to face him. "I want us to be partners."

He unzipped his coat and withdrew some folded papers, which he tore in half. "I don't need a contract to say we're partners. We want the same thing, for Sand Creek to be a success, but more important than the winery is our relationship." He cupped her cheek. "I love you, Tessa, and I want us to be partners on every level, and we don't need a business contract to make that a reality."

She tore her eyes from his. "I'm scared."

He knew that admission had been like baring her soul and she worked to present a tough façade to the world when in reality she needed to find her confidence. "Tessa, why did you want to buy Sand Creek Winery?"

She looked at him, her eyes wide. "You know why. My father gave Don the presidency of CLW and it was the job I wanted."

"But why Creek? Why not another winery somewhere in the Finger Lakes or beyond?"

"It was a good opportunity," She kicked the ground with the toe of her boot. "And I guess if I needed help, I had my family close by to turn to for advice." Softly, she said, "Oh. I see where you're going with this."

"Tee, you never had anything to prove to anyone other than yourself. Your father and Don believe in you, and I do too." He kissed the exposed underside of her wrist.

"I need to step out of Don's shadow and take control of my life and business." Her soft-brown eyes were somber. "But how do I do that?"

"Start by believing in yourself."

"It's not that simple. Working at CLW was comfortable. I knew my job and I worked with my family." She spread her hands wide. "It was easy. We supported each other."

He put an arm around her. "You know how to run Creek and we balance each other; you handle sales and marketing and I'll handle the growing of the grapes and the creation of the wines. Together we will be unstoppable."

"Is this your way of saying I need to stand beside you and work to build Creek into an amazing business and keep my family and our business separate?"

He pondered what to say next and how she'd take it. "Think of it this way. There are two vines growing from the fertile soil. One begins to overshadow the other. It becomes bigger and stronger and the second vine struggles to grow. It can, but it will never be as strong as the first. So we separate the two vines, plant them side by side with enough space between them that the two vines will grow strong independently while still sharing a common ground."

With a small laugh, she said, "And they'll support each

other and spend holidays and family meals together but business will be separate." She shoulder-bumped him. "Is that what you're trying to tell me?"

"Well, you missed one important point."

Her eyes lit up. "What's that?"

"I love you and we're in this together." The kiss he gave her could melt an iceberg. "Partners in love and in life."

*T*essa made one final walk-through of the dining room. No detail was too small to be overlooked. She adjusted napkins, tweaked vase placement, and checked wineglasses for water spots. Max was making sure the white wines were chilled and the reds were ready to be opened so they could breathe. The first seating was in less than one hour, and she was glad her dress and makeup bag were upstairs.

She strode into the kitchen, happy to see Kate overseeing the last-minute dash. The waitstaff had arrived and were plating the salads. Kate gave her a relaxed smile.

"We're all set, if you want to get dressed. I got a text from Don and the family will be here in about fifteen minutes to get the final rundown before the doors open."

A tray clattered to the floor and drew Tessa's attention. Kate hurried over and helped clean up the vegetables from the floor, all while reminding the young man to relax.

Max stuck his head through the swinging door.

"Tee, it's getting late. We should get ready."

She glanced up. "Kate, you're all set?"

"Absolutely." She was instantly absorbed in conversation with her sous chef, Tessa and Max forgotten.

He held the door for her and she crossed to the stairs.

"Hey, slow down."

"Sorry." She waited for him. "I'm focused on tonight. Thank heavens it's not snowing."

He laced his fingers with hers as they walked to their office. "The tables look wonderful. The kitchen is humming; Liza has everything organized to perfection, and Stella just got here."

"Liza has done an amazing job. I'm confident her business cards will be snapped up as people leave tonight."

He said, "I see big things for her future." At the top of the stairs, he put a hand on her arm. "Will you save a dance for me?"

"Well," with a smile, she drawled, "it is Valentine's Day. I think I can spare one dance for you."

He threw his arms around her and brushed her lips. "You're incorrigible."

"It's all part of my charm." She wriggled out of his arms. "Now, I have primping to do. In private."

She would love to have lingered right where she was, but it was time to put her business owner hat on. There would be time later to celebrate the most romantic day of the year with the man she loved. She urged him in the direction of the empty office down the hall.

"Are you looking to make an entrance?"

She could tell by the way the corners of his eyes crinkled and the slow and easy grin he wore, he was teasing her.

With a laugh, she said, "Doesn't every woman?" Then she followed up with, "Well, at least the women in my family love to make an entrance." She flicked her hand. "Now go."

She could hear him chuckling as she closed their office door. She turned around and stopped in her tracks. Placed in the center of the large table was a bouquet of deep-red roses with small chocolate KISSES candies circling the vase. Her insides melted. This was the first time in her adult life anyone had given her roses for Valentine's Day. In a few short steps, she buried her nose in the fragrant buds. A small white envelope was nestled in the midst of the flowers. Her heart quickened.

She withdrew the card from the envelope and recognized his bold handwriting. He hadn't phoned the order in, but had done it in person.

T - Everyday my life is better because of you. All my love, M.

She clutched the note to her chest. Her heart was full of love for this man. She tucked the card in the flowers and with one last sniff, she hurried into the adjoining bathroom.

⁂

*M*ax stood at the bottom of the stairs. He tugged on his jacket sleeves and adjusted his tie. He hoped his black tuxedo wasn't going to make him overdressed for the evening. When he told Tessa he was wearing a dark suit, in his mind a tux was the only option.

He could feel eyes on him. Slowly he turned and she was standing at the top of the stairs. His mouth went dry. Tessa's auburn hair was piled on top of her head. Long pearl and diamond earrings were liquid from her ears. She wore a floor-skimming, deep-red dress with a draped neckline and a long pearl necklace. The dress clung to her curves and her leg was partially exposed through a mid-thigh slit. She took her first step and he noticed the red pumps. She was breathtaking.

Her hand slid over the metal banister as she made her descent. His feet were glued to the floor and he couldn't take his eyes off her.

When she reached him, he kissed her cheek and whispered in her ear, "Is it your goal to make my heart stop beating?"

Her soft laugh was music to his ears. "It's okay. I know CPR."

"You are beautiful." He couldn't stop himself. He pulled her into his arms and kissed her breathless.

Her cheeks flushed. "Thank you for the flowers. They're beautiful."

"Anything for you." He kissed her again.

A cough interrupted them. He looked around her and saw Sam grinning from ear to ear. He too was wearing a tux. Max guessed it wasn't an original idea after all.

"If I could interrupt, we're about to open the doors."

Reluctantly, he let Tessa go and she glided across the room to a wall mirror. Sam handed her a handkerchief and motioned to his mouth. She wiped a smudge of lipstick from under her lower lip and checked her hair. She smiled at Max in the reflection. "I'm ready." She held her hand out to him. "Party time."

---

essa was cursing her heels by the end of the second seating. She had gone for the wow factor and not comfort. There was no way she was slipping them off to massage the arch of her foot, as she'd never get them back on. She casually leaned on the hostess stand as the last of the guests filed out.

Max caught her eye and strolled over. It was only as he got closer that she saw the way his eyes were shining. He was excited about something.

"Hey," she said softly, "what's going on?"

"I was working the coat room and there were a bunch of people talking about how this was the best dinner they'd been to in years and they *loved* the wine and food."

He grabbed her hand and squeezed it, out of view from

anyone who might be looking. "Do you know what this means?"

She loved seeing his passion for the winery, but this was more. "What?"

"We're a hit. Our sales are going to skyrocket. Who knows how much, but we have to do another event this summer. Maybe a barbeque or something."

"That's a great idea. We should have a meeting tomorrow and tell the family what you heard."

He gave her a slow, sexy wink. "Can we make it Monday? I'm hoping we can spend a quiet day just the two of us."

The staff was busy clearing the tables of dishes and linens. The band was packing up their instruments.

Her finger grazed his jaw. "Oh, Max, we didn't get our dance."

"Don't worry; I have a plan. Give me a few minutes."

She watched as he walked in Liza's direction. After a short conversation, he handed her what looked like his phone. She was nodding.

What were they up to?

He walked around the room, lighting candles. The lights dimmed and it seemed as if the staff melted into the shadows. She looked out the front windows and saw her family drive away. It was odd that they didn't say goodbye.

A soft guitar strain swelled to fill the room. Max emerged from the shadows and with eyes locked on her, the distance between them evaporated.

He held out his hand. "May I have this dance?"

If Tessa hadn't fallen in love with him before, she would have in that moment.

"Yes."

He took one hand in his and she placed the other on his shoulder and his rested at her waist. Their sensuous movements became trancelike as they moved to the strains of Ed Sheeran singing "Thinking Out Loud." She rested her head on his chest and could feel his beating heart. She placed her hand over it and lifted her face to him for a kiss.

He lowered his head. But their lips didn't touch. In a soft, seductive voice, he said, "Happy Valentine's Day, Tessa."

A lump filled her throat. She pecked his lips.

He held her close. The music wrapped them in a cocoon for two.

"Max." Her voice was a whisper.

He kissed the exposed sensitive spot behind her ear.

"Mmm. I love you, Max."

"Sweetheart, I love you with all my heart."

She said, "I don't want this night to end."

He slowed and, using his hand, tilted her chin up so their eyes could meet. "It has to eventually, but we can keep dancing forever and always."

"Music to my ears."

EPILOGUE

The last few months had been hectic, but tonight Max had plans with Tessa. Flowers graced the coffee table and candles dotted the room. He glanced at the clock again. When was she going to arrive was the big question. He circled the room, lighting several fat beeswax candles. He was ready to say those four little words, and he was going to show her just how much she meant to him.

A light rap on the door had him hurrying to the front hallway. Through the side window, he could see her standing on the step. Raindrops drifted down and landed in her hair.

"Tessa." He took her hand and pulled her in from the rain. "How were the roads?"

She shook off her coat and handed it to him. "Wet. The storm should be over before I drive home."

"You don't need to."

Her eyes twinkled. "Is that an invitation?"

He skipped playing the game. "Yes. I like waking up with you in my arms."

"That's settled." She pecked his lips and held up a bag. "I brought the wine."

"Come with me." He took the bag and guided her into the living room.

She gave a small gasp. "Oh, Max, the candles, the fireplace. It's so romantic. Thank you for doing all of this."

"Make yourself at home and I'll open the wine."

She stepped around the side of the furniture and tucked her shoes under the coffee table.

He carried two empty glasses and an open bottle of red toward the table and set them down, only to go back into the kitchen.

"I made a plate of appetizers." He paused when he opened the door. "Unless you'd like to have dinner soon?"

"I'm in no rush."

He couldn't help but grin. Things were very promising indeed. He passed her the plate with cheese, prosciutto, crackers, and sliced apple.

"Yummy. You've really gone all out."

He sat close to her and kissed the corner of her mouth. Softly, he said, "I was inspired."

"That is a sweet thing to say." She tilted her head so her lips met his. "I love kissing you." She nibbled on his lip with her teeth. Her breath was warm on his face.

"Ditto."

She gave a small, throaty laugh. "A man of few words." She pulled back. "Can I ask you a question?"

"Just one?" He moved in closer to continue his exploration of her mouth.

"Are you happy with the way the last nine months have gone?"

He gave a snort. "I am. I would never have dreamed a year ago, when I knew there was a serious inquiry for Creek, that I would be here, with you." He wanted to stop talking and do more kissing, and in more places than just her mouth.

"It's funny how life changed for us both." She placed a hand on his arm and he took the hint. "I'd love some wine."

He was definitely moving too fast. He switched his focus to the bottle. "I haven't tried this cab yet. It's a new startup. This is the first release and you know me, always looking at the competition."

He handed her a glass and she held it under her nose, which she wrinkled. "Take a sip."

He cocked a brow. "I saw that expression on your face and I'm guessing you don't like the bouquet."

He could see she was struggling to keep her face neutral.

"I'd like your opinion first."

He held the glass aloft in the candlelight. "Nice color." Then inhaled, sipped, and grimaced. "Vinegar."

She set the glass aside. "That is awful for them. Do you think it is their entire production of the cab?"

"That would be my best guess." He looked at the label. "I'll give them a call tomorrow or better yet, I'll go out there and see what I can do to help."

Her eyes grew wide. "I thought you didn't like being social with other winery owners?"

"Let's just say that over the last few months, I've come to realize that most owners aren't out to shut you down. Having input from one or two experts in the business could have proven to be helpful when I was the new guy in The Valley."

"You've come a long way." She placed a warm hand on his thigh. "I can't wait to see where we go from here, and I'm not just talking about Creek."

Then she kissed him like it was the first time. Full of passion and promise.

In a soft, husky voice, she asked, "What do you say we take the appetizers and a different bottle of wine in the other room?"

"Do you have a particular room in mind?"

Without saying a word, she handed him the plate and gestured to the wine rack. "I'll meet you in your bedroom."

That was all he needed to hear. He hastily blew out the

candles and checked the fireplace. He pulled the cork on a bottle of Fuse and, with two fresh glasses, hurried down the hallway. His pulse quickened, seeing items of clothing discarded in Tessa's wake. He softly chuckled. She did like to make a statement.

There she was in the middle of his bed, which was illuminated by the moonlight through the glass doors. Her smile reminded him to stop and take a mental snapshot. He wanted to remember her like this.

He carefully set the glasses and bottle on the table and stepped out of his shoes.

She ran her gaze from his toes to his eyes. "You have way too many clothes on."

※

She woke with a start, alone and chilly. Where was Max? She flicked back the covers and discovered a dark velour bathrobe laying across the foot of the bed. She slipped it on. It smelled like him. In the early morning light, she could see her clothes were in a neat pile on the chair. She smiled at his thoughtfulness. The soft sound of clattering pots drifted to her ears and she padded down the hall in bare feet.

When she came around the corner, she saw the breakfast bar was set with two place settings and candles were lit.

"Something smells good."

A slow smile graced his face as he saw her leaning against the doorjamb.

"I promised you dinner and since it's early morning, I thought omelets would be a better choice."

She folded back the sleeves on the robe. "Can I help?"

He glanced at her feet. "I have some wool socks in the top left drawer of the dresser if your feet are cold."

"I'll just get dressed."

Before Tessa could slip down the hall, he had her in his

arms. "You look better in my robe than I do. Please"—he looked deep into her eyes—"don't change."

If she looked down, she'd swear the blush started at her toes and rushed to her face. "I'll put socks on."

She floated down the hall, and right where he said was a pair of thick socks. Hopping on one foot and then the other, soon her feet were toasty warm. She paused to look out over the rain-dampened grass. It glistened like shimmering diamonds in the early sunlight.

She didn't want to linger too long, until a glimpse of her reflection caused her to stop and look closely. Her hair was mussed, her mascara smudged, and she looked relaxed. How could he have possibly thought she was remotely attractive with the black streaks and hair jutting out in different directions?

After a quick trip into the bathroom, she was pleased with the damage control. Now she was ready to rejoin Max.

"Hey, I thought you got lost." He slid a half-round omelet onto a plate and cut it in half.

"I fixed my face and hair so you wouldn't have to look at a hot mess over breakfast."

"It was a nice reminder of last night." He gave her a slow smile and passed her a plate. "They're overstuffed, so I hope you don't mind sharing."

She held the plate up to her nose. "It smells delicious. Let's eat at the coffee table."

They settled on the floor in front of the fireplace, eating Japanese style at the coffee table.

She ate with gusto, and Max chuckled. "I guess you like it."

She grinned. "You're a much better cook than me."

He ran a finger down her cheek.

Over small talk, they finished their meal. Tessa stretched out her feet to the fire and wrapped her arms around her body before yawning. She didn't want to break the mood, but she was getting chilly and tired of sitting on the floor despite the thick carpet.

Max held out his hand. "You look like you could use a short nap."

She took it and allowed herself to be swept into his arms. "How're your coffee-making skills?"

"Better than my eggs."

She went on her tiptoes and lightly kissed him before saying, "Bed, nap, and then coffee."

"Tee, before that…" From his jeans pocket, he pulled a diamond ring out and held it up. Her eyes grew wide.

He cupped her cheek. "On Valentine's night, I promised you always and forever."

"You did." She lifted her hand and he placed the ring at the tip of her fourth finger.

"I'd like to make it official. Tessa Price, will you marry me?"

She nodded. "Yes! I love you, Max. Always and forever."

He twirled her in his arms and they sealed their future with a kiss.

The End

Thank you for reading Tessa and Max's story. I hope you enjoyed the story. If you did, please help other readers find this book: **Please leave a review now!**

Sign up for Lucinda's Newsletter today at www. lucindarace.com to be notified about upcoming releases and specials just for you, my newsletter subscribers.

Read on for a Sneak Peek of
Crush, Book 2

Order At Your Favorite Retailer
The Crescent Lake Winery series
Featuring brilliant Anna Price and the handsome Colin Grant

He's just the spark she needs…

*A*nna Price is an Enologist, a world-renowned expert in anything having to do with wine. Her work at her family's Crescent Lake Winery in the Finger Lakes region of New York has her feeling as if she's treading water. There has to be more to life than just wine. Has she lost her spark? She's jolted when her father suffers a heart attack, then gets a jolt of a different kind from the man taking care of her father.

Colin Grant is a nurse practitioner, specializing in the care of cardiac patients. He'd met Anna once before, but had just ended a long-distance relationship and wasn't ready for someone new. But this time it's different. There's no denying his attraction to the curvy girl who has no idea how beautiful she is.

When Anna is offered a job in France, they may find their growing relationship crushed. How can she say no to the offer of a lifetime? Colin's job is caring for other people's hearts; he's determined not to have his own broken again. Absence doesn't always make the heart grow fonder. But is it worth the risk, for a lifetime of love?

Follow Me On Social Media

Like my Facebook page
Join Lucinda's Heart Racer's Reader Group on Facebook
Twitter @lucindarace
Instagram @lucindraceauthor
BookBub
Goodreads
Pinterest

LOVE TO READ?
CHECK OUT MY OTHER BOOKS

The Crescent Lake Winery Series
Blends: A Novella – March 2021
Breathe – March 2021
Crush – May 2021
Blush – Fall 2021
Vintage - January 2021
Bouquet - March 2022

It's Just Coffee Series

The Matchmaker and The Marine – May 7, 2020

The MacLellan Sisters Series

Old and New – June 19, 2019
Borrowed – July 10, 2019
Blue – July 31, 2019

The Loudon Series
Between Here and Heaven – June 2014
Lost and Found – November 2014

The Journey Home – July 2015
The Last First Kiss – November 2015
Ready to Soar – August 2016
Love in the Looking Glass – June 2017
Magic in the Rain – November 2017

ABOUT LUCINDA

Award-winning and best-selling author Lucinda Race is a life-long fan of romantic fiction. As a young girl, she spent hours reading romance novels and getting lost in the hope they represent. While her friends dreamed of becoming doctors and engineers, her dreams were to become a writer—a romance novelist.

As life twisted and turned, she found herself writing nonfiction but longed to turn to her true passion. After developing the storyline for The Loudon Series, it was time to start living her dream. Her fingers practically fly over computer keys as she weaves stories about strong women and the men who love them.

Lucinda lives with her husband and their two little dogs, a miniature long hair dachshund and a shih tzu mix rescue, in the rolling hills of western Massachusetts. When she's not at her day job, she's immersed in her fictional worlds. And if she's not writing romance novels, she's reading everything she can get her hands on. It's too bad her husband doesn't cook, but a very good thing he loves takeout.

Made in the USA
Middletown, DE
15 March 2021

34714809R00166